Falling Madly

ENNI AMANDA

1st Edition, February 2025

Lumi Publishing

ISBN 978-1-0670235-7-7 (ebook)

ISBN 978-1-0670235-6-0 (paperback)

Editing by Vicky Skinner

Proofread by Evie Alexander

Cover by Yummy Book Covers

Designed by Yummy Book Covers
Typeset in PT Serif, 10pt

*To Sam Heughan, on the off-chance
he one day finds this book and
feels inspired to perform a line or two...*

Falling Madly

CHAPTER 1

Teresa

I scrolled through the Valentine's Day menu of my favorite restaurant, slouched at my desk in the broom-closet-sized office I called "work," telling myself I was fine. Totally fine. It was fine that my boyfriend Richard had been too busy to book us a table, so I'd done it myself. I was a capable, modern woman, and there was no reason to feel weird about this.

We hadn't seen much of each other lately. I'd been busy with work, and he'd... well, honestly, I didn't know *what* he'd been doing. His job was both super confidential and incredibly boring, which made it easy for me not to ask questions. I was a creative, and stock market talk put me to sleep.

So far, I hadn't felt the butterflies, but Richard was nice enough. Dependable. Considerate. The kind of guy who'd hold the door open for you—a little theatrically, but still. Maybe tonight, with the help of moody lighting and the mouth-watering soufflé currently staring at me from my laptop screen, I'd finally feel the way all those women in romantic movies did.

For the first time ever.

I'd made it to thirty and still hadn't experienced that paradigm-shifting thing people called falling in love—the one that made you say things like "I can't live without you" or "you complete me" without a hint of sarcasm. Once, a guy I was seeing told me his heart was so full it might split, and I suggested he see a cardiologist.

Safe to say we weren't on the same page.

People told me that if you liked someone enough, you could partner for life and make it work. But I wanted more. I wanted the fairytale, damn it. The magic. The madness—even if it sounded a little daunting. Honestly, the idea of going slightly insane because of some hormonal imbalance in my brain scared me stiff, but I was also desperately curious.

My best friend Bess had recently fallen in love, gotten married, and was having a baby. It had all happened so fast it gave the rest of us whiplash, but I was happy for her. I was even happy for Charlie, her new husband and business partner, who I'd used to think of as a spoiled brat. I still thought he was a privileged rich boy, but he was good to my friend. He'd been good to me, too, offering me a job when the last ad agency we all worked at imploded, and he went into business with Bess. And Trevor.

Mustn't forget Trevor. The guy I once thought I could fall for,

for one magical night.

Since our relationship crashed and burned, we'd gradually transitioned into reasonably pleasant colleagues. Sharing a physical space might have been awkward, but our office was so tiny it didn't make sense for us all to be there at the same time, bumping elbows and running out of oxygen. So, we took turns working from home, which ensured I didn't see Trevor that regularly. In fact, I made sure I saw as little of him as possible.

I wasn't trying to freeze him out or anything. We talked. These days, we even had a private chat that pinged multiple times a day, which I took as a sign that we'd both gracefully moved on from what happened that night. We exchanged memes and funny stories, notes on restaurants and movies like you'd do with any colleague. We were civil.

He'd told me about a laser tag game he'd had with Charlie and some other guys, so I didn't think twice about updating him about my date night and the incredible chocolate dessert I was going to consume. I was at work, after all, and he was a colleague. It was Wednesday—my office day—so Trevor was working from home. Charlie and Bess were on a family trip to New Mexico, which also meant I was there by myself and feeling a little lonely.

Trevor: You sound more excited about the soufflé than the date.

Teresa: If you've never tried this soufflé, your opinion is irrelevant.

Trevor: They deliver, you know. You could enjoy it at home without watching Richard dab his mouth like a 19th-century duke.

Why did I tell him things? He despised Richard, for whatever reason. And now the image of Richard dabbing the corners of his mouth, looking like he was sucking on a lemon, played in my mind. Could I get to the restaurant early and confiscate all the napkins? Could I encourage him to order a dish that required no mouth-wiping of any kind? What would that be? Cardboard?

Teresa: You're a jerk.

Trevor: Obviously.

Teresa: You going out tonight?

Trevor: Nah. I'm ordering soufflé online.

Teresa: Ha ha.

I'd leave it at that.

Another message popped up—a picture of a woman devouring a soufflé larger than her head. I minimized the window.

My stomach growled. It was way past lunchtime, and I'd run out of office snacks I could nibble on to skip lunch. Looking at pictures of food was not helping.

I threw on my jacket and ventured out into the cool winter air. My growling stomach guided me down the road to the only restaurant within a hundred-yard radius that served ready-made food. It was an Indian place with samosas so hot they made your eyes water, but I kind of liked it. They left an impression, which was more than I could say about the stale pretzels and crackers I'd been munching all week.

My mouth watered in anticipation as I hobbled over puddles and patches of dirty snow in my Italian leather boots. Technically, the winter conditions in Denver called for more practical footwear, but I loved my boots. They made my whole outfit feel more expensive than it was. And if a piece of clothing gave you even an ounce of confidence, I firmly believed it was worth it.

As I was about to reach the entrance of Noon 'til Naan, a giant puddle blocked my path. I halted at the edge of it, just before the dainty ends of my shoes hit the water. I could already smell the spices. Chili, cinnamon, cardamom...

The restaurant had large, decal-adorned windows and a battered awning that leaked at the seams, creating the small lake that now stood between me and my spicy food. To get to the door without soaking my feet, I'd have to leap.

Contemplating my options, I glanced through the restaurant window, and that was when time slowed down. All the way down. I'm talking about one of those movie scenes where bullets hang suspended in midair. There he was—Richard, my boyfriend of nine months—with his arm around a blonde woman.

My brain went into overdrive. In two seconds flat, I'd cataloged everything: the way he guided her to the window booth, all protective-like, and the way he brushed his nose against the collar of her oversized coat. It was intimate. Familiar. And nauseating.

I was in no way clairvoyant, but I knew what would happen. Yet, I couldn't look away.

"Why're we watching your boyfriend snogging another woman?"

I jumped at Trevor's Scottish baritone. My head whipped around to confirm it really was him. Yes. The colleague I avoided like it was an Olympic sport stood right behind me, witnessing my humiliation.

My heart pounding like a jackhammer, I turned back to the window where the mortifying scene was developing into an X-rated show. Richard wasn't just kissing the woman. He was gobbling her up like a cartoon character attacking a lamb shank. They sat on the same side of the booth, both still in their overcoats, clawing at each other like they'd been waiting for this opportunity all day.

How was this possible? I'd talked to him this morning, confirming the reservation for tonight.

Thanks, babe. Let's meet up there. Hope you got a good table.

What was I missing? Was there a hidden meaning to that text? My eyes burned and legs felt like fence posts, bolted to the sidewalk, as I continued to stare at the window. They didn't even come up for air. People needed air, right?

I was vaguely aware of Trevor clearing his throat, but I couldn't move. My brain had connected another dot: I knew the woman. It was the ex—Carolyn. The one he always complained about. But I could tell he wasn't thinking of her flaws now. He didn't really care how she loaded the dishwasher (front to back, the maniac) or randomly pumped the gas pedal. He was probably obsessed with her perfect blonde waves and talon-like white nails. She looked like a dying bird clawing at his ponytail.

For her, he'd probably cut off the ponytail, his symbol of rebellion among the finance guys. She was tugging at it with borderline violence, so maybe Carolyn and I agreed on this one detail. If you'd had a ponytail since you were sixteen, it was a symbol of inertia, not rebellion.

"I thought you guys were exclusive." Trevor's voice cut through my thoughts.

I shut my eyes, wishing to erase his pesky existence. Of all the days in my life, most of them filled with work and nothing else, why did this have to be the day Trevor appeared in the flesh? He belonged in my chat window. I could handle him there. I almost liked him there—a friend I could ignore at will and bring up when needed.

I took a breath, keeping my voice level. "Me, too."

There was no way for me to save face, even if I avoided looking at him. Also, it wasn't my fault Richard was currently cheating on me, was it? He was cheating on me one block away from my office, which felt deliberate. Was he trying to get caught?

Maybe I should have seen this coming. He'd talked about Carolyn a lot. But people talked about their exes. He'd always framed it as a compliment to me, comparing me to this woman who couldn't parallel park and cried over doing taxes. I'd stood up for her, reminding him that we each had our weaknesses, slightly terrified of what he'd say when he learned about mine. But I'd never thought he'd been hung up on his ex. That's how blind I was.

"Sorry." Trevor glared at the window, eyebrows drawing together.

I scoffed. "Save it. I know you hate him."

"I'm not sorry for Dick. I'm sorry for you."

"Dick?"

"Ach! I was going for his nickname."

"Nobody calls him Dick."

Trevor arched his brow. "I do, in my head."

I blew out a breath. "You know what? From now on, I'll join you."

"Would you like me to…"

"What? Kick his teeth in?" I huffed, half-laughing at the absurdity.

Not because he couldn't—Trevor could probably send the guy to an early grave with one hand tied behind his back. But we didn't have that kind of relationship. At least, I didn't think we did.

Trevor looked unfazed. "Aye." He peeled off his gloves and cracked his giant knuckles. "Dinnae think of it as a favor. Think of it as somethin' fun I've always wanted to do."

"You hate him that much, huh?"

"Nae." He looked like he was about to say something else but changed his mind. "Just happy to help."

I sighed, glancing at the window again. My boyfriend—strike that, my *ex*-boyfriend—was now talking to the waiter, gesturing at the menu. "That's okay. He's not worth it."

Part of me had always known we'd part ways, eventually. Either that, or we'd magically fall in love. How delusional had I been to even think that earlier?

My sister Suzanne had once told me I was probably too independent to fall in love. She might have had a point. I'd never slept over in Richard's apartment or left my things behind. He'd poked fun at me for my "crime scene cleaning," but I didn't care. That was why they were called personal belongings—they belonged in my home.

In the nine months we'd been together, we'd only ever talked about the future in vague terms. Before Thanksgiving, he'd suggested a trip to his parents' place in Connecticut, but I'd carefully steered us off that topic. If you weren't madly in love, why would you meet someone's parents? So, maybe this was all my doing. I'd been holding back.

Of course, he could have done the decent thing and broken things off before sucking the tonsils off another woman. Even Suze couldn't say *this* was my fault. Not that I had to worry about my sister saying anything like that. She might have been in a blissfully co-dependent relationship, but she didn't want me to give up my independence for the wrong guy. And now I knew Richard was exactly that.

"Are you sure?" Trevor pressed on. "I'd very much enjoy helping him see the error of his ways."

A small part of me wanted to see Trevor march in there, lift my useless boyfriend by his fake-fur collar and shake him for loose change. For entertainment, or closure. Maybe both. But did I really want a favor from Trevor?

I cast him a warning look. "If you think that using your fists to defend my honor will make us even, think again."

He dropped his arms to his sides, feigning defeat. "No, my darling dragonfly. Nothing could ever make us even."

He'd taken to calling me that sometime in the last few weeks. I pretended to be offended, but it was hard, because dragonflies were awesome.

"And you can drop the hurt bunny look with the fists," I instructed him, keeping my voice calm. "Don't do the crime if you can't do the time."

His eyebrows lifted. "How much time are we talking about?"

That playful spark in his eyes hit my insides, causing a slight wobble. This is why I didn't want to see him in person. Everything about him threw me off balance and brought back memories. I'd friend-zoned him for all eternity for a reason.

I'd first met Trevor about two years ago, when I'd taken the designer job at Wilde Creative. We'd flirted from day one. Inside jokes, looks, and glances, a bit of friendly competition. We'd kept bumping into each other in the tiny printer room, bonding over our frustration with the complicated machine and its constant paper jams. By the time the Fourth of July party rolled around, my panties were already halfway to melting off. But I was also in the middle of a huge campaign. A career-defining one. I'd pitched my idea to Charlie, our Creative Director, and he'd liked it. All I needed was the blessing of his team, and I'd be designing a massive blockchain game.

Nope. Trevor vouched for Boris, and they appointed him. What was worse, I stood right there, behind a potted palm tree. I heard his words, loud and clear.

Maybe Teresa isn't the right fit.

I guess I'd been lucky to hear those words and see his true colors. Just like I was lucky right now to find out the truth about Richard. I didn't *feel* lucky, though.

Trevor hadn't just cost me the job. He'd cost me my big break. As it turned out, the client was so happy with their work that they each got gifted a whole lot of tokens, the internal currency of the new game. In six months, the game tokens were upgraded into a crypto currency and the value of the coins skyrocketed. And yes, they used my ideas. Not exactly as-is, but not any better either. If anything, they butchered those graphics.

I could have used the money. I'd been saving for a deposit to buy my own place, scraping it together. I'd still managed to buy a small condo, but on a tight budget, at the worst possible time.

I didn't know Wilde Creative was going to implode, causing us both to look for new employment. As expected, Trevor had followed Charlie like he was the pied piper. And I'd followed both because I had no choice. I still wasn't sure why they'd offered me a job at their new venture, but it must have had something to do with Bess. She had pull with Charlie, and Charlie had pull with Trevor. So, here I was—working with the guy who'd so casually betrayed me, trying to avoid him in person for the sake of my fragile equilibrium.

"Why are you even here?" I asked, my voice sticking to my throat.

He glanced to his left, and I noticed his blue Volvo parked in front of the restaurant. "I'm off to check out a vacant office in Cozy Creek."

"Cozy Creek?" My insides flipped. "I thought we talked about this! The clients are here, it doesn't make sense…"

I tried to quell the swelling panic. My job could not be moving to a small mountain town in the middle of nowhere. There was no way.

"Bess and Charlie seem to think it could work. We cannae stay in the current one and everything else in Denver is too expensive. Plus, the company is already called Cozy Creative."

I groaned. "That name is so misleading! Someone called us today asking if we do baby accessories."

Trevor's mouth twitched. "Well, in Cozy Creek it'll make sense."

At the last meeting, we'd agreed that the company would stay in Denver for the time being, which I had hoped meant at least for a year—or however long it took me to find another job. I'd been distracted though, happily working on exciting new briefs that Charlie kept hauling in. For all his faults, that man could attract quality clients.

When I got excited, I got absorbed, telling myself that I'd just finish this next job before updating my portfolio. It had been months and the only thing I'd done was idly browse job ads on my lunch breaks while snacking on yogurt raisins and pretzels.

It was exciting to be part of something new, away from our old boss's looming presence. We played music as loud as we liked, took breaks whenever we wanted, and celebrated every win.

I'd even toyed with the idea of becoming a shareholder, since Charlie kept that option on the table. But that would have meant owning a piece of the same company as Trevor. He and our developer, Lee, had jumped onboard from the start, and I'd become the only full-time employee. I had a good deal. I wasn't sure how they could afford it, but I didn't want to question it. Not while I was saving up for a vacation in Bali. One I would now have to take alone, if at all.

Planning that trip with Richard had been fun. We'd talked about March or April. Had he already been seeing Carolyn behind my back? If I hadn't stumbled on them, would he have told me? Or would he have booked tickets to Bali and a third one for Carolyn so he could see her in the neighboring hut behind my back? There were too many questions. Nausea swelled in my stomach, momentarily overtaking hunger.

I took a breath, hiding my face from Trevor. "Why are you here?" I asked again, narrowing my eyes. "This isn't on the way to Cozy Creek."

"I came to pick ye up."

I frowned, suspicious. "You think I want to come with you to see some stupid office?"

His smile was infuriatingly casual. "Call it a courtesy kidnapping."

He raised the collar of his winter coat against the cold. His beard looked tidier than I remembered, and his skin had a healthy pinkish tint. It must have been the cold teasing his capillaries. The Trevor I knew had more of an ashy complexion and a revolting smoker's cough. But he was handsome, I had to admit. Built like a tree, with wildly curling dark hair and smoky teal eyes. A man I could easily imagine with an axe, even if I'd only ever seen him with a laptop.

"I can't go for a joyride in the middle of a workday. It's hours away!"

"A hundred and fifty kilometers." He loved annoying me with the metric system.

My breath was shaky and my hands trembled, but despite myself, I laughed. "Fuck you all the way back to Scotland!"

I shouldn't have raised my voice. As if in slow motion, Richard turned to look out the window, and his gaze landed on me. I'd never seen a deer in headlights, but I finally understood the reference. Even through the glass, I could tell his face went white as his mouth dropped open. We stared at each other. I wasn't sure how much time passed. It might have been a nanosecond, or ten minutes. But eventually, I felt Trevor's hand on my shoulder, guiding me away from the window.

Before I turned around, I saw Richard getting up. Was he coming outside? Bile crept to my throat. I didn't want to talk to him. I couldn't stomach the excuses or explanations.

I launched towards Trevor's car, stumbling over a pile of dirty snow. I heard the double beep of the central lock, and I scrambled inside. Trevor slid into the driver's seat and started the engine, steering us away from the restaurant. Away from Richard and that woman.

"Thank you," I whispered. "I can't handle talking to him. Do you think I should?"

"No," he grunted with an air of finality.

He changed lanes, and my gaze fell on the highway signs. "Wait! Where are you going?"

"Cozy Creek. I told ye."

CHAPTER 2

Teresa

Why the hell had I gotten into his car?

"I'm not going to Cozy Creek," I snarled. "I only wanted to get away from him!"

"It's not a taxi."

I grabbed the door handle. "Fine. Pull over. I'll find an actual *taxi*." I mimicked his accent, out of spite.

"No." He sounded annoyingly unbothered.

"What do you mean, no?"

"Ye can have yer wee hissy fit in the car while I drive. By the time we get to Cozy Creek, ye'll be done. Saves time, aye?" He flashed me an infuriating smile. "Also, ye should put on yer seatbelt before the car starts beeping."

As if on cue, the seatbelt alarm went off. Huffing my disagreement, I buckled up to make it stop. "I'm not throwing a fit. I told you I have no interest in any office space up there and I have work I need to finish."

"Sure. But ye also need a break. We've been working nonstop for weeks. Might be a good idea to put some distance between you and Dick." He threw me a searching look. "And I know you'll want to have a say about the new office. D' ye want Charlie and Bess only hearing my take on it because ye never saw it? I can be convincing, and they're already big fans of that town."

Trevor was right. What if Charlie and Bess got onboard? They were currently out of town on a short holiday. She was pregnant and they were both so in love their brains were probably mush right now, marinating in a cocktail of hormones that made kittens, ice cream parlors and small mountain towns irresistible.

I had to resist. I couldn't move to Cozy Creek. I'd have to resign, which would leave me struggling with my mortgage.

Even if I amped up my job search, it would take a while. It was so much easier to look for a new job when you still had one, without the smell of desperation.

I had to join Trevor and make note of everything that was wrong with that office to ensure this idiotic move never happened.

Trevor glanced at me. "I'll take your facial cramp as a yes."

I huffed. How did other people play it cool? I didn't even have micro expressions, only macro ones—obvious, overwhelming emotions I couldn't hide.

Outside the car, suburban Denver blurred by in shades of gray under a cloudy white sky. I took a deep breath. No cigarette smell. Odd. Was it masked by some car fragrance? Trevor didn't look exactly like I remembered, either. When had I last seen him in person? It had been so easy to avoid him at the tiny office with a timeshare desk.

We'd both been smokers once. I used to tell myself I was just a social smoker, nowhere near as bad as Trevor. But I'd been addicted. After his betrayal, when we still worked at Wilde Creative, I was so desperate to hide from him that I'd finally quit smoking. I didn't want to risk bumping into Trevor on the balcony or other usual spots.

But now, he smelled different. It must have been a while since his last cigarette, or I had polyps in my nose and needed surgery. Anything was possible. Either way, I was grateful for the relatively fresh air, given I'd be trapped in the car with him for two hours.

Being increasingly hungry was probably a bigger issue. After my stomach audibly growled, I spoke on its behalf. "Can we stop for food? I'm not picky. I'll eat anything that isn't nailed down."

Trevor's lips tugged into a smile. "Open the glove box."

Casting him a suspicious look, I released the latch, letting the lid fall on my knees. There, on top of a pile of car manuals, sat a plastic container and on top of it, a fork. I opened it and my eyes widened. It was a huge portion of fresh Niçoise salad with tuna, beans, potatoes, and boiled eggs. My favorite.

How could he have known? I hadn't ordered it with the team, had I? I only bought it from the corner deli on my days off when I was too lazy to cook.

"Thank you," I mumbled, shoving a forkful into my mouth. It was delicious. In fact, it tasted exactly like the one from my corner deli. "Is this for the both of us? There's a lot in here."

"I already ate."

"Oh. Well, thank you. I'll pay you back."

The suburbia turned into occasional farmhouses, and the snowcapped mountains glowed on the horizon like pointy, cream-covered chocolate cakes. I was clearly in the mood for dessert.

"Can ye reach behind my seat?" Trevor asked as I finished the salad. "There's a bag."

I pulled out a small cooler bag, unzipped it and discovered an individually packaged piece of chocolate cake covered with sticky ganache. "What's this?"

"I thought it'd make the road trip a bit more special."

"Special?" I narrowed my eyes in confusion. "Why did you even pack me a lunch? It's way past lunchtime."

"Ye said ye were off to grab lunch. And it's always that Indian place, isn't it?"

I gave a slow nod, thinking back to our chat history. I might have occasionally mentioned my guts being on fire after those samosas.

"It's the only place within reasonable walking distance."

"I know. I planned to catch ye just in time." He frowned, staring at the road. "I didn't mean to catch the... ye know... the Dick show." He was quiet for a moment. "Are ye okay?"

I let out a wobbly huff. "Of course not."

"No, I mean, do you think ye gonnae be?"

"Probably. It's not like I dreamed of marrying him and having his babies."

In fact, I'd never dreamed of that with anyone.

"You didn't?" He sounded genuinely surprised.

"No. We were just... dating."

"Exclusively?"

"I thought so. He wanted me to meet his parents. We were planning a trip to Bali."

He shook his head in slow motion. A tendon on his neck twitched. "That's messed up. Did ye already buy the tickets?"

"Not yet."

Thank God we hadn't.

My phone rang, and I jumped at the sound. Richard. I stared at the screen, contemplating my options. Did I need to talk to him? Did I need to know how long he'd been seeing her or how and when he'd been planning to tell me? Nothing would change the outcome. There was nothing he could say that would lessen the pain. There was plenty he could say to make it worse.

Trevor glanced at the phone in my hands. "Ye don't have to talk to him. Ye can block his number. Or does he have a lot of yer stuff?"

"No." I rejected the call, feeling a tad lighter.

I didn't need anything from Richard. I could imagine how badly he wanted to explain himself, justify his actions and part amicably. That was his MO—calm and rational. "We're all adults here," he'd always say. If I didn't give him a chance, he'd be left without closure. He'd be judged by his actions—actions he couldn't caption with his version of the truth. Denying him that was a small act of defiance, but it gave me back an ounce of control and I almost smiled.

Trevor drove in silence as I sanitized my phone of all things Richard—blocked his number and email, blocked him on all social apps, and finally, entered my photo gallery. I browsed the evidence of our time together, wondering if it had all been a lie.

The trips to the farmer's market for the perfect focaccia. Movie nights with wine and low-calorie snacks, watching the latest art films so that Richard could "keep up". He didn't want to see them in the cinemas though, so we watched bootlegged copies. I'd hated it, but I'd loved sitting on his comfy couch, eating three flavors of popcorn and feeling like I wasn't a lonely weirdo, because I had a boyfriend.

We'd only taken one proper trip, to a bed and breakfast in Maine where he'd had food poisoning and I'd bought him a bottle of Moxie neither of us could finish. After that, he'd wanted me to join his family on Thanksgiving, planning a long journey to their suburban home in Connecticut, where we were to sleep on the couch and possibly babysit his little sister I'd never met, so that his parents, who I'd also never met, could have a date night. Maybe I should have agreed, but it had felt like too much. Something you should only do if you were deeply in love and fully committed.

I'd let him down as easy as I could, and maybe that had been the beginning of the end. He'd traveled by himself, stayed away for a week, calling to catch up only once. After that, he'd never again brought up the possibility of visiting family—mine or his. The only trip we'd talked about was the Bali one.

In November, my life had been swallowed up by the end-of-year rush. In advertising, the last months of the year were something to be survived rather than enjoyed. I'd made it through, leaning on my online chat with Trevor. After all, he was always there and claimed to have no life outside work, something I could relate to. In January, things had calmed down for me, but Richard had become busy, working late nights on a job that was so high profile and top secret he couldn't tell me any details.

Cold sweat prickled on my neck. Carolyn. She was the late-night job, and I was an idiot.

With my phone Richard-free, I expelled a deep sigh and leaned my head against the seat.

"Ex-boyfriend digital bonfire?" Trevor asked.

"Yeah."

"I'm trying to figure out when it started," I confessed. "I don't want to think about him. He doesn't deserve my attention. But I can't stop going over the timeline and trying to spot anything suspicious. Anything I should have noticed."

"Ye wouldn't notice anything. Cheaters are too good at acting normal."

"You think he's been at it the whole time?"

"Uh-huh." He sounded so sure that my stomach tightened.

"Why? That could have been their first meeting we saw," I argued.

"You need some build-up for that kind of PDA. Unless he's paying her."

"It's his ex."

His eyebrows shot up. "Really? Well, maybe they didn't need that much build-up, then. Old flames…" He bit his lip, giving me a quick side-eye, and my breath seized.

Old flames.

Something twisted in my gut. Maybe not an old flame, but something old. And no matter how hard I tried to stop it; my mind drifted back to that night.

CHAPTER 3

Teresa

18 MONTHS AGO

I arrived at our client's penthouse apartment in my sequin-adorned little black dress, ready to impress. The party was in full swing, with the thumping bass and laughter reaching my ears before the elevator doors even opened.

I'd heard stories of Gavin Buckland and his crypto millions (we called him Crypto-Gavin), but it was fun to see it with my own eyes. He'd invited the entire creative team to his Fourth of July gathering. Maybe he hadn't expected everyone to show up, but I couldn't pass up the opportunity, and it seemed neither could anyone else.

I was gunning for the lead designer role in the crypto game creative team, which meant sucking up to him and his minions. Not that I was succeeding at that. Sucking up didn't come naturally to me.

I waved at a couple of colleagues, who looked as baffled as I felt surrounded by the huge, opulently decorated apartment featuring multiple seating areas and the nighttime panorama of Denver. Seeing familiar people relaxed me a bit, but my eyes scanned across the drinks and nibbles, searching for Trevor. I didn't even question it. Being near him relaxed me more than anything else, and I needed to chill.

After a moment of searching, I spotted his broad shoulders out on the balcony. Dark hair curled on his neck and the cigarette burned in his hand like a tiny red beacon, pulling me closer. Underneath the beard, I imagined he looked like James Dean. A handsome legend. But I kind of preferred him with the beard—a forest ranger version of a movie star with striking blue-green eyes framed by dark lashes, his slanted, sexy smile partially hiding behind the scruff. Like he couldn't care less, yet always brought his unshakable calm and disarming wit. An ego that gave everyone else enough space without curling in on itself.

This must have been Denver's tallest building. An occasional firework pierced the sky, countless parties in progress around us. The heat of the day still lingered in the air and the wooden banister felt warm to my touch. He smiled, his eyes lighting up. They were usually so relaxed he looked almost sleepy, entirely unaffected by the drama around him.

His beard looked freshly trimmed, and I gently scoffed at his vintage *One Direction* T-shirt. I knew he wore it to taunt me. You should never reveal your childhood crushes to anyone.

"Happy Fourth of July!" He offered me a cigarette.

"Thanks. How was Charlie's meeting?"

We'd been dancing around this attraction for weeks, but it felt safer to talk about work. I was also desperate to find out about this one job—I'd put everything into designing concepts for the crypto game, and I needed to know if Charlie had presented any of my work to the client.

Trevor leaned on the banister, gazing at the city lights flickering below us. "Heard it went well, aye," he said, taking a drag of his cigarette. "Do ye really want to talk about work?"

I did, but it didn't seem like the right answer. "I guess not."

"Have ye met Crypto-Gavin yet?"

"No. Where is he?" I glanced over my shoulder, trying to remember what the guy looked like. I'd seen his picture on the website, but only Trevor and Charlie had met him. Charlie was the boss's son and met everyone. Trevor was a copywriter, which didn't give him a high status, but as Charlie's sidekick, he was always there. Not that I was jealous, I told myself. Just a little frustrated.

What would it take for me to be invited into a meeting one day?

"That crypto game might crash and burn, you know." Trevor's voice held a warning.

"But if it doesn't..."

He gazed at the dark horizon. "Then it'll be an exception."

"I heard that our team could get tokens. Is that true?"

He shrugged. "I always felt fireworks were for winter. Not when it's hot enough to fry an egg on the pavement."

I felt like he was keeping something from me, but he seemed so pessimistic I decided to drop the subject. I wanted to believe it was possible.

The faint sound of my favorite song drifted in through the open glass doors. It was by an underground indie band and hardly ever on anyone's playlist. I finished my cigarette and wandered back inside. If Trevor was going to sulk and shit on my dreams, he could stay where he was. We were just flirting. I owed him nothing.

I spotted Charlie amongst the partygoers, surrounded by three blondes. He offered me an unsure smile and I veered toward the bar. Me and Charlie didn't mix that well, so it was best I stayed away. I grabbed one of the red, white and blue cocktails set out on a tray and downed it too fast. It must have been pure vodka and food coloring.

I hated flirting at work, no matter how well it might have served me in certain situations. I wanted to impress people, not lead them on or stroke their egos. For the sake of my career, I should have occasionally positioned myself in the vicinity of Charlie and the gang to nod and smile at their jokes. I should have giggled and looked at them with starry-eyed adoration. But there was something wrong with my brain, and I couldn't flirt without genuine interest. And that's why I only flirted with

Trevor.

I grabbed a second drink and looked for another familiar face, someone I could talk to. The crowd was more friend-of-a-friend than close acquaintance. The one colleague I truly liked, Bess, was home with her daughter. She hardly ever made it to parties. I should have put more effort into befriending my colleagues, but George kept hiring and firing temps with such frequency it felt pointless. Plus, I'd recently caught two newbies making fun of Bess behind her back and didn't feel like knowing any of them that closely. People like that were not worth my time.

I saw a curly-haired woman who I'd talked to at a couple of industry events and tried to recall her name. When it finally came to me—Angie—she was pulled away by someone and a man I'd never seen before appeared in front of me.

He was clean-shaven and had too much product in his stiff hair, but I liked the way he smiled. Confident and friendly, with a hint of nerves. "Hi! I don't think we've met. I'm Kyle."

He offered his hand, which hardly anyone did at these casual cocktail parties, and I took it. "Teresa."

"You're from Wilde Creative, right?"

"Yes. And you are from…"

"XYZ."

XYZ. Crypto-Gavin. My posture straightened automatically, and I tried to relax my face. Was I looking too eager or creepy?

"So… you're here with Gavin?" I scanned the room, hoping he'd point out the mythical CEO.

If nothing else, I could try to avoid him, which would ensure I didn't embarrass myself in front of him.

Kyle looked over his shoulder, gesturing so vaguely it was no help. "Yeah. He's here somewhere. Gavin's hard to pin down. But we're very excited to work with Wilde! None of us are creative like that. It's so cool what you guys can do."

"It's a fascinating project."

His eyebrows lifted a fraction. "Are you... working with us?"

I caught Trevor's tall frame in my peripheral vision, in the doorway to the balcony. I could feel him approaching, like a shadow casting across the floor.

"I hope so," I said, draining my drink.

"Reese!" Trevor's giant hand landed on my shoulder. "I need to show you something. Excuse us." He offered Kyle a quick smile, pivoting me away from him, out of earshot.

"Reese?"

"I'm user-testing nicknames."

"Where's the feedback form?" I was hyper aware of his hand on my shoulder but tried not to show it. Trevor was touching me.

He laughed, walking me across the large living room, weaving between people. "Is it not working? How about Rizz? Rizzler?"

"Are you twelve?"

"I have the sunny disposition of a twelve-year-old boy, hormones of a teenager and lungs of an eighty-year-old man."

I had to laugh. "Sounds like a winning combo."

I didn't pay attention to where he was taking me, and suddenly found myself outside the apartment, waiting for an elevator. When it arrived, Trevor pulled me in.

"Where are we going?"

"You'll see."

In the close quarters of the elevator, his broad frame seemed to take up all the space. Our faces reflected off the mirrored walls like a kaleidoscope of drunken smiles. He'd been teasing me for weeks. But always in jest. Always keeping his cool so that if I shot him down, he could step away smiling. No harm, no foul.

Trevor fascinated me. He seemed so even-keeled that I gravitated to him every time the slightest bit of drama erupted in the office. Next to him, I felt almost invincible, protected by that unflappable smile and tree-like physique. But I couldn't figure out if he was really that chill, or just dissociating somehow.

I knew that I shouldn't date a colleague. It was messy and could easily backfire. But he wasn't my boss, so nobody could say I was trying to sleep my way anywhere. My tipsy brain loved that argument, hanging onto it as I leaned a little closer. I caught a whiff of his aftershave, something spicy and woodsy and all-man, and I wanted more.

I must have leaned a little too hard because my elbow brushed the alarm button on the wall. A loud ringing hit my eardrums.

"Shit! Shit!" What had I done?

The ringing continued for a moment as I stared at Trevor, my brain spinning in panicky circles, generating wild scenarios. Was this like calling an ambulance when you didn't need it? Would they charge a call-out fee? Would they tell Crypto-Gavin since it was his building?

"What is your emergency?" A tired male voice rattled through the speaker on the wall.

Trevor bent down to speak to the microphone. "Apologies. False alarm." There wasn't a hint of shame or panic in his voice.

"Copy that." The guy disconnected and the elevator came to a stop.

I took a deep breath, trying to settle my nerves. I could usually keep my inner chaos and spikes of anxiety to myself and appear somewhat collected. I'd been perfecting the act for years. But Trevor was the real deal. No elevated heart rate or rapid breathing. He seemed to have no physical reaction of any kind.

Sure, it was only an alarm button. No big deal. But I'd never accidentally hit one.

"Do you play show tunes in your head?" I asked as we stepped into a dark hallway.

"Show tunes?"

"Reruns of the Simpsons?"

He blinked slowly, trying to follow my runaway thought train.

"How do you stay so calm?" I clarified. "You must have a solid happy place. Like, on another planet. None of that babbling brook shit."

He chuckled. "You're a babbling brook."

An uncontrollable laugh erupted from me, and I leaned on the wall to keep my balance. "It was so loud. I seriously jumped out of my skin."

Finding my center of gravity, I adjusted my dress to make sure my bra wasn't peeking through the plunging neckline. I might have been feeling a little drunk, but there was no reason to look trashed.

His eyes dipped to my cleavage. "I'm used to it. My family home had a smoke alarm that went off every time anyone made toast."

I pulled a face. "Sounds awful."

"Then one year, I bought my mom a new toaster for Mother's Day."

"Instead of cleaning the old one?"

"That's what she said!"

A moment of sadness lingered in the air. I knew his mom was long dead and all those stories of his family had taken place years ago in Scotland, which made them sound like fairy tales to me. Sweet and nostalgic.

He led me down the hallway to a frosted glass door labeled "spa."

"There's a spa?"

"Sort of." Trevor produced a swipe card from his pocket and tapped it on the reader. The door slid open with a beep. "Take a look."

Crypto-Gavin lived a life of luxury, so I'd already expected something grand. Still, the massive swimming pool surrounded by huge indoor plants took me by surprise. Like a jungle-themed holiday destination on an international space station if NASA had the budget.

We found a bench under two potted palm trees overlooking the silent pool. Ornate lanterns hung overhead, creating an eerie atmosphere. I heard a faint tip-tip-tip of water dripping somewhere far away.

I let out a reverent sigh. "This is impressive and unreal, all at the same time."

"Aye. The ultimate controlled environment." His hand brushed against mine and stayed. "I prefer wild nature with all its discomforts. You?"

I glanced at our hands. At work, we never touched, not even by accident. Tonight was different. The skin on my shoulder still glowed from where he'd placed his arm around me. That first touch had woken my nerves, making me hyper aware of him. Of us. He'd claimed me in front of Kyle like I wasn't just a colleague but... something more.

"Sure. Overly controlled and manicured is a bit creepy. But I also like coffee shops and movie theaters and occasional concerts that don't involve line dancing, so I prefer civilization over small towns or total wilderness."

He was quiet for a moment, as if gathering his thoughts. I knew he disagreed, which was fine. It wasn't like we were getting married and deciding where we wanted to live.

"I love the mountains. I'd happily give up lattes and concerts for a cabin in the woods, if I could convince George to let me work from home."

I smiled at the thought. "Cabin in the woods, huh? What would you do there all day long?"

"Hunt and fish, build things..."

"And split logs and make fire and push the snow?"

"Aye. O' course."

The mental image of him wielding an axe flashed behind my eyes. Why was it so easy to imagine him as a mountain man? A laugh bubbled in my belly, and I couldn't resist poking fun at him. "Every day, you buy your coffee from that pretentious master barista. You get your beard trimmed and waxed at that place downstairs from the office. I've seen them give manicures..."

He wedged his fingers under his legs, grinning. "What? Lumberjacks can't have oiled cuticles?"

"Not unless it's motor oil."

He revealed his hand, studying his short and rough nails. "Well. Good thing I've never tried a manicure. They sell a nice beard oil, though." He brushed a hand over his dark facial hair and grinned.

Our hands were no longer touching, but he shifted slightly, and our elbows made contact. My skin tingled and I held still, not wanting to break the connection.

He chuckled. "You know what, Teresa?"

"What?"

He turned to look me in the eye and the laughter fizzled away. The air vibrated between us. "I lied. I could work from home most of the time. George is a dick, but he's not a dick about attendance. He'd much rather keep all humans out of the office and deal with machines. So, I could buy a cabin in the mountains and commute once a week. But I haven't..." He held my gaze. "Because then I wouldn't get to see you."

I swallowed, waiting for the punchline. This was Trevor. The one with all the jokes and the loudest laugh. But he wasn't joking.

"You wouldn't get to see *me*?" I repeated, searching his eyes for a clue. Was he serious? Was this the moment I'd been waiting for when we finally talked about this thing between us? When we finally admitted there was something more than harmless flirting going on?

His voice was low and warm. "Seeing you is the best part of my day."

"Because my freak-outs are so entertaining?"

Last week, he'd witnessed me running my head under the faucet to cool off after a client who'd asked to see twenty-eight iterations reverted to version one.

Trevor ignored my deflection, looking at me in a way that woke up every nerve in my gut. They vibrated like someone was plucking a mandolin down there.

In the privacy of my bedroom, I'd imagined this moment, and sometimes a little further. I'd imagined him cornering me in the office, late at night, and each of us confessing to what was really going on in our minds. Giving in to passion that replaced the need for words and cut through all the uncertainty.

I'd been ready to take that first step. Maybe tonight. Maybe here. But I'd never imagined his words quite like this—subtle and vulnerable. I felt off kilter. The only part of his body touching mine was that elbow, his hands now wedged under his thighs like he was trying to keep them from misbehaving. "Everything about you is fascinating," he said.

My breath turned ragged, but I tried to smile. "You don't think I'm scary?"

He shook his head. "I'm not easily scared. Also, I'm not looking for a subservient woman."

"So, you're looking for a challenge?" I'd been that to some. A mountain to climb. A bet to win. I shuddered.

"You're not a challenge. More like a… mystery. I like mysteries."

My shoulders dropped a little and the bubbly feeling in my center returned. "Do you think I'm hiding something?"

"Everyone's hiding something. To be honest, I think most people are mysteries, but you're the best kind of mystery."

"*Best* kind?" I chuckled, thoroughly entertained by his musings.

"Aye. The kind of mystery that raises juicy questions on the first page, so you must keep turning the pages."

"What kind of juicy questions?"

He tilted his head. "Why do ye work so hard? Why do you pitch ideas for campaigns that you aren't assigned to? I mean, they're great ideas, but most people wouldn't have the interest or capacity. So, why?"

My body clenched. "If I have an idea, why wouldn't I share it?"

He narrowed his eyes. "That's the thing. Ye don't randomly get ideas for other people's jobs unless you think about them. So, why do you think about them?"

My cheeks heated and I turned away from him. I'd always tried to do it in a casual way, saying something like, "Hey, I saw you guys are working on that cheesecake campaign and I had a thought…" But it was true. I browsed the job board, read all the briefs, and dreamed of being assigned to the higher profile, challenging jobs. And when I wasn't, I inserted myself. It felt better than being completely on the outside, even if they just grabbed my ideas and took credit for them. Which happened regularly.

Trevor's voice was gentle. "I'm not trying to embarrass you. I can tell you're bored and need challenges. And your ideas are brilliant."

"But…" I helped him out, sensing the word on his tongue.

"But… some of the lads find you intimidating."

Of course. "So, that's why nobody wants me on their team?"

"I do. But I don't have that much say."

"Ha!" I yelped in protest. If anyone had say with Charlie, it was him.

I kicked off my heels and launched off the bench, tiptoeing to the pool's edge. Careful of my short dress, I sat down, dipping my legs into the water. It felt warmer than I'd expected, almost like a hot tub. I spread my toes and moved my feet, relieving the ache and numbness caused by the not-so-sensible three-inch heels.

After a moment, Trevor joined me. He'd removed his shoes and rolled up his jeans. "Now it feels like a beach trip."

He took a deep breath that somehow made him sound like an old man, tired of life.

"What were you like growing up?" I asked. "I have a hard time imagining you climbing trees and riding highland horses or whatever you did."

He chuckled. "Is it the rattling lungs? I've had a chest infection for two months, and I know I need to quit smoking. I *really* know it. I used to be quite fit. I still lift, but I don't run that much anymore. When I was a lad, our house was on a hillside, and I'd run up and down all the time. Down to the loch, to town to buy sweets, bum cigarettes... Fuck, I felt invincible." He huffed.

"When did you start smoking?"

"At sixteen. I had a friend who was hooked already, and I didn't want him to feel alone."

"That's the craziest reason to smoke!"

He nodded in agreement, hanging his head. Something about him always made me feel safe. As if I knew, without knowing, that he'd lay down his life for me. It made no sense and probably wasn't true, but a deep, dark part of me craved that feeling. Being that important to someone.

"Looking back, I wish I'd been more of a lone wolf. Could've saved my life."

"It's not a bad thing that people want you around." My voice was as quiet as a whisper. "I'm sure it makes life a lot easier."

I could count with one hand the people who truly wanted me around, with no agenda. Mom, my sister Suze, and Bess. And Trevor, it seemed. I told myself I didn't mind. People were generally shit sandwiches, and I had no time to weed out the good ones amongst those who were just waiting to stab you in the back. But I also knew I would have been a lot further in my career if I were popular, like him.

It was hard to be friends with colleagues, though. Bess was different, but many others simply saw me as competition. If I'd been a little wary of people before, working in advertising didn't help.

"Who wouldn't want you around?" he asked. "You're a delight."

"Ha!" The laugh launched out of my chest like a cough induced by a crazy tickle. "That's a new one."

"Wha'? I mean it!"

I kept laughing, even if the sound fizzled into something a bit sad. "It just doesn't sound like me. Sounds a bit fake."

"Hey! If thinking of someone makes me want to get out of bed, put on clothes and go to work, that person *is* a delight."

Something in his voice gave me pause. It wasn't a light comment.

"Do you often feel like... not getting out of bed?" I finally asked.

He chewed on his lip for a moment before answering. "I've had seasons when... it's been hard. Hard to remember why you'd do anything. Why you'd try."

"Was that when your mom died?"

"And long after. I think my decision to skip town came back to haunt me. First, I was happy to get away. My family is noisy and involved and everyone was dealing with it in their own way, sort of dragging each other down. So, when I left, I felt like I'd escaped and could start over. New place, new job. No reminders. And I had to work hard, so I didn't have too much time to think. But over time, the questions start drifting across the ocean. Why're you still there? When are you coming back? It's been long enough. And it's hard to justify staying, even if you feel like you've built a life. They don't see it. They see that I'm single and unattached and having a bit of an extended trip. Time to grow up, Trevor."

"But your life is here. It's valid." My words rushed out too fast. I didn't want to think of him leaving. Knowing he was there made going to work a lot more attractive to me, too.

"I think so," he agreed. "And I don't *want* to be single."

"You want to live in a cabin in the woods with someone who skins the deer you shoot and bakes lots of cookies, right?"

He chuckled, knocking my foot with his under the water. I pushed back and our feet locked together in a battle of wills under the surface.

"They'd have to be some disgusting keto cookies. I'm trying to get back into shape." He slapped his stomach.

As far as I could tell, Trevor didn't carry a lot of extra weight. I'd never seen him shirtless, though. Maybe he had a bit of padding around the middle. Not that it bothered me. I found ultra-fit guys a bit obnoxious. Nice to look at, but dreadful to listen to. Maybe because maintaining that look in your thirties took so much effort that it easily became your whole personality. Or I kept running into the worst kind—fitness nuts who thrived on the dating apps.

"They'd be disgusting, keto or not. I'm not much of a baker," I admitted.

"All good. For the record, I'm not looking for a woman in an apron to fatten me up to an early grave. My dad went down that path. The reason he's still alive is that Mom died, and the baking stopped. He existed on beans on toast for a couple of years, then learned to cook. Now he's on a healthy diet, so I guess it saved his life. His cholesterol used to be through the roof."

"Oh, wow. That's... terrible."

He huffed. "A bit morbid, I guess. Life's funny. I'm lucky my cholesterol is fine. Must be my mom's genes."

I tilted my head, amused. "Now I'm starting to think you're not twelve, but fifty-five."

He ran a hand down his face, grimacing. "Fuck. I need to start moisturizing."

"It's not going to help if you keep talking like that."

He grinned back. "Would you like to hear about my colonoscopy?"

I laughed, kicking his leg again, splashing water. "I feel like the whole cabin in the woods dream is something you develop in your sixties. You know, after the kids move out and you don't have to worry about living near the schools."

"Well, I've always had that dream. Maybe I need to find a sixty-year-old woman to join me if you... youngsters are not interested."

I tried to laugh, but his words made my stomach clench. Was he asking me to move into the mountains with him? I wanted to breeze past the odd comment, keeping things light and funny, because if he was for real, what did that mean? Were we really having a serious talk about our future? We hadn't even kissed.

"Trevor?" I said, my voice a little strained. "What are we really talking about?"

He smiled, looking a little uncertain. "I'm scaring you off, aren't I?"

I shook my head. "I'm not scared. I'm confused."

"About what?"

I turned so I could look him square in the eye. "About your intentions."

He looked at me for a moment, as if debating with himself. His beard shifted as the corner of his mouth tugged. "Well, that's no' good. A man should always be clear about his intentions."

"I agree."

"Okay," he said slowly. "I intend to win yer heart. And love you so well, no one else comes close."

My heart, hearing its name, pounded frantically in my chest. Under the surface, my feet paddled the water as I looked away from him, trying to compose my thoughts. I loved flirting with him. I loved the way he looked at me. But no one had ever dropped these sorts of words, not even after months of dating. We weren't flirting anymore, and I didn't know the lines to this play. My mouth opened and closed and opened again, trying to form words that felt completely foreign.

"Trevor, I—"

"It's okay," he cut me off. "I know you're not ready. I shouldn't have said anything. I should have waited."

"You should have kissed me first," I choked out.

"I should've." He tilted my chin up, his fingers warm against my skin. "Let's fix that, eh?"

CHAPTER 4

Teresa

18 MONTHS AGO

A kiss had never hit me like that before. The moment his lips touched mine, a barrage of tingly heat poured in, melting every part of me, liquifying all things solid. The room spun and my heart pounded like it was supplying blood for ten people. He tasted of rum and Coke, with a woodsy scent that pulled me into a cabin-in-the-mountains daydream. Lying down on a sheepskin rug in front of a fire, devoured by the lumberjack who was out to win my heart.

The kiss grew hungrier, and he grabbed my waist, pulling me closer. My fingers curled into his One Direction shirt, crunching Harry's face as I anchored myself against the storm stirring inside. My pulse settled lower, throbbing between my thighs. I squeezed them together, trying to control the overwhelming sensation. I couldn't. Trevor's tongue swept in to meet mine. Fire shot through me, and my body shivered with need. If he wanted to love me, I was here for it. At least for tonight. The bench didn't look that uncomfortable.

But as I ran my hand down his chest to his thigh, Trevor pulled away. "I need to chill." He blew a heavy breath.

"Why?" my horny brain demanded.

He took my face in his giant hands, sending confusing waves of warmth down my spine. "I've been thinking about ye constantly for weeks. I've dreamed about this, and our first time's no gonnae be at Crypto-Gavin's space station spa."

My eyebrows gathered into a frown. "What does it matter?"

He coughed, looking flushed. "I want this to be right."

"I don't mind the location," I insisted, smiling, trying to get him to smile. "We're both adults, Trevor. We can hook up. Unless you don't want to."

He took a breath, as if hitting the reset button, and adjusted the crotch of his jeans. "Let's play a game. Never have I ever..."

"Slept with anyone on the first date," I said. "But I'd break my rules for you."

"Appreciate it." His voice was throaty. "But this doesn't count as a date."

I could see the battle behind his eyes, and it excited me. "Why not?" I argued. "Drinks, a romantic walk, a bench make-out session—sounds like a date to me. And now we're going for a night swim."

"A what?"

"You heard me." A laugh bubbling in my tummy, I unzipped my dress, then peeled it down to my waist.

Trevor stared at me, his mouth ajar, eyes glossed over. I'd never felt so beautiful. I stood up by the edge of the pool and pulled the dress all the way to my ankles. I wanted to feel like a queen and not care, but my eyes instinctively scanned the room, checking the entrance we'd used. What if someone walked in? Gathering my courage, I unfastened my bra and dropped it into the same pile as the dress, then jumped in.

For a moment, I heard and saw nothing, completely enveloped by the warm water. My hair would be wet, and I'd have to reapply my makeup, but that was a small price to pay for this sense of freedom. I let my full lungs pull me up to the surface. My feet didn't touch the bottom, so I swam to turn around.

When I looked up, I saw Trevor standing by the pool in boxer shorts. I gasped at the sight of him. I knew he was a big guy, but seeing his thigh muscles flex, I could really appreciate how big. My gaze zeroed in between those thighs. Yep. Big.

His mouth stretched into a wicked smile, and I braced for impact. As his body hit the water, I dove under, approaching him from behind.

"Shit!" he yelled as I grabbed his shoulders. "Don't spook me like that!"

He spun around to face me, and we both swam in place, wiping our eyes. "Never have I ever gone swimming on the first date."

"Me neither," I said. "I don't think I've ever gone swimming with a… date."

"Good. This is not what I had in mind, but as long as it's memorable."

"Are you worried about not being memorable?" I had to laugh. Even without tonight, I would never be able to forget Trevor.

"I'm largely forgettable," he insisted. "Most of my old friends in Scotland have forgotten all about me."

"What about girlfriends?"

"They're all happily married by now," he said in a surly voice.

"Did you ever propose to anyone?"

"That's not how you play." He grinned. "Never have I ever…"

I rolled my eyes and splashed his face. "Never have I ever proposed to anyone."

He turned away from me. "And if I have…?"

"Then I get a point, right?"

"You get a point." His voice sounded heavy.

There was a story there, I thought, but I wasn't ready for it. I swam toward the shallow end, and he followed. When my feet reached the bottom, I stopped and let him catch up to me.

He stood in front of me, close enough to touch, water lapping against his chest. I couldn't stop staring at the dark, curly hair covering it. I was so much shorter that the water reached my neck, obscuring my body. A part of me wanted him to see me.

"Never have I ever kissed anyone in a pool," I said.

I wondered if it was true, or if I'd momentarily forgotten most of my life, singularly focused on this connection with him.

"Me neither," he replied.

"And you know anything that happens underwater doesn't count?"

"Is that the case?" He smirked, raising one eyebrow.

"Yes. The case is… watertight." I smiled, sliding my fingers under the waistband of his boxer shorts.

With our bodies hidden under the rippling water, it was so easy to misbehave. I pulled myself closer until I could feel his erection against my belly. His eyes were shiny, lips parted, and he wrapped his hands around my lower back, holding me against him. I felt his heavy breath on my forehead, his lips brushing my skin. I raised my chin to bring our mouths together. We molded together like clay, our tongues tripping over each other in a desperate frenzy. There was no hesitation in him or me. Only burning need.

Under the surface, my nipples grazed against his chest, sending sparkling desire down between my legs. The hard-on was growing between us, pushing us apart. I couldn't resist touching him. But as I trailed my fingers down his length, he gasped and released me. I stumbled backwards, as if carried away by an undertow.

"I'm sorry," he ground out, a little out of breath. "It's not safe… They'd have to drain the pool."

My face felt warm. "Really? We haven't even…"

He looked so torn my gut twisted. "You're the hottest woman I've ever met. I… I can't…" He dragged a hand down his face, letting out a groan.

Feeling flushed all over, I swam to the pool ladder as he pulled himself up to sitting on the edge. I couldn't wrap my mind around having this effect on anybody, let alone someone as sexy as Trevor. I wanted to get close to him—so close that he couldn't hold back.

I wondered who he'd proposed to. Considering he wasn't married and, to my knowledge, had never been married, he must have been turned down.

"Do you think they have towels here somewhere?" I asked.

He stood up without a word and walked around the pool to a door that probably led to the showers. I noticed he'd folded my dress next to his clothes on the bench, outside the splash zone.

After a moment, Trevor returned with a fluffy white bath towel. I climbed out of the pool, and he wrapped it around my shoulders. I made no move to cover myself, enjoying the way his gaze dipped to my bare chest. The cool air pinched my nipples into hard peaks, and I bit back my smile. "Fuck," he muttered, swallowing hard, and finally pulled the towel to cover me up.

Even if he didn't want to sleep with me here, I knew he wanted to sleep with me, and the anticipation made my limbs feel like jelly. We'd both been playing this game for weeks.

He walked me back to the bench, holding my shoulders in a way that sent trembles down my spine. We were finally touching. My work crush was turning into something real.

I dried up and after a while, I tried to offer him my towel.

"I'm happy to air dry," he claimed, sitting down next to me.

The glowing lanterns reflected off the droplets of water on my skin. I felt beautiful and desired, even if I was aware of my nudity. "We should probably get dressed in case anyone comes."

"Everyone's at the party and I nicked Gavin's key tag. Doubt it's the only one, but it should keep him from barging in."

My breath caught in my throat. "So, you know him?"

"We had drinks with a bunch of them last week." His voice had an ominous tone.

"Do you not like him or something?"

He frowned. "I have a bad feeling about him. I can't explain it. It's—"

"You think he'll be a cringe client?"

He shook his head. "Not the way you're thinking."

"Not an indecisive, condescending dick?"

He took a moment to consider. "Not indecisive," he said slowly.

I laughed, then swallowed. "I still want the job."

"Me, too," he admitted. "It's a good gig. But if I were a woman, I might steer clear of him."

"Why?"

"He's already rated all the ladies at our office."

"Rated, how?"

Trevor sighed, staring at his toes. "Face, ass, boobs."

"What, like separately? Face five out of ten, boobs seven?"

"Pretty much."

He wouldn't look me in the eye anymore. My gut twisted at his words, but I'd worked on the art concepts for two weeks, and I felt more than a little stubborn. We sat on the bench, closer to each other than before.

"Okay. I appreciate the heads-up," I said, securing the towel so it wouldn't slide down. "I'll carry mace to meetings and hide a spy camera between my five-out-of-ten boobs."

Trevor didn't laugh. "Ten out of ten," he finally said, staring at the pool.

"What? My boobs? Is Gavin into B-cups?"

"He hasn't seen them. I have."

Silence filled the air for a beat. "Thanks for the top rating," I eventually said, now feeling very naked under the towel.

He shook his head. "I don't like the way they talk about you. Or I mean... any woman."

"That's okay. You should hear how I talk about your gender with my sister. We can really trash it out."

"Fair enough." He smiled. "Are you close with your sister?"

"She's my best friend." I paused, wondering how much I should share. If he cared. "She moved to Colorado Springs two years ago, but we call or text every day. She gives me an update on family life, and I have to tell her one thing I did that day that wasn't work." I smiled to myself, thinking of our conversation before the party. Today had been easy. Some days I was scrambling, talking about my lunch.

"That sounds good. Healthy."

"We talk about other stuff, too. She did the whole marriage-and-kids thing. It's perfect for her, and she's really happy. I know she's worried I'll never get there, working the hours I do."

I felt him tense a little. "Do ye... want to get there?"

"I don't want to be alone for the rest of my life. I haven't thought any further than that."

"So, ye have no plan? No two-point-five children, a dog, and a house in the suburbs... near the good schools?"

I smiled. "No plan. Honestly, I don't see myself as a housewife. You build your whole life around a husband and a marriage with no backup. What if it doesn't work? He carries on with his career and you do... what? I mean, my sister found a good one, so maybe it'll work for her. But there are no guarantees."

"Life no' big on guarantees."

I kicked my foot, making the towel fall off my knee. "I guess not."

"People don't make those decisions rationally, either. They fall in love." His voice sounded wistful.

"Suze says I'm too independent to fall in love."

"You say it like it's a good thing."

I jerked back at the suggestion. "It *is* a good thing, isn't it? Kids are brought up to be independent. That's like the main goal, right?"

"Sure. But I think independence is overrated."

"Says he on Independence Day."

He smiled at my joke. There was no judgment in his eyes. They were open and searching. "We're a tribal species. Back in the caveman times, the worst punishment was being shunned by your tribe. It was a death sentence. And we're not that highly evolved these days. Maybe ye can technically survive on your own, but that's not how we thrive."

I thought about Suze. She relied on her husband for so many things. She didn't even know how to start the lawnmower.

"I guess you're right, but it's a huge risk, too. Every time you enter a co-dependent relationship of any kind, you're risking a lot of hurt."

"So, you never take a chance?"

I smiled, letting the odd, warm feeling gush through me. "I didn't say never."

We sat there for a long time, chatting. Most of it was innocuous and light, a stream of consciousness that would later fade from memory. But I knew I'd always remember the feeling of bathing in his undivided attention. I'd never felt so fascinating. I talked about my house-buying dream, about the suburbs I liked and the layouts I hated. I showed him my Pinterest board, featuring my absolute dream living room decor and other interior designs I couldn't afford but still drooled over. He asked why my username was DragonflyDreams and I told him I loved dragonflies.

At some point, Trevor pulled on his jeans and T-shirt, but I was oddly comfortable under my fluffy towel, in no hurry to squeeze back into my tiny black dress and heels. I told him that.

"You're adorable," he said, straddling the bench.

I turned my back to him, and he pulled me into his chest, kissing my neck. My body vibrated from his touch, the rough of his beard scratching against my skin. "I love these curls." He nuzzled his nose into my short, dark bob.

"I think they have more personality than I do."

At the start of the evening, my hair had been sleek and straight, but after the impromptu plunge, the ends were curling again. I'd have to go back to my usual messy style. I'd never been the adorable one. The word didn't seem to fit. It was something people said about my fairer sister. She was the embodiment of adorable. I was something between intimidating and sexy, depending on the day.

"Do you want to go somewhere?" he whispered into my ear. "I know I said we shouldn't do anything here, but it's becoming hard to control myself."

"*Hard*, you say?" I giggled. The way he pronounced the word, with the soft yet distinct Scottish 'r', was doing things to me.

"Very, *very* hard," he rasped.

I felt something solid against my lower back, and it sent a zing through me. I wanted so badly to sleep with him, but now I knew it meant something. It wouldn't be the grand finale of our weeks of flirting. It'd be the beginning of something, and the thought made my gut wobble.

"It's not my fault," he argued. "You're basically naked. You *stripped* in front of me."

"And I got wet," I teased.

He shifted a little closer with a low growl, that hard-on now fully evident, pulsing against me. "Fuck. What are ye doing to me? Where can I take you?"

"I have a roommate and she's having friends over. I couldn't... Is your place disgusting or something?"

He shook his head, scratching his beard on my neck. "No... but I just moved, so it's basically a pile of cardboard boxes."

I sighed. "Well, it's the only option. Unless you want to sneak into the office?"

He kissed my neck, sending thousands of tingles down my spine. "And do it on Rhonda's couch?"

I laughed, wondering how serious he was. I knew he had the key fob for after-hours access, but it was the worst idea. "Recording a surveillance camera sex tape sounds like a spectacular way to leave our jobs."

"You're right, aye." His voice rang with disappointment.

"Were you really considering that?" I laughed, enjoying the bubbly lightness in my belly.

He inhaled deeply and groaned, his hands around my waist, fingers digging into my hip through the towel. I imagined them underneath, slipping a little lower, and held my breath. Every part of me was agreeing now, my insides glowing like hot embers, waiting for him to stoke the fire.

"I was thinking a limo, a hotel room... the office is way down the list. I promised myself I wouldn't rush this. I don't want ye to think this is a hook-up. There's something here, Teresa—something I can't stop thinking about. You've been in my head for weeks, and now... now I can't think straight. Everything about ye..."

My back arched without any conscious thought, and I let my head drop against his shoulder. I may have moaned. His fingers brushed lower, teasing the edge of my underwear, frustratingly distant through the fabric, like a beautiful song muffled by a wall. I placed my hands on his, guiding them lower. The growl of frustration rising from his throat was my reward.

"Teresa," he rasped into my ear. "Not here. Not like this."

Yet he made no effort to extract himself. Instead, his fingers brushed small circles on my lower belly, reaching a little lower each time. My breath hitched, and I tilted my hips to meet his touch.

"Then you better make sure you don't accidentally slip under my towel." I lifted the edge of it so that his hand could slide in.

It did. He groaned into my ear like a man torn between his best intentions and desires, and I loved it. My underwear was still wet from the pool, sticking to my skin.

"I thought my panties would dry on me, but I don't think that's happening." I took his hand and inched it to the waistband.

"Oh, God. Teresa. You play dirty." He sounded breathless, his fingers holding still. Not advancing, not pulling away.

I loved having this effect on him. It was intoxicating, and I would have found a way for us to go on. I would have done something stupid and gloriously enjoyable if it weren't for the faint beep across the room.

Someone was at the door.

I sprung up from the bench, gathering my clothes, shoes, and clutch. "Where do I go?"

"Showers." He pointed at the door behind me, looking far more relaxed than I felt.

I ran. To my relief, I found a large bathroom with a lock on the door. I could get dressed and make myself as presentable as possible before re-entering. The hand dryer looked powerful enough to dry my hair.

After fifteen minutes and using every bit of makeup in my clutch, I was looking good enough. I could only pray nobody noticed my hair wasn't straight anymore. Guys hardly paid attention to that sort of things, I told myself, before stepping out of the bathroom and trailing past the showers and through a spacious changing room.

When I turned the knob on the door leading back to the pool, I heard laughter. Whoever had come in was still there. Multiple people. I recognized Trevor's baritone chortle in the mix. It was the most distinct laugh I'd ever heard. The infectious kind you couldn't help but join. He must have been with the other party goers.

I pushed open the door and approached them, hidden by a huge potted palm tree. I recognized Kyle, the guy who Trevor had led me away from and to his left, a dark man with an air of importance. It must have been Crypto-Gavin.

I almost announced myself, but something held me back. I had an opportunity. I was close enough to hear them without being seen. If Gavin really was as horrible as Trevor had made him sound, he'd reveal himself. This was my chance to gather evidence.

Gavin's voice rang with confidence. "This thing will skyrocket like you've never seen. First, we build up the platform, get the gamers hooked, trading tokens, winning big. Then we go fully decentralized and listed. It's going—"

"To the moon!" Kyle bellowed.

"No one makes a move until we're at hundred million market cap. We've got big backers on this—you have no idea. You're gonna look back at this moment and think, shit, that was the seed of my first million. Trust me, nothing beats that feeling." Gavin sounded both high and drunk, and like a giant douche.

"I'm happy to work on it," Trevor replied mildly.

"Charlie vouched for you, so you're in. But we still need a head designer."

My stomach turned into a ball of fire.

"Well, there's Boris and Teresa..." Trevor said, his voice careful.

My breath caught, heart pounding.

"The dark one? I bet she's a firecracker in bed! Girls like that don't hold back."

I barfed in my mouth a little but held still. Okay, Trevor was right. The guy was the worst. I'd pack my mace, but I'd also complete the most brilliant, career defining artwork.

"The whole team gets in on the initial token allocation," Kyle enthused. "They could be worth millions."

"They *will* be worth millions," Gavin announced. "We need the right guy on this, and Charlie thinks it's Boris. But we wanted to get your take on this. I don't know much about your kind of creativity, but I want to hit that magic zone. When the planets align, and we squeeze the pure essence of your sweet brain juice." He made a squeezing gesture with his hand, and I quietly gagged. It'd be challenging to keep a straight face around this guy.

Trevor's voice sounded strained. "I think Charlie's right—Teresa isn't the right fit. Boris has more experience with this sort of thing."

The fire in my stomach turned ice. I could barely hear anything else they said. Something about how excited everyone was and how they were going to make millions.

Trevor had sold me out.

That was it. My biggest dream, down the toilet.

Tears stinging behind my eyes, I stormed to the exit, leaning my whole weight on the green button that made the sliding door open. I heard Trevor's alarmed voice and footsteps, but I was faster—straight into the elevators. The door shut before he reached me, and the elevator plummeted towards the ground floor.

This was why I couldn't trust anyone. Not Trevor, not anyone. My independence wasn't just a choice—it was survival. And tonight, I'd been stupid enough to forget that.

CHAPTER 5

Trevor

Fed Teresa looked a lot more settled than hungry Teresa, and I congratulated myself for my foresight. Not that one car picnic solved our problems. I had a long way to go before she'd trust me again. Even longer before she'd give me another chance. But I'd get there.

I'd loved Teresa for eighteen months, ever since the night we'd spent by the quiet swimming pool in Crypto-Gavin's apartment building. Mostly talking, mind you. We'd been rudely interrupted just as things started heating up again, which was probably for the best. I'd been at the end of my tether, self-control-wise. Yet, she meant more to me than some random hookup, and I was glad we hadn't slept together in that weird spa, no matter how desperately I wanted her.

That night had changed everything for me. Before, she'd been my office crush. Someone I flirted with every day. Someone I thought about, constantly, imagining what it would be like to act on these desires, wondering if she saw me like that. If I was just a bit of fun or someone she could be with.

After that night, I knew she was my soulmate, who no longer spoke to me. I deserved it, too.

Later, I decided it had been a blessing in disguise. On that Fourth of July night, I hadn't been ready for us. I'd been lost and floating, gambling with my health and wasting my life. A directionless man who'd left his home country to get away but hadn't yet figured out what I wanted to get *to*. Fleeing had been more important.

As much as Teresa had hated me, I'd hated myself more. And I'd finally gotten myself in motion. Bit by bit, I'd changed my life. I'd fixed my health and was finally chasing dreams I'd been sitting on for years. Eighteen months on, I felt so much better that it almost made up for the fact that she'd written me off.

Almost. Because I couldn't move on. We still worked together and chatted every day. Even when I didn't see her in person, Teresa was always there. The living, breathing, gorgeous reminder of what I'd lost.

When the highway withered into a smaller, winding road and the last remnants of suburbia turned into forest, her posture tensed. "Do you have any music?"

"Maybe on the radio?" I suggested, turning it on.

A mattress ad with an irritating jingle filled the silence between us. Teresa killed the volume. "I'll just connect my Spotify to your car stereo."

I let her work it out as I drove, wondering why I'd never thought of doing that. I listened to the ads and accepted them for what they were—one of life's little uncontrollable annoyances.

"I've been working on something," I confessed. "Many things, to be honest."

I only had this little trip and limited time with her, sharing the same space. Things between us probably couldn't get any worse, so I might as well go for broke. But it was surprisingly hard to put any of this into words. I was a copywriter. If I couldn't put things into words, what the hell was I good for?

Teresa turned up the volume, and a melancholic guitar created an instant mood—not one I'd expected. Wistful. "Working on what?" she asked.

"On myself," I said, gripping the steering wheel. "I wasn't happy with a few things, so I've been making changes."

Her eyebrows traveled up. "Like what?"

"I quit smoking."

She chuckled softly.

"I'm not joking." I huffed a frustrated sigh.

Me quitting smoking had been a running office joke for a long time. Nobody had noticed when I'd quit for real. I guess they had all assumed it would never happen.

Teresa's smile faded. "For real? You?"

"You quit months ago, right?"

"Almost eighteen months now." She sounded a little hurt.

Of course. It had happened right after that night.

"So, why is it so unbelievable?" I asked. "I've been smoke free for nine months."

Her eyebrows furrowed. "But... you go out for a smoke. On Fridays. I know it's been a while since we shared the office, but it hasn't been nine months."

I nodded. I'd been trying to mentally prepare for this, but I still didn't know how she would take it. "I replaced one activity with another."

Her eyes were huge. "So, what do you do? Crossword puzzles in the rain?"

I swallowed. "I knit."

I smiled at her shocked expression, watching the disbelief slowly morph into sparkling amusement. "You knit? Like... socks?"

"I'm not that confident with the heel yet, so it's been mostly scarves."

She blinked a couple of times, then sucked in her lips as if to stop grinning. "Okay. I was thinking your skin looked healthier, but I didn't connect the dots."

I rolled my eyes. "You're allowed to laugh."

She didn't. Instead, she looked genuinely impressed. "Why would I laugh? I mean, I'm dying to see you work those needles. I hope you brought them... but honestly, I think that's amazing. I never thought you'd get there."

I smiled back but couldn't help the heavy sigh. "Never say never, right?"

CHAPTER 6

Teresa

I shifted a little closer and inhaled deeply, to confirm what I'd noticed earlier. Trevor smelled different, and I was here for it.

"Check behind your seat." He nodded behind him.

I pulled out a striped shopping bag with needles sticking out of it. "Bamboo needles? Man. This is next level."

"They're less noisy." He grinned.

"So, you could knit in secret when we all thought you were having a smoke outside?" I stared at him, trying to rewrite those memories.

"I suppose."

"I thought you might switch to vaping or something."

He shook his head. "I've given Big Tobacco enough of my hard-earned quid."

I pulled out a long purple scarf and wrapped it around my neck. "This thing is nearly finished, right?"

"Looks like it." He gave me an assessing glance. "Suits you."

"I love the color." It was my favorite shade of purple—deep and royal. I was currently wearing a sweater in the exact same shade.

The scarf smelled like him. A mix of cologne and something more organic, like salt and wood. It must have been made of pure pheromones, since my body reacted by the delicious sensation of flow—blood rushing up and down, every cell alive and tuned in. I buried my nose in the wool, breathing in the feeling. It intensified, funneling between my thighs.

How easy it would be to come, inhaling him.

The thought smacked me in the ribs, and I leaned away from the source of that scent. I had no business lusting after him. Not because I hated him. I'd forgiven him, for my own sake. I was a busy woman—I had no energy to hold grudges or hate a guy I had to work with. But he'd shown me who he really was. That was core stuff, and it never changed, right? We could be friends, but that was the extent of it.

He'd apologized later, claiming he did it to protect me. I would have hated that job. I would have hated that client. He had so many excuses, but nothing could change reality. He'd known how much that gig meant to me, and he'd killed my dream.

Trevor was the easy-going guy who got along with everyone. The guy who always sided with his superiors and never rocked the boat. So, of course, he'd gone along with Charlie. By sticking his neck out for the woman whose boobs the client had rated, he would have risked losing their respect. And anyone who craved the respect of such douchewads was a spineless coward.

I needed someone in my corner who truly had my back. Maybe I needed a guy who was a bit of a caveman. I probably should have figured that out before the whole dating-Richard fiasco because he was as far from a caveman as one could be, other than maybe in the sense of spreading his seed around town—now that I knew what he was really up to.

No. Richard was more likely to offer helpful statistics and inspirational quotes than defend me. "There are two sides to every coin," he'd say. When someone had stolen my bicycle, he'd berated me for not investing in a high-quality lock and eventually argued that the thief might have been in great need. We simply didn't know all the facts, and he was obsessed with gathering information and looking at it from every angle like he was shooting for an 'A' with a college essay.

I should have run.

I shook my head as if to rid myself of the unwelcome thoughts. There was no point in dwelling in that chapter. All I wanted to do was close it and move on.

I removed the scarf and folded it back into the bag. "Very impressive."

"Do you knit?" he asked.

"Not well. I never had the patience for crafts."

"But you have the patience of a saint when it comes to creating graphics."

I shrugged. "I like having the Z key. It's hard to go from that to creating in the physical world. Every time I try drawing or painting, my left hand does that involuntary Apple-Zed twitch."

He laughed. "Undo. Undo. I get that."

"It's terrifying when you can't undo!" I exclaimed, laughing along.

"You like keeping your options open, eh?"

His voice held a deep vibration that delivered more meaning than I could handle. I bristled a little but smiled. "How else can I find what works the best? I have to try lots of options. If you commit to anything too early, you might get stuck."

"Is getting stuck the worst thing you can imagine?"

I bit my lip. I sensed he wasn't talking about work, but I was not ready for this. My throat felt tight. "Who the hell enjoys being stuck?"

He gave a slow nod, keeping his eyes on the road. The lighting had turned moody, with tall trees shadowing the winding road from both sides. I felt each curve in my belly, like on a roller coaster.

"Are you saying I have commitment issues?" I asked, fixing my eyes on the road.

"No, but it sounds like I touched on something." He flashed me a quick smile. "I didn't mean it like that. If it helps, I'm way more messed up. My therapist would back me up on this if he didn't have that confidentiality thing."

"You're seeing a therapist?"

"Aye." He took a deep breath, his shoulders tensing in a way that made my whole body tighten. "Ever since... what happened wi' us, you know, I've been aware that I need to change. So, I've been working on that. And I wanted to thank you."

"For what?"

"For showing me I was on the wrong path. I could have followed it to my grave and never taken charge of my own life."

"Are you talking about smoking, or..."

"I'm talking 'bout everything. And I know I don't have a lot of time with ye, so I want to get it oot."

I frowned. "You already apologized. I forgave you. There's no need to rehash it."

"You wrote me off, Teresa. I'll regret that night for the rest of my life."

"That's a bit dramatic." I tried to smile, but the joke fell flat.

"I mean it."

Something stirred in my chest, and I tried to breathe through it. I couldn't open that door. That night had been pivotal in my life, but I'd never thought it meant that much to him. "I get you wanted to quit smoking, that's great. But what do you have to regret? You got the job and the payout. You're set for life."

"I took the easy way out." His voice cut through my thoughts and every layer of clothing. "I had this ill feeling about ye working with Gavin... I told you that, right?"

I nodded.

"But I knew how much it meant to you. Ye told me," he continued.

"Yeah," I admitted.

"I did what was easy. I did what served me. It wasn't fair to you. I thought I was protecting you, but I could have protected you by being there *with* you."

I forgot to breathe and my mouth dried as I stared at him, my heart in my throat. I'd never expected him to say those words. I hadn't even known I *needed* to hear them until now.

His fist squeezed the steering wheel, skin tightening over white knuckles. "In the end, I was a coward, going with the flow because it suited me, and I did it behind your back. You didn't deserve that."

I finally resumed breathing, trying to process his words. I noticed we were both out of breath, panting like we'd just sprinted a hundred yards.

"Wow," I finally said. "I don't know what to say."

Deep down, I'd thought I deserved it. That there was something wrong with me. I was a bit too much. Intimidating. Not fun to work with. Trevor might have been attracted to me, at least back then, but I'd genuinely believed he didn't want to work with me.

"Don't say anything. It's me who needed to say something. You didn't do anything wrong."

My throat felt like I'd swallowed Trevor's woolly scarf. "Maybe, but I know I'm not... likable. I don't know how to play the game. Or maybe I do, in theory. But I don't want to because it feels inauthentic. You have to fake so much. It's exhausting."

He lifted a shoulder. "It's part of the job, aye? Ye know how it is. We massage the truth until it takes a new shape and form.

This incredibly attractive—"

"Lie."

"Sometimes. But I get so swept up in the work that truth becomes almost meaningless. It's never about the product. It's about crafting that emotional response. That takes skill."

I nodded, recognizing the feeling. "It's an addictive game. It's weird that we can put all this effort into selling an organic cola that tastes like dishwater and somehow that doesn't bother me. I mean, it's irritating, but nothing compared to people being fake or two-faced. That gets me every time."

"No wonder you hate me, then." He let out a sad laugh.

"I don't hate you," I insisted. "I told you, we're good."

It had been more than a year. None of this was fresh, and I didn't particularly want to dwell on it.

"Dragonfly. That night at the pool, we weren't just 'good'. We were on fire."

He left the sentence hanging in the air, and I didn't know how to respond. I still thought about that night sometimes. A memory would surface, out of nowhere, of something he'd said, or I'd told him. We'd been so vulnerable. So naked.

"You know we can't go back to that, right?" I said. "I appreciate your apology and it's amazing you're making positive changes... But we can't be like that ever again."

He huffed. "You sound like my therapist."

"You talk about me in therapy?" I wasn't sure how I felt about that.

"It's all confidential. He says something else, though."

"What?"

"That even if you can't get back what you lost, ye can build something new."

The town sign of Cozy Creek caught my eye, and I pulled in a sharp breath. I wasn't ready for this.

"And, who knows," Trevor went on, smile on his lips, "Maybe some small-town magic will melt yer icy heart and you'll find room in it for one reformed Scot with healthy lungs?"

He slowed down, turning onto Cozy Creek Main Street. Snow had started to fall, turning the already cute-as-a-button street into a children's storybook illustration, complete with snow-capped mountains.

I blew a measured breath, taking it all in. The cafes, Bookers bar, the beautiful old library building. Copious amounts of pink hearts hung from the lampposts, reminding me of what day it was. My heart, not icy at all, squeezed in my chest.

"Come on. I know you're not a Hallmark movie character, but you must admit this is fair lovely!" He pulled over, parking in front of a bookstore with pink paper hearts hanging across its window.

I swallowed. "If your plan was to use small-town adorableness to win me over, you should have chosen another small town. Literally any other town."

He blinked at me. "Why?"

"Because I grew up here."

CHAPTER 7

Trevor

Teresa's words felt like a blast of cold water. How did I not know this about her? Countless details I'd carefully curated about her flashed through my mind as I searched for a clue.

"Are you sure?" I finally asked, like a true moron.

I fully earned the eye roll she gave me. "No, Trevor. I'm not entirely sure where I grew up. Maybe it was another cute, backward-ass town in the Rockies called Cozy Creek."

She glanced at the row of pretty lampposts with their pink decorations. I'd killed the engine, but neither of us was making a move to get out of the car.

"I thought you were born in Colorado Springs," I said.

"I was. Mom moved me and my little sister here after my dad left. I was thirteen. She was worried about the big city influences and thought the wholesome, small-town environment would stop me from turning into a hard-to-handle teenager."

"Did it?"

She laughed, but it wasn't a mean laugh. A little sad, maybe. "It's the magic fix. Instantly balances teenage hormones." She nibbled at her lip, her jaw tense.

"Have you been back?"

"Only when I found out I was getting fired from Wilde and I drove here to pick up Bess." She looked down at her fingers, blushing. "And scream at Charlie."

"If it helps, I've wanted to scream at him many times."

"He's like your best friend."

"I love him like a brother, but the man can be a right eejit... I mean an idiot."

"Anyone can."

I grabbed the door handle, trying to adjust my expectations. The pretty-as-a-picture small town was Teresa's old hometown. What I associated with my future, she associated with her past. And if her formative years had been anything like mine, the memories were a mixed bag. Judging by the stiffness in her shoulders, maybe even worse.

Ye heart wants whit it wants.

It was one of those infuriating, tautological statements my dad overused, but it was true. I couldn't turn off my feelings for her. I had to go on hoping and trying to win her back. And if I had to, I'd do it all on my own, without any small-town magic.

I flung open the door and launched myself out onto the sidewalk, then circled the car to help Teresa out. Not that she accepted my help. She downright fought it, but somehow, we both ended up in front of the right door at the right time.

Annalise Higgins, the realtor I knew from earlier, appeared from behind it, opening the paneled blue door with a huge smile and a flourish. She was in her fifties, wearing a pink pant suit, her carefully coiffed dark hair perfectly matching the Valentine's Day decorations and the 'we-go-all-out' vibe of the town.

"Hi Trevor! Great to see you again. Welcome, welcome!"

I introduced Teresa, and we followed Annalise up a narrow, squeaky staircase. At the top, she opened another door and led us into an unfurnished office space overlooking Main Street.

Three old-fashioned cable poles pierced the open floor, supplying power and internet connections to where the workstations had been. There was nothing to see, per se. The couple of windows were the pretty, paneled kind, casting a pattern of filtered daylight across the floor. The walls were white and blank, punctuated by two doors leading to other rooms. It was a perfectly functional space, and many times larger than what we had right now. And it cost about the same.

I could tell Teresa had noticed the size. She circled the room as if measuring it with her steps, her head tilted.

"I like the natural light," I said, to appease Annalise. "Is there an ethernet connection?"

She fussed about showing me a little cupboard with wires sticking out of the wall inside it. "Right here. All good to go. The previous tenant ran a call center. They never had any issues."

"Why did they move?" Teresa asked.

She cleared her throat. "The business... um, closed down."

Teresa cast me a meaningful look, and I acknowledged her with a brief nod. Businesses went under every day. It happened in big cities and small towns alike.

"Let me show you the kitchen!" Annalise powered on, opening another door. "It's quite cozy, but there's space for a coffee maker and a microwave here. And you could fit a small table by the window."

We followed her to the end of the narrow space, where you could just about fit a bistro-style table and two chairs.

"We can always take turns eating lunch," Teresa muttered, pointedly backing out as if there wasn't enough space to attempt a one-hundred-eighty-degree turn.

"Like we take turns right now to use our current office?" I shot back with a grin.

Annalise's professional smile never wavered. "There's also a small storage space, but that's about the size of it."

"Could you leave us here for a bit to talk shop?" I asked her. "I have a few things to discuss with my colleague."

"Sure thing!" She beamed, handing me the key. "I have some business down the street. I can collect this later. Just give me a call."

"Thank you so much."

She wiggled her fingers at us and wobbled away on her pink heels.

Teresa had settled by the window, leaning her forehead

against the glass, staring outside. I shifted a little closer, trying to read her mood. "Okay. I know this isn't what you had in mind for Valentine's Day."

She jerked back, as if thrown by my sudden appearance. "I told you we had a dinner reservation at this small Italian place. My favorite restaurant. I was going to have the creamy mushroom risotto." Her voice was dreamy, yet depleted.

"And soufflé," I added, not very helpfully.

Her voice echoed off the blank walls. She sounded sad. "He never canceled on me. He would have gone out with her for lunch, then met me for dinner." She pushed away from the window and shuddered. "Who does that?"

"Dicks who like to keep their options open."

Her mouth twisted, lips pink and plump from all the biting. I wanted to soothe them with mine. I wanted to make it all better. If I could climb over this wall between us.

"Does it look the same?" I asked, gesturing at the view behind the window.

"By and large. A lot prettier in some ways. Everything looks freshly painted and I can't remember there being this many decorations, ever."

"I was here around Christmas time and the whole place was lit up and bursting with tinsel. Their holiday budgets have probably gone up with all the tourism," I said.

"It doesn't have that dwindling feel anymore. So many small towns have that sadness about them, like everyone's just bracing for the next person or business to pack up and leave."

I took a tiny step forward. "I honestly think our business could thrive here. We'd need to work remotely with some clients, but there are also some we could tap locally. There's a real sense of community and people want to work with local businesses. They only have a couple of freelancers offering design and marketing, but no companies. Ye wouldn't have to fight over every job."

She nodded slowly, her gaze still at the window. "If it was any other town…" The sentence trailed off, and I tried to give her space, staying quiet.

"Yeah, I get that," I finally replied. "But you've changed. The town has changed. Maybe it won't be the same."

"Let's go get coffee!" She threw out her arms and smiled, a little forcefully, like she was shifting gears without a clutch. "My brain needs a strong cup of something."

"Sweet," I said, following her to the door. "Cozy Creek Confectionery?"

Her head whipped around. "Is that still here?"

"Sure is. Bad coffee, great baking."

"Perfect. I want a coffee that slaps me in the face and calls me names. And something insanely sweet to wash it down with."

Her smile was quick. Too quick. Like she was plastering it on to cover the hurt. I wasn't about to push her, though. Not when she was barely holding it together.

CHAPTER 8

Teresa

The Cozy Creek Confectionery looked exactly as cute as I remembered, but also fresh and trendy. The place must have been renovated many times since my youth. The tall, paneled windows gave it a gingerbread house charm my mother once thought was the answer to her prayers. Nothing bad could happen in Cozy Creek.

The bell above the door jingled as we stepped inside. The smell of fresh baking was so intoxicating I felt like I was absorbing calories through my lungs. I wanted to live in this room. For the first time, I saw it through Mom's eyes. She'd been through a divorce, with two kids in tow—one of them a moody teenager. Cozy Creek must have felt like the safe haven she'd been looking for.

A pretty woman in a pink apron smiled at us from behind the counter. "What can I get you?"

Trevor ordered us coffees and pointed at a tray of heart-shaped pink cookies in the cabinet. I nodded my approval. They did look sickly sweet, which would help if the coffee really was as bad as he claimed. I had no memory of it since I'd only picked up a coffee habit in college.

The cafe was packed with a mix of pensioners and high school kids, along with a couple of tourists on winter break. You could always spot them from their expensive snow gear and the fact that they photographed everything they ate.

Each table had a vase of pink roses. Pink hearts and garlands hung on the window. Valentine's Day had obviously thrown up all over this town. I remembered Cozy Creek having a slight obsession with festivals and decorations, but this was next level—like a movie set.

"In my defense," Trevor said, taking a sip of coffee and grimacing. "At Christmas, the color scheme was a bit less obnoxious."

"What's wrong with pink?" I asked, grinning at him as I took a bite of my cookie. It helped with the motor oil of a coffee blend.

He emptied three creamers into his coffee and stirred. "Ach, I'm ashamed to admit I tend to forget about Valentine's Day. It's not exactly a big deal when you've no one to buy chocolates for. And it's not like Denver will paint the whole town pink for it."

I looked at the paper hearts currently obscuring my view through the window. "Yeah, this is something else."

His eyes twinkled with mischief, mouth tugging into a smile.

"So, when I said I was going to win yer heart and smack you in the face with small-town magic—"

"That's not what you said."

"I'm sorry, lass. When I said I was going to transport you into a Hallmark movie and turn into an irresistible lumberjack. Flannel from head to toe. Flannel underwear and—"

"Not even close." I laughed so hard my eyes watered.

"Well, whatever I said I was going to do, I had no idea I'd be taking you into this theme park of commercialized romance. I swear this was not part of the plan! I've just been looking at office spaces and then this one popped up. I had a quick chat with Charlie and since they're out of town, he asked if I could take a wee look." He blushed, which made me smile.

"What?" I looked at him in mock horror. "Are you saying you haven't been crocheting pink hearts for weeks on end in preparation?"

I liked seeing him a little flustered. He wasn't playing it cool. I was so used to seeing Trevor with his unflappable smile and that nothing-can-get-to-him attitude. Here, he was different. A little on edge, like all of this meant something. Almost like he was worried.

That made no sense. We were friends, or at least friendly colleagues. We messaged daily. We joked and chatted and argued and never got mushy about... feelings. We never talked like he'd talked to me in the car.

I thought I'd been the only one grieving what I'd lost that night: my respect for him. Our connection. I'd lost my bonus reason to go to work—the spark that kept me going. The months after that had been dreary and hard, even though it was summer. I'd focused on my house hunting and had eventually bought my condo. Miraculously, really. And then I'd lost my job.

A thought hit me.

"Did you know about the restructuring at Wilde? Did you know before everyone else?"

Trevor's eyes widened, and he froze for a second, staring at me. "Ye mean, before the first email?"

"You know what I mean."

He looked me straight in the eye, his voice steady. "I knew the production team was on the chopping block. I knew Charlie was trying to fix things. I didn't know they'd fire you."

"I bought my condo that week. No one warned me."

"I'm sorry. I didn't know about your job, I swear. But I also didn't know you were buying a place. Ye weren't talking to me much around that time."

I'd always thought Trevor had been part of it, keeping secrets with Charlie. But maybe he hadn't. It was true I'd been actively avoiding him back then.

"When I found out they were firing you, I went to George and told him he was making a huge mistake."

"You did?"

"I did. Ask him, he'll tell you how he gave me a twenty-minute lecture on being a bleeding-heart softie, just like his son."

I bristled. "I'll take your word for it."

"Because you don't want to contact George?" he guessed,

grinning.

I nodded. Nothing could make me voluntarily approach my psychopathic ex-boss.

"Great! Then I also punched him in the throat for you." His eyes sparkled with mischief.

"No, you didn't."

"No, I didn't," he admitted. "But I thought about it. Vividly. I thought about the sound his windpipe would make as it crushed under my knuckles, and he let out a choked whine—"

"Thanks, poet. Have you ever actually punched anyone?"

"The boxing sack at the gym," he confessed, shrugging. "I'm more of a hit-them-wi-ma-words kind o' guy."

I could easily imagine him at the gym. Nobody's shoulders got that wide by holding a pen. But I couldn't imagine him in a fight. Who would even fight him? Trevor was too likable. Too ac-commodating. I could barely imagine him raising an issue with George. If he'd really stuck his neck out for me... what did that mean?

"I appreciate you talking to George. But right now, I'm glad it didn't work. I'm glad I don't work there anymore."

"Me, too."

I finished my cookie, and my gaze drifted back to the cabinet. So much fresh baking.

"I think I'll buy some to take home. Can I have the keys? I left my wallet in the car." I rummaged through my purse, coming up with nothing.

I'd been charging my phone on the drive, and since my cards

were all held in the phone case, I'd come to the cafe with nothing to pay with. But Trevor had been so quick to order and pay, I hadn't even noticed.

"What do ye want? I'll pay for it." Trevor shot up, but I motioned him back down.

"Seriously, the car is down the road, it'll take a minute."

I should have added a dramatic "what could go wrong?", because in the next five minutes, everything did.

I took Trevor's car keys and skipped out of the cafe, hurrying down the road as if to prove to him this little trip would take no time at all. The temperature was just above freezing, and I didn't account for the slick ice hiding underneath the freshly fallen snow. I also didn't account for my Italian shoes with their smooth soles sending me flying. I lost my balance, my hands flailing until they found an anchor—an iron lamppost covered in pink hearts.

As my hands gripped the iron pole, the car key became airborne, and I watched in horror as it landed on top of a storm drain. The slats were wide enough for it to go through, but so far, the key was sideways, sitting safely on top of the grid.

I inched closer, reaching to pick it up as carefully as I could. I didn't see the dog before its nose touched my bottom, and I fell forward, slamming my knees on the ground and palms against the iron grate, unwittingly launching the car key into the town sewage system.

"I'm sorry, he's not usually this excited," a friendly voice behind me said.

I turned and saw a woman my age with a round face and a friendly smile, tugging at the leash of an excitable border collie. "Harry! Heel!"

Harry? The dog's name was Harry? Where had I heard that before?

My mind shot into a million directions, chasing its tail. I'd just permanently lost Trevor's car key, and the woman whose dog kept nuzzling my bottom looked oddly familiar.

Her gaze caught mine, and she beamed. "Teresa! Oh, my God! Now I understand why he's going nuts. Harry was a puppy last time you met, but he must remember you."

I smiled back, a little startled. "Peony!"

I stood up, and she hugged me. She'd always been a hugger. Even when we'd seen each other daily, she'd always hugged me goodbye. We'd spent countless hours in the garden room behind her family home, dreaming about the life we'd live when we finally escaped Cozy Creek and went to college. And she was... here?

"You... live here?" I stammered. "And Harry... It's been fourteen years."

"He's a senior, but still going strong." Peony scratched the dog's ear. "What brings you back? Where have you been? I tried to look you up on Facebook once or twice, but—" She smiled apologetically.

"It's okay. I'm not on Facebook. And I really needed to get away."

"Yeah, I get that."

"I'm sorry I didn't stay in touch. It was easier that way."

She nodded, and I fought back tears. I wasn't ready for this. I didn't want to relive any of it.

"The cafe is closing." Trevor's voice made me jump, and my stomach wound itself into a tighter knot.

There he was, standing behind me, smiling, not knowing what I'd done.

"Hi! Sorry, Trevor. I bumped into a friend from high school. This is Peony."

Trevor smiled and introduced himself, and Peony pulled him into a hug. I waited for them to finish the pleasantries, the bad news burning a hole in my throat.

"I dropped your car keys!" I blurted as soon as there was a lull.

"Dropped them?" Confused, Trevor looked at the ground, until his eyes found the storm drain. "Do you mean..."

I nodded, my throat so dry I couldn't even speak anymore.

Peony's hands flew to her mouth. "Oh, my God! Did that just happen when Harry gave you a shove? I was trying to hold onto his leash. He's never that excited anymore, but I guess he recognized an old friend and summoned all his energy. Oh, no!"

She looked as white as a sheet. I probably looked the same. Trevor stared at his car, a couple of yards away, his mouth open as if he was still processing the news. Finally, he pulled a phone from his pocket. "Okay. What can we work with? I have a phone, a wallet, and the keys to the office. What do you have?"

I swallowed, opening my purse. "My phone and cards are in the car, so... nothing."

I browsed my measly belongings: makeup, a used tissue, home keys, several receipts, half a packet of mints and an antacid. What a great survival pack.

"I'm so sorry." I looked at Trevor, then his car, which I now realized was my only way out of Cozy Creek. "Do you have another key?"

"Aye. In Denver."

Of course. Who walked around with two car keys?

"Can we call someone? A locksmith?"

"They won't be able to do anything. It's not like those old cars you could wiggle your way into with a bit of wire. They'll tow it to the dealership. It'll cost a fortune."

"I'll pay," I said, my voice wobbly.

"Nae. That's silly. I'll have someone fetch the spare key and drive here. Maybe Charlie. He has a key to my place for emergencies."

"But they're not even in town!" I cried.

"They'll be back this weekend."

"I feel like this is my fault," Peony piped up, her smile so pained she looked like she was about to cry. "How can I help? What can I do? Do you need a place to stay? I know the town is fully booked on Valentine's."

Trevor's eyes flashed with alarm. "I don't. But Teresa might."

"Great!" Peony smiled, twisting the dog leash around her fingers. "My place is a bit crowded... three kids and the dog... but my couch is yours if you want it!"

"Thank you," I stammered. "Three kids? You've been busy!"

"A set of twins!" She smiled, her eyes sparkling. "I actually need to head home to make dinner, but I'll give you my number…" She pulled out her phone, then halted and turned to Trevor. "I guess I'll give it to you if her phone is in the car?"

Trevor took her number before we waved goodbye.

"Even if you decide not to stay on my food-stained couch, please message me! I'll take you out to Bookers for drinks and reminiscing! Promise me we'll do something. I need to get out of the house!" She laughed breathlessly.

"Let's!" I promised, and she powered down the street, dragging her dog.

Harry had done his sniffing and lost interest in me, moving so slowly I could tell his age. Back then, he'd been an excitable puppy we'd named after Harry Styles, of course. I'd been away for fourteen years, and so much had happened. I couldn't believe my old friend had three children. She'd always been the maternal type, but still.

I turned to Trevor. "What did you mean you don't need a place to stay?"

He gave me a sheepish smile. "I bought a little cabin a while back. And I have the keys in my pocket."

"You have a place in Cozy Creek?" I stared at him in utter confusion.

Why hadn't I heard of this? News of this magnitude tended to travel.

"I bought it on the down low," he added, jingling the keys in his pocket. "It still needs work, but it's livable.

I narrowed my eyes. "And only accommodates one person?"

"What? No. It's... under construction."

"It must be pretty bad if you think I'm better off fighting over a couch with a giant border collie, breaking crayons every time I turn."

He scratched his beard, looking flustered. "I thought you wouldn't want to share a house with me since ye didn't want to come here in the first place."

"I didn't," I admitted.

I kept my gaze on my shoes, trying to calm the brewing storm in my chest.

Part of me wanted to reconnect with Peony, but I knew I'd have to ease into it—start with a couple of beers and a chat, not by crashing on her couch, surrounded by her family. Relying on Trevor didn't feel right either, especially since he didn't seem thrilled about inviting me to his cabin. So where did that leave me? Where could I go?

"The office! It's unoccupied. I can sleep there." I held out my hand. "Keys, please."

"I don't know if it's safe to give ye any more keys."

"It wasn't my fault. The dog pushed me," I said defensively.

It probably *was* my fault I kept buying shoes designed for a gentle Mediterranean climate, but that was beside the point.

He gave me a lopsided grin. "I'll let the realtor know that we'll go back tomorrow morning for one last check or something. Maybe she'll let us keep the keys overnight."

He stepped away to make the call, and I leaned on the car,

emptying my lungs. This day couldn't get any worse, right? We'd reached the pinnacle of awful now, and it had to be plain sailing from here.

Tomorrow, I could try to convince Trevor to contact someone other than Charlie to pick up his spare key and bring it over. If they had to break into his apartment to do that, I'd cover the cost. That way, I didn't have to sleep on the floor for more than one night. One night I could handle.

Trevor returned with a smile. "It's all sorted. Do ye need some money for dinner? Then I'll leave you alone."

He put the office key into my hand, curling my fingers around it. He stood so close, leaning in, that I could smell him. Sometimes, those pheromones were real pesky bitches, stirring trouble. What had Richard smelled like? I couldn't remember feeling like this with him. I couldn't remember feeling like this for such a long time I had blissfully forgotten this rush. Why did I have to be this susceptible?

I tried to swallow down my discomfort. "Some dinner money would be great."

"I'd take you oot to dinner, but I doubt we'd get a table with such short notice on Valentine's Day."

"You're right! We'll have to buy something from the general store."

He looked defeated, handing me a credit card. "Here you go. Get yourself something to eat."

I stared at the card, a hollow feeling spreading through me. As much as I wanted to be independent and look after myself, staying the night in an empty office building made me feel uneasy. And when I thought about him leaving me here, by myself…

My voice wobbled with need. "You're not going shopping? We could go together."

CHAPTER 9

Trevor

It sucked to lose my car keys, but I chose to see it as an opportunity. I'd always been a glass-nearly-full kind of guy, and this seemed like divine intervention.

It just as easily could have happened to me. I occasionally dropped things, although I didn't wear shoes that resembled slip-and-slides. I'd seen the way she walked, carefully balancing on the uneven, icy surface. But I could have lost the car keys without her help, and she might have thought I'd done it on purpose.

So, I quietly thanked the universe for letting her lose them. Now I didn't have to worry about what she thought of my plans. I didn't even have plans beyond checking out the office. I hadn't planned to keep her here overnight, let alone several nights. And

I definitely hadn't planned to show her the cabin.

I'd put a lot of effort into renovating it, and I'd been planning to one day introduce it to her. But I'd done something stupid. Something I needed to rectify before she set foot in that house. Which meant it couldn't happen on this trip.

But I also didn't want her to sleep on a couch with three children and a dog or lie alone in an empty office space. There were no good options.

"Let's have a wee look at those two first," I said, pointing at a couple of restaurant signs down the street. "You never know. Maybe a couple broke up and canceled their reservation."

Her anxious expression melted into a smile. "You mean, like one of them was found cheating earlier today and their plans fell through?" She twisted her mouth.

"Exactly! Or maybe someone died," I added on a more hopeful note.

She laughed. "You're such an optimist."

I loved seeing her relax. Maybe she really wanted to hang out with me. At least she preferred me over an empty office. How could I get us that restaurant table? We were here, in the most romantic town imaginable, on the most romantic night of the year. Such opportunities should never be wasted.

We walked down Main Street to the Italian restaurant and were waved away from the door. Down the street, I recognized the next place, Bookers. The line was so long several people stood waiting outside. The delicious smell of cooking drifted through the open door, along with music. It was so inviting, but

I could tell there'd be a long wait.

We kept walking, first around the town square, then down various side streets. Everything was fully booked. When we returned to Main Street, the sky was already deep blue, almost black. One glance at Teresa told me she was tired, cold, and hungry.

"Sorry," I said. "It turns out I'm not an optimist, but a daft fool."

"It's okay."

"Let's go find the general store, eh?"

"It's a couple of blocks that way," she said.

As we walked down the road, back towards my car, my phone beeped. Charlie. He'd gotten my message and promised to sort things out as soon as they got back home. Two nights in this town, with a woman who didn't want to be here. It was either an opportunity to finally reconcile, or destroy whatever goodwill was left between us.

"If we find somethin' edible from the store, we can take it to the office to eat there," I suggested as we reached my car.

Her lips quirked. "You mean, like a Valentine's Day dinner on the floor?"

The streetlights took that moment to flicker on, reminding me of the importance of lighting.

"Sure!" I grinned. "If that wee gift shop is still open, I'll buy a candle and we'll camp like two hobos in love."

The gift shop I'd spotted right underneath the office was indeed still open, and as we reached it, I wandered in. Teresa remained on the sidewalk, until I returned to the door and held it open for her. "Milady."

She stepped over the threshold gingerly, scanning the shop like she was expecting a jump scare.

"Teresa? Is that you?" A gray-haired woman in her sixties appeared from behind a tall shelf, carrying a giant bouquet of flowers. "It *is* you, isn't it?"

Teresa stiffened, her face a little paler than usual as she attempted to smile. "It's me."

The lady leaned closer, cupping Teresa's face in her hands. "It *is* you! I thought you had a doppelgänger, and I was going to make some poor stranger really uncomfortable."

I felt like pointing out that she was currently making Teresa really uncomfortable. I'd never seen her like this, and I could barely contain my curiosity.

"No, it's me," Teresa confirmed, glancing at the door as if she was going to make a run for it. "Just passing through town."

The lady released her cheeks and smiled the most disarming smile I'd ever seen. "You must be going skiing then! It's been a busy season on the slopes. So much snow."

Teresa shook her head, looking sheepish. "We're not passing through on our *way* anywhere. I just meant..."

"We're looking at an office space upstairs," I offered.

"Really?" The woman's eyes widened. "The vacant one up there? It's a lovely space. What's your business?"

Teresa shot me a murderous look, which I ignored. Whatever her history with this town and this woman was, she'd been nothing but lovely and I needed all the inside information I could possibly get. "We have a small design business. Teresa is one of our brilliant designers. Do you know anything about that space? We heard the business went bust. What happened?"

The lady leaned in, smiling conspiratorially. "I heard they were breaking labor laws."

"Well, that's good. I mean, not a good thing to do. But great if it wasn't the location."

The lady looked offended. "Can't have been! Main Street is prime real estate. This side gets more natural light, too. It's perfect." She set down the flowers and offered her hand. "I'm Selma. Nice to meet you!"

"Trevor McAllister," I said, shaking her hand.

"Are you… Scottish?"

"Can't hide it, can I?" I gave her my best smile and wink combo, the one that worked like a charm with older ladies.

Selma blushed, shoulder-bumping Teresa. "Where did you find this one?"

"On the street," she deadpanned. "Can't seem to shake him."

Selma laughed like she'd dropped the most hilarious line, walking off to organize another shelf. "Well, be careful. Did you hear about the missing tourist? Vanished without a trace outside her cabin! They say she might have been picked up by someone. Someone charming, I bet!"

"Wasnae me," I assured her, raising my hands. "I've been with Teresa the whole time."

She laughed again. "Well, that's good. You've got an alibi. Excuse me, I have to go close the register. But please pop in tomorrow if you're still here! We need to catch up. It's been too long."

"Will do," Teresa promised.

"And I hope the office works out. I'd love to have you for neighbors!"

She waved at us as we left, led by Teresa. Back on the sidewalk, she cast me an annoyed look. "Can we go to the grocery store now? I don't know how long it's even open for. Everything closes super early in this town... What time is it now? I don't have a watch. I always use my phone." Her voice was a little breathless.

"We can go as soon as you tell me what just happened there."

She folded her arms. "What do you mean?"

"Why were you acting like she'd just caught you shoplifting or something?"

She jerked at my words as if I'd slapped her across the cheek. "What?"

I studied her for a beat, and a faint picture begun the emerge. "You did something in your wild youth, didn't you?"

She stared at me, her jaw jutting forward. "What's it to you?"

"I'm endlessly fascinated by you. I'm collecting Teresa trivia and I'm willing to play dirty."

Her eyebrow sailed up, suspicious. "Dirty, how?"

I folded my arms to match her stance, flashing her a wicked smile. "Either you tell me about the discretions of your youth, or I won't buy you dinner."

"That's okay, I'm not that hungry." She punctuated her words with a scoff.

Unfortunately, her stomach took that opportunity to growl. I burst out laughing and after a moment, she followed.

"Fuck, I can't..." She cast her eyes at the sky, or rather the awning we stood under. "I skipped breakfast, and it's been a hot minute since that salad."

"Come clean, lass! You'll feel a lot lighter. For every confession you make, I trade you one of mine. They're embarrassing, too, I promise. I was quite into acting in my earlier life. Did various audition tapes for roles I never had the slightest chance to land, and my eejit brother uploaded them to YouTube. So, I've got visuals."

"Holy shit!" She raised a hand to her mouth, trying to suppress a cackle. "I've seen you on stage, though. I bet those tapes are totally brilliant and not embarrassing at all."

CHAPTER 10

Teresa

He pulled out his phone and tapped on it, then stuck it in my face when a video started playing. It was a young Trevor, holding a prop gun, dramatically and insufficiently lit from the side, speaking in an awful, fake American accent.

"A scene from Casino Royale," he told me, but I wasn't listening to the movie lines. I was staring at his face—Trevor without a beard! He had a nice, strong jaw and full lips. Nothing that could be drastically improved with facial hair. Why had he grown a beard?

"Thank you," I said, passing the phone back to him. "I appreciate that."

"Your turn," he said.

My throat felt sticky. I wanted to tell him. I wanted us to be this close, just like we'd been that night. But how could I trust him with my secrets? He'd already betrayed me once, and I wasn't made of Teflon like him. We worked in the same industry, in the same city. If my past transgressions became common knowledge, it could affect my career.

"I did naughty things in my youth. Can we just leave it at that?"

He cocked his head, staring at me like he was trying to extract something from my brain using telepathy. "Everyone does naughty things in their youth... Are we talking about drinking, drugs, crime..."

A muscle in my face must have spasmed on the last word since he smiled. "Crime! I would have never thought." His voice was almost reverent. "Tell me more. I don't think you're a killer..." He kept watching my face, eyes narrowed. "Nae, ye not violent, and ye far too driven to waste time on drugs. My money's on shoplifting."

I glanced at the shop we'd exited. "Selma is my mom's old friend. They still keep in touch, and I heard she'd opened a gift shop. She used to work at the school and keep an eye on me... and she saw me do something stupid... I know she means well, but you know how seeing someone reminds you of something you'd rather not think about?"

"What did you do?"

I stared at my boots. "Stupid teenage stuff."

"That's it?" His voice rose in suspicion.

"That's all you're getting until I get fed." I spun around and marched towards the general store. Hopefully, it was still there. "And if they don't have anything ready-made and I have to live on cold Pop Tarts and soda, no more secrets."

I already knew the store was tiny and overpriced. I doubted the selection had expanded to include anything highly exciting in the last fourteen years. So, my secrets were safe. For now.

As we reached the store, Trevor spotted another restaurant down a side street. "I'll just quickly check that one, aye?"

He jogged down the alley like it was a race and that last available reservation was going to be taken in the next sixty seconds. I trailed behind, careful not to slip on the icy sidewalk. When I made it to the restaurant, he appeared in the doorway, grinning at me. "We have a table!"

"What is this place?" I peered at the green sign.

"Dinnae… Something Irish. Coddle and stew? Does it matter?"

"No," I admitted, following him inside.

I had no memory of this place. It must have been a new establishment. Round tables were covered with green tablecloths, and cheerful folk music played faintly in the background. We were seated in a corner, partly behind a see-through partition that gave an illusion of privacy, but only on one side.

My stomach growled again, and I grimaced.

"D'ye want me to order for us?" he asked, and I nodded, suddenly too tired to even think.

My feet ached from all the walking, and my toes felt numb from the cold. Too much had happened today. Too much to even process. Sinking into the luxuriously padded green chair, I suddenly felt like crying.

"Are you okay?" Trevor leaned over the table, taking my hand. "You've been through an awful lot today. I guess I've been trying to distract you... and I think you've done a great job with that yourself. But I get it if you don't feel like holding it together right now."

His kindness almost cracked me open, and I bit my lower lip, stifling a sniff. "When is that ever an option? When can I ever *not* hold it together?"

He squeezed my hand. "Wi' me. Ye feel free to fall apart. I can handle it."

"Can you now?" I let out a sad laugh.

"I can handle a lot of stuff. And I'm not angry about the key."

"You're not?" I looked up, blinking away tears.

"I'm glad to be stuck with you." He smiled like he didn't have a care in the world.

I tried to smile back. "You roll with the punches, don't you?"

"Still waiting for the punches, Dragonfly. Any time you feel like it."

The waiter arrived with a tall glass of beer and a glass of red he set in front of me. I hadn't even paid attention to what he'd ordered.

"I remember you ordered pinot noir once before. Is it okay?"

I took a long sip, sighing deeply. "It's perfect."

A moment later, two huge bowls of stew and a basket of bread appeared in front of us, filling the air with a meaty, spicy aroma. I'd entered some sort of comfort-food heaven. It tasted as amazing as it smelled, and for a moment, we ate in silence.

"I'm so glad you found this place," I finally said. "The general store is dire. Or at least it used to be."

"Happy Valentine's Day!" He raised his glass, clinking it with mine.

I couldn't help laughing. This was so not what I'd planned for today, but things were so far out of my control I had no choice but to go with it. Maybe I could roll with the punches, too, if I really tried. "Okay. I think you've earned another secret."

He leaned in, a sly smile crinkling the corners of his eyes. "*Another* secret? Ye haven't told me anything yet."

"Okay, a secret. But it must stay between us. Can I trust you?"

"Have I ever betrayed your trust?"

I jerked back, thrown by his question. Surely, he had. He'd betrayed me. As I watched him, his mouth twitched, that relaxed exterior cracking a little.

"I trusted you to recommend me for that job," I finally said, stating the obvious.

He nodded, weighing his words carefully. "I made the wrong call, and I hurt you, but I didn't go back on my word. You didn't ask me for a recommendation."

The statement hung in the air, like an invisible note floating above our breadbasket.

"You knew how much it meant," I argued, but I had little air left in my lungs and the words died on my lips.

It was true. I'd told him I wanted that job, but I hadn't asked him for anything, even though I'd known he had pull with Charlie, and probably all of them. I'd simply assumed he'd be on my side.

"I'm not saying this to let myself off the hook," he added. "Only to point out that I wouldn't break a promise. I've also never passed on anything personal you told me that night. I don't blab about anyone's business."

I nodded, hiding behind my wineglass. It was probably true. I'd never caught him gossiping. Was it possible my anger over the game design job had distorted the image of him in my mind? I'd been so convinced Trevor had shown me his true colors that I'd never stopped to study those colors more closely.

Something occurred to me. "Is this why Charlie calls you 'fortress'? I thought it was just because of your size."

He huffed a laugh. "Maybe it's both. I hold a lot of dirt on a lot of people." He tapped on his temple.

"You sound like that Sherlock villain! Have you ever blackmailed anyone? Do you have a mind palace?"

He rolled his eyes. "I'd rather be worth the trust placed in me. And most people's secrets are nothin' exciting. Once they work up the courage to share, they're just embarrassing stories."

"So, you receive confessions?"

He met my gaze head-on, and my smile wavered. He was so serious, like this was something he'd really thought about.

"I enjoy deep conversations. I share about myself, and others do the same. Where I grew up, it wasn't the norm. Men didn't open up. But I wanted to find connections that go beyond hanging out and watching sports. I don't mean ye sit in cafes staring into each other's eyes." He gave me a comically long and intense look. "With guys, it's easier to do something and talk at the same time. Side by side, not face to face."

I chuckled. "Like parallel play? Toddlers do that."

He gave a solemn nod. "It's been important to me since I was three."

As my laughter fizzled out, I considered his point. "It makes sense. I remember my dad being like that. Even though he's an academic, I still never saw him talking to a friend without some kind of activity. They'd be barbecuing, or even working on a research paper, but there was always a reason. Mom would go out with a friend, sit in a cafe and talk. I do the same."

"An' where's yer dad now?"

"In California. He had an amazing career opportunity a long time ago. It didn't turn out to be that amazing, but it ended their marriage. And that's how we ended up in Cozy Creek with Mom."

"You, your mom and your sister..."

"Suzanne," I offered. "She's five years younger than me."

"Do you still call every day to tell her one thing you did that wasn't work?"

I finished my wine. "You remembered." My head was spinning a little, in a nice way.

"Do you need to call her? You can use my phone." He slid it across the table.

"Thank you. That's not a bad idea. Especially if we're stuck here overnight. It's not like she'd call the cops if I don't, but..."

"You'd rather she doesn't worry," he finished for me.

I nodded. Suspicion crept in again. "Is this how you get people to confess their deepest, darkest secrets?"

"By asking questions?" He laughed. "You say it like I'm playing mind games. I'm fascinated by you, Teresa. The questions pop up from me brain, I can't help it." He turned his palms up as a show of innocence.

"I'm going to need another embarrassing audition video to keep going."

He unlocked the phone he'd set on the table between us, and obligingly fetched me another video. In this one, he looked a little older, his dark, wavy hair nearly shoulder length, brown kilt fabric draped over his shoulder. I recognized the monologue from Braveheart and my cheeks warmed.

He tried to close the video after a couple of lines, but I snatched it from him. "I'm not done."

"At least turn down the volume," he begged as a couple at a nearby table halted their conversation, listening.

I dialed the sound to its lowest setting but kept watching. This was the role he was born to play, complete with the thick Scottish accent I couldn't get enough of.

"Your accent doesn't sound like this."

"Aye, ma accent doesnae sound like this these days." He smiled, sounding perfectly Scottish to me. "I swore I wouldn't change, but I've never been that good at accents. Turns oot I've got verra little control o'er it. Wish I'd figured it oot sooner." He nodded at the phone.

I couldn't stop smiling, staring at the phone. I would have

watched him on the silver screen for hours.

The scene ended, and I set the phone back on the table. "Thank you. You've earned one secret." I leaned over the table until my top was nearly swimming in stew, whispering so quietly that the couple at the next table would have needed hearing aids to understand. "Before that night at the swimming pool, I had a crush on you—"

He cracked up, belting out his signature laugh that made our eavesdropping couple jump. "That's no' a secret! I had a massive crush on you. We were flirting every single day."

"That's not the secret part." I glared at him, waiting for his laugh to settle before I whispered again so quietly, he had to lean in, our noses nearly touching, our breaths mingling in hot gusts. "I kept having the same sex dream about you."

There was a beat. His brows knitted together. "What?"

"What do you mean, what? I told you a secret."

"That's not a secret. That's a teaser. What was the dream?"

"What, like details?" I assumed a look of absolute innocence and confusion.

"Come on!" He huffed in frustration, and I grinned.

I leaned in again, forcing him to meet me halfway, my nose accidentally brushing his beard. His breath tickled my cheek, and I was suddenly hyper aware of his lips, so close to mine. "I will only tell you if you guess it right. There are three parameters— the position, the piece of clothing, and the location. If you guess all of them right, I'll tell you."

"Wait... a piece of clothing on you, or me?"

"On you. I'm naked."

His cheeks reddened. "I like the sound of that."

"Of course, you do. What man doesn't enjoy starring in a sex dream?"

"So, have you had this dream since then?"

"Nope."

"D' ye even remember it well enough? It's been a while." His eyes sparkled.

"Yes. Dream you was very memorable," I added generously.

"That's what I'm talking about!" He beamed at me, so ridiculously pleased with himself I couldn't help laughing.

I shook my head, trying to decide if this was a huge mistake or a fun game I didn't want to stop playing. His smile pulled at my belly, so deliciously, so deeply. My body hummed.

He tilted his head, watching me, his mouth now permanently curved. That pull centered between my legs, intensifying. I had needs, but now was not a good time to become aware of them. I needed to stay in control.

"I'm not sure about the other two, but the piece of clothing is easy." He held my gaze, looking very pleased with himself.

"Easy?" I lifted my eyebrows.

"It's obviously a kilt. And yes, I do have one."

I tried to keep a poker face, but it was a good thing I'd never tried that type of gambling.

"Thank you for confirming that." Trevor chuckled. "Now, let's see about that position..." He drained his beer, keeping his intense gaze on me like he was trying to extract the truth telepathically.

"Okay. You do that, I'll go call my sister. Be back in a sec." I grabbed his phone, had him unlock it for me, and made my way to the restrooms.

Good thing my sister had had the same number since we were teenagers—the only one besides my own I'd memorized.

CHAPTER 11

Teresa

Suze answered on the third ring, a little out of breath.

"Hi! It's Teresa. I—"

"Teresa? Do you have a new number?"

"This is my colleague's phone. I'm stuck in Cozy Creek. We came to look at an office space and I lost the car key, and my phone is locked inside the car."

Her voice rose in alarm. "Oh, no! What are you going to do?"

"It'll be fine. We'll get the spare key tomorrow, I think. But we have to spend the night."

"Where are you going to sleep?"

"Oh, don't worry. There's a cabin..."

I'd talk Trevor into letting me stay at that cabin. It had to be a better option than the empty office.

"Wait. It's Valentine's Day! Wes is taking me out tomorrow because we couldn't get a babysitter for tonight. But weren't you supposed to go out with Richard?"

"Yeah…" I took a deep breath and explained the situation. I had to find the volume buttons on Trevor's phone when the expletives began flying. My sister was the sunny one compared to me, but she could be quite expressive.

"How are you?" I asked, to get us back on track. "How're the kids?"

She gave me a quick update on her two toddlers before jumping straight back into our earlier topic. "I told you, didn't I? That guy was as dry as a piece of toast. No passion! Nothing. You can't fall in love with someone like that. He doesn't have the necessary parts."

I almost laughed at her choice of words, despite the bitter taste in my mouth. "He seemed plenty passionate with his ex."

She sighed so forcefully the speaker rattled. "Okay, fine. But you guys had no zing! I don't understand why you waste time on anyone who's not crazy about you. You can't fall in love unless you're both ready to jump, headfirst. Why would you settle for anything less?"

The memory of Trevor and me jumping into the pool resurfaced, and I pushed it down. "Well, you found it straight out of school, so I don't think you realize how rare it is."

I didn't even feel like defending myself. She was right. After their first night together, Wes had stayed up to learn Suze's favorite song on the guitar so he could play it to her before breakfast. After our first time, Richard had ordered me an Uber before ordering himself a pizza. I'd settled for a lot less.

"It's out there! And you're a catch!" Suze insisted.

I heard the soundtrack of a kids cartoon in the background.

"And what did you do today that wasn't work?" she finally asked. "Quite a bit, I assume, since you're out of office."

"I've done absolutely no work since one p.m.," I announced proudly. "I'm freaking out over the emails I've missed."

"Oh, right! You locked your phone in the car! *That's* why you're not working." She laughed as if she'd figured out a mystery.

"Pretty much."

"I guess this is the only way for you to vacation." I heard the smile in her voice. "Even if it is in Cozy Creek. Is it... awkward?"

"I've already run into Peony, and Mom's nosy friend Selma. She runs a gift shop now."

"Peony? Oh, my God! How is she? Did she ever... graduate?"

"I don't know. She seemed well. Married. Three kids."

"Oh." Suze sounded surprised. "After what happened with Julian, she seemed so quiet and depressed. I was worried she'd never be okay."

There it was. Julian. She'd casually dropped the name I'd been trying to block out for such a long time. Julian Neville. The guy I never wanted to see again.

"I don't want to talk about him," I pleaded. "I'm only here for one night, maybe two, so I'm really hoping I don't run into him."

"I'm sure you won't," Suze said in a soothing tone. "Just stay in the cabin of... who're you with again?"

I swallowed. I'd been trying to not say his name. "Trevor."

"What? The Scottish jerk who ruined your chances on that design job?"

I sighed. "Yeah. But I don't know. He's been… nice."

"Nice?" she repeated, her voice oozing suspicion. "Maybe he's gathering more information to ruin another aspect of your life."

"What other aspect?"

"Fair enough." She laughed.

"Honestly, I think he's changed. He's quit smoking and picked up knitting and—"

"Knitting? Dear Lord."

"It's sweet," I insisted. "I'm the one who lost the key, but he's been so good. He even found us a table at this restaurant and—"

"Hang on. You're in a restaurant, on Valentine's Day, with the guy who betrayed you?"

"Well, he didn't betray me… I mean, he was misguidedly trying to protect me—"

"From making a shitload of money?"

"He didn't know it was going to be so successful."

"Teresa." Suze switched to her mom voice. "You bitched to me about this guy for months. Months. He was the reason you almost didn't take that job with Charlie and Bess. I had to talk you into it. I didn't want you to lose your condo."

"And I appreciate it. I needed this job, and it's been good."

"You told me that you were doing your best to avoid this dude at all costs. How did you even end up in Cozy Creek with him? Did he kidnap you?"

"No," I said, but my voice faltered.

"Listen. It sounds like you're warming up to him, and I don't want you to get hurt. You've just broken up with someone. You're in a vulnerable state, right? Anyone would be. And I know the Scottish accent is irresistible, and it's probably tempting to have this rebound thing. But I want you to find something real! That'll never happen if you keep picking these terrible guys."

I wanted to argue that Trevor wasn't a terrible guy, but how could I possibly know that? I'd been wrong about Richard. She'd watched my sorry dating history for a long time. I couldn't blame her for being concerned.

I ended the call, promising her I'd be careful, and returned to the table, my thoughts a jumbled mess. Suze was right. I *was* warming up to Trevor, and if I let myself get any more comfortable... if I got myself invited to his cabin... who knew what would happen? I was feeling too vulnerable, and Trevor was being too nice.

I had to tough it out on the office floor. It was the only option. But I'd try to make myself as comfortable as possible.

"Do you know if Cozy Creek sells any clothing these days?" I asked. "Anything at all? I don't want to sleep in my jeans."

"You don't sleep in the nude?" He looked disappointed. "So, the location in your dream was not a bedroom, then?"

We were still on the sex dream, then? I had to smile. "I don't think that dream scenario would ever happen in real life."

"Are we talking about an alien planet or just in the supermarket aisle?"

It had been a scorching-hot dream, one I hadn't thought about in a long time. He'd never guess it, which was for the best. I'd take that one to my grave.

"I'm not giving you any hints. You must guess all three things correctly."

I thoroughly enjoyed the frustration on his face as he got up and settled the bill.

When we stepped back outside, it was pitch dark. The streetlamps glowed along Main Street. We walked towards the lights, and I noticed myself huddling closer to Trevor than before. It felt safer. With my body still warm from the meal and my head a little light from wine, I didn't feel like questioning it. In extenuating circumstances, even enemies had to work together. For survival.

Trevor kept throwing me wild guesses, mostly locations around Denver, and I kept laughing him off.

"I don't think it's even possible to have sex on an escalator."

"Oh, you'd be surprised. There was a news story..."

"Seriously? Like, how?" I hiccupped.

"I think it starts with being under the influence of something that removes any shred of shame."

"Obviously."

"And then... they probably got turned away from every other establishment."

"People are insane."

"I couldn't agree with you more." He scooped a hand around my waist when I missed our turn. "This way."

I felt the warmth of embarrassment on my face, but the warmth of his hand quickly overpowered it. I got so flustered that my foot slipped on the icy ground, and I nearly went down. But Trevor was faster, catching me between his giant hands, holding me upright. "D'ye want me to carry ye the rest o' the way?"

"Yes, please," I laughed. "I'm clearly not fit to walk."

I meant it as a joke, but he swept me into his arms with such force I nearly dropped my purse. "As you wish."

The sudden loss of contact with the ground sent me into a full-body flush, panicked and aroused at the same time. We were so close to the office entrance it only took him a few steps to get there. But as he lowered me to the pavement, I felt hot and out of balance, as well as weirdly out of breath.

"Here we are."

"Thank you." I leaned on the door, rummaging through my bag for the key he'd given me. Dear God, don't let me lose that one! After a moment of frenzy, my fingers curled around the jagged shape, and I sighed with relief.

"Are you sure you're okay to sleep here?" His voice was soft.

"I think it's for the best."

"We could call your friend... Peony?"

"No. She... we... have a history. It's a bit complicated."

He nodded, quietly watching me work the key. Not a word about that cabin of his. Did it even exist? And if it did, why didn't he insist that I stay there with him?

The door creaked open to the dark staircase, but I didn't step in. "What if something happens?"

"Like what?"

"Like... an alarm going off. Or a fire... Or a friendly ghost who starts turning on the faucet in the kitchen?" I tried to joke as a cold sensation crept up my throat. Why was I trying to scare myself?

"Hmm. We know you don't like loud noises. But a friendly ghost like Casper—"

"How far is your cabin?" I finally blurted, holding onto the doorknob, my fingers stiff from the cold.

"It's about three kilom... two miles, I think." He bit back a smile, gazing down the street, into the darkness that continued beyond the row of streetlamps. "No, three miles. Three and a half."

"Is it moving away from us?"

He huffed an awkward laugh. "It's a blimp. Did I no' mention that?"

Okay. He clearly didn't want me in his cabin.

The air felt colder, nipping at my cheeks. The snow on the ground had crystallized into a blanket of diamonds. I could only hope the office had some sort of central heating. My toes, which had thawed nicely during our dinner, were going numb again. There was no way I could walk to his cabin in them, even if he invited me.

He took a step back in his sensible winter boots, rubbing his hands together. He didn't have gloves, either. They were probably in the car, just like the scarf he'd been knitting. "Well, I better get on the road. Good night."

Looking a little torn, he turned around and headed down the street.

"Wait!" I cringed at how my voice chimed with alarm.

He halted, looking over his shoulder.

"Are we meeting here in the morning? What time?" I asked.

"Does it matter? You don't even have a watch."

Dread shot through me. I didn't have a change of clothing, either, or a toothbrush. What if the office toilets didn't work? We'd never tested them. It was going to be a long night.

He turned around to fully face me, waiting. I stepped a little closer and filled my lungs, gathering my nerve. "I know it's awful and I shouldn't even ask… but could you stay with me? Just long enough to make sure the alarm doesn't go off." I suddenly felt like crying, and it took a lot of effort to keep the tears at bay.

He closed the distance between us, grabbing my arms and rubbing them up and down. "It won't. I already checked with the realtor. There is central heating. The power is connected. The toilet works. I wouldn't leave ye here for a minute otherwise."

"Thank you. I should be fine then. You don't have to—"

"I want to," he cut me off, looking at me openly. "I've wanted to be with you for a long time, but I couldn't. Not with Richard the Dick in the picture. Not with you avoiding me at every turn."

I swallowed a lump. "I was just protecting myself."

"I get it. And that's why I never want to force my company on you. I know I practically kidnapped you to bring you here, and I already feel awful about that. But I was never planning to keep ye overnight. So, it's your call. D' ye want me here?"

"I do," I choked out.

"Then I'll stay."

A big fat tear let loose, running down the side of my nose. "Why are you so nice? I haven't been nice... You don't even know me. There are more secrets. Worse secrets."

He peered into my eyes like he was looking straight into my soul. "I'm counting on that." He caught the tear with his thumb before it made it to my lips. "Okay, let's go inside, crank up the heat, and see if that office is survivable overnight."

CHAPTER 12

Trevor

The remote for the heat pump hung helpfully on the wall underneath it, and I cranked it up to a higher setting. "It'll be good to test if this works, in case we want to consider this for an office."

"It would be an upgrade," she muttered.

Our current office only had a small space heater with no cooling option and got very hot and stuffy during the summer.

"Everything about this is an upgrade," I countered with a smile.

Her eyes narrowed. "Everything? Only having a handful of restaurants, a constant stream of tourists and paying three times as much for a gallon of milk?"

"We'd have to stock up in Denver. That general store is for emergencies only," I said.

"And if you want a hobby, the only options are hiking and skiing."

"What are you talking about? There's hunting, fishing, woodworking..."

"Yeah. There's a lot of stuff for *you* to do," she said, but her mouth curved up.

"There's a gym!" I countered. I'd seen the sign earlier.

She took a step closer, looking at me with slightly unfocused eyes. A little drunk. Happy. "There's a gym for dudes, full of iron, that smells like feet."

"And what you need is..."

She stood right in front of me now, her fingers hovering over my chest. "A pole dancing studio."

"You mean a strip club?"

She shot me a hurt look. "No! I mean a pole fitness and dance studio. I love pole dancing."

An image of her in clear heels and body glitter flashed in my mind and I tried to shake it. "And you need a special studio for it?"

"And an instructor."

My dick had stopped listening to her clarifications, getting more excited by the second. All I could think of was Teresa in her underwear, spinning around a pole.

I shuffled to my side to grab one of the cable poles in the middle of the floor. "Poles like this?"

She followed me, wrapping her hand around the pole and leaning back. "Not quite."

"I'll install a pole for you. Here, or in my cabin. Wherever. As long as I get to watch."

"It's not striptease," she insisted.

"If it involves you and a pole, I'm good."

My mind was already busy undressing her. She had incredible posture. I'd always sensed Teresa was fit, and that realization had further motivated me to get back in shape. I wanted to be good enough for her.

The heater worked its magic, and we both removed our jackets.

"I think I'll survive the night," she concluded. "I only wish I had something comfortable to wear. These jeans feel like a prison." She grimaced, trying to lift her leg as she spun around the pole. "This pole isn't half bad! In different clothes, I could practice my routine."

"Okay. Stay here." I said, heading for the door.

"Where are you going?"

"Hunting."

♥ ♥ ♥

Ten minutes later, I shoved open the cabin door with my shoulder, cursing my frozen limbs. The night temperature had dropped well below freezing and the walk had felt way longer than half a mile—the actual distance to my cabin.

I hated leaving Teresa behind, even if it was only for a short time. She'd put on a brave face, but I could see right through it. I'd been able to read her moods ever since that night, yet she held onto all those secrets. I would uncover them, I promised myself. I'd get there. Even if she decided she didn't want me as more than a friend.

I closed the door behind me and resisted the urge to crank up the heating since I wasn't going to stay the night. I packed quickly, prioritizing her comfort over mine. Unfortunately, I didn't keep a lot of clothes, and had no bottoms that could possibly fit Teresa's slender frame. But I could make her more comfortable to sleep on the floor and provide snacks.

As I walked around the cabin, I tried to see it through her eyes. Would she appreciate what I'd done with the space? Or would she freak out? I couldn't risk it.

I hoisted the bag of camping supplies onto my shoulder and headed back outside, traipsing down the road back to the town and the office. But there was one quick stop I wanted to make on the way.

CHAPTER 13

Teresa

I collapsed on the low-pile carpet, letting out a deep sigh. The empty room felt creepy, but the office was warm and safe. There was even a little wall light in the kitchen that wasn't a terribly bright halogen tube. I sat in its faint, warm glow, right outside the kitchen doorway, slowly eating every breath mint in my purse. I even popped the antacid, just to fill the time.

I took off my shoes and rubbed my feet, trying to bring them back to life. This was the strangest Valentine's Day I'd ever had, and it wasn't even over yet. With no phone, no way to tell the time, and nothing at all to do, my mind raced a million miles a second, my legs and arms twitching restlessly. What was the deal with Trevor's cabin? What was the deal with all the apologies, personal questions, and the way he was looking after me? We were suddenly back to where we'd been eighteen months ago. Flirting. Touching. Looking for those excuses to get closer. And right now, I was missing him like crazy.

He'd said he'd be back soon. What did 'soon' even mean? Why hadn't I stopped him at the door and demanded a timeframe? By the time I heard a faint knock on the door, I was lying on my stomach, convinced that I'd grown at least an inch of leg hair and lost two ounces of muscle mass from lack of exercise.

That knock made me pounce to my feet like a dog waiting for its owner. I raced to the door and threw myself into Trevor's arms. "Oh, my God! That took a year."

"Hello." He sounded amused, and a little surprised, dropping two bags on the floor to free up his arms. "It's been forty minutes."

By the time he hugged me back, I'd regained some of my emotional resilience and pulled away. Why on earth had I thrown myself at him? What was wrong with me?

"It's just that there's nothing to do and when I sit down, completely idle, my thoughts go crazy." My voice wobbled.

He smiled compassionately. "Of course, they do. You've had a rough day. A really rough day."

"I wish I could exercise. I need to move my arms and legs. I need to do something." Anxiety was quickly getting the best of me, but I couldn't hide it with him. Not this time.

"Well, you're in luck, because I found a laundromat that was open late, and I managed to get you some clothes that might fit better than mine."

"Really?"

"There's a catch, though." He bit his lip.

"What? Did you bring me someone else's dirty laundry?"

"Oh, God. No." He laughed so hard that his shoulders shook.

He followed me into the office, carrying his huge rucksack and another overnight bag across the floor. I guided him to what I'd now decided was the homeliest corner, right by the kitchen doorway with its glowing warm light, framed on one side by a cable pole. It was a nice enough spot to sit.

I hated sitting on the floor in my high-waisted jeans, though. Thanks to the late hour and the hearty stew, they felt like a corset. I'd already opened the button and the zipper to be able to breathe.

"I wouldn't mind changing into whatever you have for me, as long as it's stretchy and washed." I glanced longingly at his bag.

"I'm so glad you put it like that because it is stretchy and washed. But it's also... themed."

"What do you mean?"

He unzipped the bag, pulled out a small plastic bag and handed it to me, his eyes filled with glee. I opened it, unearthing a pair of striped leggings. What was that color? I shifted closer to the kitchen light source. Oh, yes. Red and green.

"There's also a matching top." Trevor helped me pull out the second item.

It jingled. Of course, it fucking did. Because it was the top half of an elf costume, complete with a hem and sleeves that were cut in a zigzag pattern. I raised an eyebrow at him.

"It's a laundromat. They obviously don't sell clothes, but they can donate items that haven't been picked up after eight weeks."

I nodded, staring at the odd outfit. Sure. It was about eight weeks since the height of Christmas season, and God was clearly on a mission to see how much humiliation I could take in one day. I could only steer into the skid.

"Wow," I said. "This is not from Temu. I think it's homemade." I rubbed my thumb across the material. "Feels like cotton."

"That's the spirit!" He grinned.

"You didn't happen to bring an extra T-shirt or anything I could drown inside? Because I don't mind mixing and matching. And it is a bit cold, even with the heater on. I can always put my jacket back on, but I'd rather use it as an extra blanket."

"I have a couple of Henleys," he said, pulling one out of his bag. "But neither of them is fresh out of the laundry, I'm afraid. That's another reason I went into that laundromat and begged them to find me something." He grimaced. "The cabin doesn't have a washer yet, so things have been piling up a wee bit. But now that I know where the full-service laundromat is…"

"Great!" I grabbed the Henley and retreated into the kitchen to get changed.

Which one was worse? Looking like a fully kitted elf or a half-elf that smelled like Trevor? Or rather, who had to inhale Trevor's smell all night? I brought the sweater to my face and concluded that it didn't smell bad. On the contrary. It was a mix of laundry powder and something so masculine it made my body jolt awake, fueling a need that had to go unmet, especially tonight. Tonight was about survival.

To my surprise, the elf costume fit me like a glove. "Was there a hat or shoes that go with this?" I called through the door. "Maybe a belt with a giant buckle? I feel like it's missing something."

What I would have given to be able to slide my feet into warm slippers… or, better yet, crawl into a real bed in a warm home.

"I left the shoes and the reindeer behind. Too bulky."

"Ah, okay."

"But I did bring you a toothbrush if you'd like?"

"Yes, please!"

I cracked the door, and he handed me a toothbrush that was still in its packaging, along with a tube of toothpaste. As I brushed my teeth, I wondered at how normal it felt, being wrapped up in soft, stretchy clothing while cleaning your teeth. My body responded with an overwhelming wave of tiredness.

When I stepped out of the kitchen, I nearly gasped out loud. Trevor had set up a bed with a surprisingly thick-looking camping mattress, a sleeping bag, and a pillow. In my bone-tired state, it looked like a four-poster bed in a Vermont B&B. But there was only one.

"It's for you," He quickly announced, stepping away from the makeshift bed.

"Where are you going to sleep?"

"In my own bed, tomorrow."

"What about tonight?"

"I'll keep watch."

"Of what? The heater?"

He shrugged. "Santa coming to haul you to his workshop?" His eyes roamed my body.

I spun around, making the bells jingle. "I should buy more clothes with an auditory aspect. This is fun!"

He sat on the floor, leaning on the wall next to the mattress. "Whenever you feel tired..." He gestured at the bed.

I took a breath, glancing at the pole. I was tired, but he'd freed my legs from their denim prison, and they longed to move.

It was a two-second decision. Three or four seconds of hard thinking would have killed the idea. A little more time to metabolize the wine I'd consumed at dinner might have also done the trick. But Trevor had topped up my glass twice... no, wait. Three times? That's probably why the lightheaded, impulsive feeling lingered, allowing me to grab the cable pole and pull myself up to the first pose.

"Holy shit!"

He whistled as I swung around the pole and transitioned into the next move, hanging upside down with one leg bent around the pole, then secured my arms around it to do the splits. I'd never done this in elf leggings. I wondered if *anyone* had.

Moments later, I heard music. Trevor was playing 'What Makes You Beautiful' by *One Direction* on his phone. I smiled but kept dancing, following the routine I'd been practicing for the last couple of weeks.

I felt his eyes on me at every turn, even when I couldn't see him. The way he looked at me was both unnerving and reassuring. I had good reason to hate him, but Trevor had never looked at me with anything other than devotion. The thought hit me hard as I did my final spin, my striped legs whirling in the air.

I'd been blocking him out, refusing to see it. But it had been there the whole time.

When I slid off the pole and onto the floor, he turned off the music and gave me a standing ovation. "That was incredible! Also hot, but I'm not supposed to find an elf sexy, right? That'd be weird. Like fancying hobbits."

"Totally," I agreed.

"But when you do that... Bloody hell! It's just..."

"What?"

He shrugged. "I mean... You know..."

"Seriously," I said. "People who don't finish their sentences drive me mad."

He flashed his winning grin. "Fine. I'm so hard for an elf right now it's an absolute disgrace. Despicable!" He slammed a hand over his face, as if mortified.

I laughed, taking a step closer, almost within a touching distance. All this time trapped together in this alternate universe, and he hadn't tried to kiss me once. Not even at dinner, when we'd both been drinking, sitting in the secluded little corner, discussing sex dreams.

He must have refilled my glass at least three times, because I still felt drunk. And I felt like testing him. "That night at the pool... how well do you remember it?"

He shifted a little closer, sticking his hands into his pockets. "Pretty well. But only because I wrote it down shortly after."

"You wrote it down?" It was my turn to take a step.

I was close enough to touch now, but kept one hand on the pole, like an anchor.

He shrugged. "I'm a writer. I didn't want to forget."

"I remember we talked for hours," I said. "I remember the swimming, and making out…"

I felt a blush rising to my cheeks and hugged the pole, resting my cheek against the cold metal. I wanted to touch him again, more than anything, but I couldn't make that move. Could I? I glanced out of the window, wondering if anyone out there had seen me dancing. Thank God we were on the second floor. The windows across the street were dark.

"I remember you once had a pet gerbil named Sybil," he said.

I blinked at him. I had no memory of ever discussing childhood pets.

"And that ye love dragonflies." He stepped back, leaning on the wall, smiling. "Later, I heard you had a dragonfly tattoo. I can't remember seeing it when we went swimming, so I have a theory about where it's hiding. It's been driving me crazy."

The glint in his eyes made my cheeks hot. "Do you have any tattoos?"

"No. My mother didn't approve. And now that she's dead, it's even harder to go against her wishes. But I appreciate body art."

"You want to see mine?" My pulse raced. What was I doing?

"Yes, please!"

I crossed the floor until I stood right in front of him, then slid my leggings down until the tip of the dragonfly on my hip became visible. As I turned to give him a peek, Trevor's hands flexed, hovering briefly above mine, before he tucked them back into his pockets. He was trying so hard to do the right thing. To not cross a line.

I peeled the leggings down until he could see the whole tattoo. "I thought about getting a fly right on my butt cheek," I said, biting my lip.

"What, a housefly?"

"Yeah." I grinned, my face hot and flushed, waiting for him to connect the dots.

Trevor swallowed, the realization dawning on his face. "Are your boyfriends not interested in swatting a dragonfly? Because I reckon a fly is a fly. I'd be happy to spank it." His voice was thick.

I stood so close now I could count his eyelashes, but it would have taken me all night. His eyes were hypnotizing. "Trevor?"

"Yes, love?"

"I didn't think I'd ever say this to you, but I think you're a good guy."

He held still, watching me. "Are you drunk?"

"A little," I admitted.

"Are you saying… you forgive me?" He flashed me his sad, lop-sided smile.

"I told you I already did."

"No, you didn't. You put me in the shit basket and moved on."

"Shit basket?"

His voice was a little heavy. "You know, the 'shit I don't want to deal with' basket."

I coughed, looking away. It was annoying how accurate that sounded.

"Are you ready to take me out of the basket?"

As he stared at me, the moment became weighted with meaning. "Yes," I finally rasped.

His gaze dipped to my lips, and I swallowed to lubricate my throat. Somewhere along the way, my mouth had lost all its natural moisture.

"Thank you," he said. "It was a shit place to be."

He spoke so casually I could have almost been fooled. I might have thought he was in no danger of losing control, his body not calling for mine. But I'd heard his earlier words and picked up on the evidence. At least I thought so.

I felt bold, glowing from the adoration I saw in his eyes. I stepped so close my shirt brushed against his sweater and I placed my hands on the soft fabric, looking up at him. His chest felt hard underneath, harder than I had expected.

"Have you been working out?" I blurted. "You feel... I mean you look different."

A sly smile spread across his face. I don't know how he managed to look embarrassed and proud at the same time, but he did. "A wee bit. I won't try the pole, though. In case they have that 'you break it, you buy it' policy."

"Honestly, it feels a bit wobbly. Probably not meant for dancing."

He closed his hands around my wrists, holding me in place.

His voice was a rough whisper. "What are you doing, Teresa?"

"What do you mean?"

"You're pole dancing for me. And now you're... touching me."

I sunk my teeth into my bottom lip, trying to arrange the conflicting thoughts and emotions swirling in my mind. "I don't know what I'm doing."

"Don't do anything you'll regret." His voice sharpened to deliver a warning, but I felt brave and beautiful. I'd had an awful day, and my sister was right about one thing. A rebound with a sexy Scot was a very tempting idea. Even if it was a mistake.

I grasped at his shirt, feeling the solid muscle underneath. "Are you worried about our inter-species pairing? An elf and a human. What if the elders find out? Imagine the scandal!" I raised my brows for emphasis.

"Elf elders?" He watched me so intensely I nearly backed out.

My gut hot and churning, I doubled down on the joke. "Sure! Or your human peers. What if they find out you've had relations with an elf?"

"I'll explain it was a pole-dancing elf. They'll understand."

"No! It'll be a scandal. You'll be shunned by the community. Someone once told me human beings are herd animals, and we need to stay with the tribe. Otherwise, you'll die in the wilderness."

Trevor bit back a smile. "Then I'll die happy, knowing it's all been worth it. Besides, if we both get shunned, we can be together. I'll build you a hut, hunt for buffalo and we'll make beautiful half-elf babies."

"Buffalo? Where is this taking place?" I asked as my hand crept up his chest, fingernails reaching his beard.

He leaned a little against my touch, lifting an eyebrow. "*That's* what you find unbelievable?"

"Yes. I draw the line at buffalos. I think you should hunt mountain lions and gather nuts and seeds and wild goose eggs."

His voice was a low growl. "I'll hunt whatever you tell me to hunt. And I'll kill anyone who threatens your survival—"

I rose onto my toes and pressed my lips against his, cutting off the prehistoric babble.

It wasn't a big move, but it gave him permission. Trevor captured my face between his hands and kissed me back. *Fire.* That's all I could think of. Wild and unruly. He held me like he'd captured diamonds in his hands he couldn't lose. My body turned into hot jello, throbbing in desperate need. I was kissing Trevor. I'd started this. What was I doing?

I pulled away to catch my breath, so disoriented I wondered which way was up.

"I'm sorry," he panted. "I—"

"Don't be." I kissed him again, this time setting the pace.

He tasted minty and hot, and fresh. Nothing like before. He felt different, too. Reverent. Desperate. Gentle and a little rough all at once, and it took me a beat to truly relax into his touch. The kiss grew in intensity, and my tongue met his halfway, releasing a flurry of sensations down my spine. His hands were on my waist, jingling the bells as his thumbs rubbed my lower back, waking up every nerve ending.

He kissed along my cheek, all the way to my ear, his fingers diving into my curls, until he finally pulled me into a tight hug, drawing a deep inhale.

"Teresa," he whispered, like a prayer. "Teresa."

A part of me questioned that tight grip and the slight shift in the mood, but I didn't want to move. I didn't want to push him away because that would have meant losing the feeling. Being aroused and safe. Loved. I'd momentarily outrun the disappointment and hurt. Maybe I could hide from it tonight, hide from all the confusing thoughts and questions. If I just stayed here and didn't let reality in.

CHAPTER 14

Trevor

I'd almost given up hope on it ever happening. Almost. I'd imagined it so many times—first as something fun and playful, like laughing in relief when you woke up after a bad dream. I imagined finding Teresa with me, like she'd been that night by the pool, sharing a connection I'd never had with anyone else. It was too good to throw away, so of course, she'd come around.

But she hadn't come around. The bad dream had continued, and I'd begun to doubt our connection. It must have been in my head since she'd been willing to throw it all away over a few words. I'd tried to explain myself, explain away my actions, and I'd made it so much worse.

Then she'd started dating Richard the Dick, closing the door on us. My explanations no longer mattered, even after I finally understood how badly I'd hurt her. To me, it was just another job. For Teresa, it was her ticket, an opportunity to break new ground and become part of the A-team. And, of course, win big. That one I hadn't expected, but I had to admit it looked bad. When I'd cashed in my coins and seen the money in my account, I'd known what I had to do.

It wasn't that I wanted to clear my conscience. I wanted Teresa happy. I needed to see her eyes shine with joy like they did tonight, a smile crinkling the corners, desire relaxing her eyelids, making them dip.

Part of me couldn't believe it, and I might have held her a little too tight. A little too desperately. When she pulled away, I wanted to kick myself. I apologized, and her eyes softened. She kissed me again, melting against me like she meant it, and when I hugged her, she stayed, squeezing me back.

My heart ached. I didn't even know it could do that, but in that moment the entire beating muscle sent signals of pain, and all I could do was hold on and hope she didn't change her mind.

I tried to wipe my eyes, so she didn't see the moisture gathered in the corners when I finally released her.

"Are you okay?" she asked.

I gave up on masking and smiled through tears. "This is a big moment for me."

"Dang. I was just going to say, can we please not make a big deal out of this?"

"Too late."

She looked at her feet, speaking quietly. "I guess it's a big deal for me, too. I never thought I'd kiss you again."

"And now that you have...?"

She looked up, a little surprised. "I'm not done." She took my hand and pulled me down onto the makeshift bed. I sat down, leaning against the wall, and she straddled me. We were finally face-to-face, perfectly level.

"We can analyze it later, but right now, I'm feeling hurt and horny and confused, and you'll just have to take me as I am. I need to feel loved and seen and okay. I need to feel like I have my shit together, even if I don't. Like I'm good enough."

I sensed the frantic energy behind her words. The picture they painted wasn't what I wanted for her, or for us, but I was grateful that she was with me. "Whatever you need, Teresa."

She crashed her mouth onto mine, rocking in my lap. Her tongue swept in, hungry and electric. I was painfully hard in seconds, my body switching gears to match her mood, even when my mind fought back, arguing that this was not right. She was upset, not thinking straight. But it felt so good I could hardly think at all.

She pulled away on a moan, moving over my cock. "Fuck me, Trevor. Make me forget everything."

I almost asked her how she liked it, but I could feel her frustration. She'd danced for me. She'd thrown herself at me. She didn't want to think or direct this. It was my turn. I laid her down on the sleeping bag and peeled up the jingling elf top until I saw a glimpse of her black, lacy bra. She was so smooth and perfect. I counted four little moles, like a constellation, surrounding her belly button. I kissed each one, drawing my tongue down to the edge of those striped leggings. She moaned again, raggedly, tilting her hips toward me.

With one swift movement, I yanked the leggings to her knees, discovering more black lace. I dragged my tongue over the silky fabric, and she shook. "You can just fuck me, Trevor," she gasped. "You don't have to—"

"I want to. More than anything."

I followed her lead, feeling my way through the maze of the body I hoped to never stop touching and learning. Every whimper and shiver I coaxed out of her took me one step closer to losing control. I wanted to drive into her with all I had, but now was not the time.

I kept my touch light, eventually pushing aside those soaked panties until my tongue was right on her bud, teasing with feathery kisses and light taps until she made a wailing sound, pushing for more contact. I sucked her clit, and she cried out, gripping my hair with her fingers, jerking against my lips. It was the most beautiful moment of my life. Transfixed, I watched her ride it out, waiting for those muscles to relax.

I'd never felt happier with myself, even if my balls were turning blue.

"Do you have a condom?" she rasped.

"No." I stretched out next to her on the floor. "I thought I could just give you this... but I might have to do something. I'll go to the bathroom."

"Stay right there." Her voice sleepy and warm, she reached for my cock.

"I didn't mean—"

"I did," she replied.

Her touch was the sweet relief my body had been waiting for all these years. I didn't want to direct her. I'd take what she gave me. Anything. Nothing. Everything. I was hers. But I'd been waiting so long my body didn't listen to reason. I could still taste her in my mouth and every stroke hit me like lightning. It was all too much. So much more than I'd dared to dream. I fought back, trying to hold onto that moment. Make it last.

"You're fucking huge." She shuffled down my body and took me into her mouth. *Oh, God.* This was it. I couldn't hold back any longer. I nearly blacked out as the powerful release rolled through me.

When I came back to earth, she was lying beside me again, watching me with a sleepy smile. "I love the sounds you make."

"Same," I said, although I had no idea what sounds I'd just made. I'd pretty much had an out-of-body experience with no audio track.

She rubbed her nose on my shoulder, smiling.

"How do ye feel now?" I asked, brushing a curl off her face.

"Mellow."

"That's good. I told ye, whatever you need."

She rested her fingers on my bicep, and I resisted the urge to flex. "I honestly thought you'd tell me to behave myself and tuck me in bed."

I huffed, amused. "You think I'm capable of such self-control with you?"

She sighed. "I don't know. At the pool, you said you wanted our first time to be just right. You had these high ideals."

"That was back then. Things change." I wondered why it had ever mattered in the first place. All I wanted was for her to be happy. To give her what she needed.

She lifted her head and peered at me with a sense of wonder. "I basically told you I needed a no-questions-asked orgasm, and you delivered."

"Well, a few months ago, when I tried to apologize, badly... you asked me to jump up my own ass and die. So, this was an easy request."

"Yeah. A slight improvement." She laughed, hanging her head. Her curls fell on my shoulder and I inhaled the scent

My heart squeezed so hard I felt that ache again, and words poured out. "And... how're ye feeling now? I fear you might run away."

She gave me a soft, sleepy smile. "My shoes are really slippery."

"Good."

"And I kind of want to see about us. Who knows?"

My achy heart leapt with joy, and I held her face, kissing her lips, cheeks, the tip of her nose. "Thank you!"

She laughed but eased into my touch. "I only said I'm willing to see about it. Cancel the skywriting proposal."

My heart lurched a little, but I held onto hope. "That's a win, trust me. I'd never ask you to marry me unless you had "yes" written across your forehead. It may not seem like it right now, but I have some pride." I might have been exaggerating, but it was probably best not to come across as totally desperate.

"Good. So, who did you propose to who turned you down? It's been bothering me."

My stomach clenched almost instantly. "It was a long time ago."

She touched my arm, her fingers gentle. "It sounds incredibly brave. Scary brave."

My heart pounded so hard I could almost hear it. Her eyes flickered with countless emotions, and I braced myself. I'd take the rejection. I'd made a pact with myself to not be a coward. Never again. I'd lay my heart at her feet and let her stomp on it. It was the bravest thing anyone could do. But fuck, it was hard.

I'd done it once and, in that moment, the old scars felt as fresh and sore as they'd been seven years ago. I still remembered the sting of rejection. It was a different ache. Not from a heart full of hope, glowing warm, but a radiating pain that made your insides curl up and tighten.

It had taken a long time to relax again, to feel good enough, no matter what I told myself. And here I was, looking into the eyes of a woman I wanted more than anything. I had to lay it all out.

"Her name's Hannah. She was the girl next door. Dark curls like you. Pretty. We'd always been friends, but after my mom died, she was there for me. I think I confused that with love. I mean, she loved me, but more like a brother. After two years of sickness and sadness and death, I was so desperate to build something good. Start a family and make new memories. And I'm so grateful she said no. Because I don't know if I loved her either. It didn't feel like..." I clamped my mouth before I could say "this," but I saw Teresa's nostrils flare as she drew a breath. "It was familiar and nice, but I've since learned that's not good enough for me."

"Me neither," she said quietly. "It was nice with Richard. Until it wasn't. Nice can go fuck itself."

I raised my hand, and she high fived me, her eyes like storm warnings. "Once more with feeling," I said.

She hit my hand so hard the pain rang all the way to my shoulder. "I'm sorry," she whispered. "I think I have anger issues."

Tears sprang to her eyes, and I quickly drew her into a hug. "Hey! Hey... you were just betrayed by someone you trusted. Hit me as many times as you need."

The irony wasn't lost on me. She was being comforted by someone else who'd betrayed her. Teresa deserved better, but I couldn't let her go. What if nobody else could see how amazing she was? Richard the Dick certainly couldn't. For all my failings, I saw it. I saw her brilliance, her beauty and her bravery. She was fiercely independent, yet guileless and honest in her battles. My dragonfly.

CHAPTER 15

Teresa

Trevor held me tight as I sobbed against his chest, cursing the injustice of my life. Maybe I hadn't loved Richard, but I'd trusted him. I'd trusted him to never hurt me because he was so dependable and boring and logical. He was supposed to be the good guy, nothing like the two-faced Trevor. And yet here I was, crying in Trevor's arms.

I allowed myself one more deep breath, inhaling the scent I was developing an addiction to. My body's reaction was so visceral it scared me. And what happened if I fell for a man I couldn't trust? Where would it lead?

I finally peeled myself away from him. "Thank you. I wish I was with my sister, or Bess. I don't want to burden you with this."

"It's a privilege."

Despite feeling overwhelmed, I forced myself to look him in the eye. To really look. "You look at me like I hung the moon. Please stop. I'm not that amazing. You don't even know me. If you did... you'd spit me out like this town did."

He smiled like he knew something I didn't. "I won't ask you, but one day you'll tell me, and it won't be that bad."

"You don't know."

"I know yer heart."

"You have a lot of trust, Trevor."

He shrugged, and we sat there for a moment, staring at each other in wonder. Finally, I felt my eyelids getting heavy.

"Sleep. I'll keep watch," he said, scooting off the bed, making room for me.

"You can't stay up all night! There are no wild animals or anything to make you produce enough adrenaline. You'll just fall asleep awkwardly on the floor and be sore tomorrow."

"That's fine."

I didn't protest. I was too exhausted. Too grateful for the way he was looking after me. I crawled into the sleeping bag, feeling like a little elf slipping into my warm cocoon under a mossy rock or a grassy hill or wherever elves huddled at night.

"Thank you, Trevor."

"My pleasure." He sat so close my hair brushed against the light blanket he'd pulled over his knees, leaning against the wall. Having him here made me feel safe, but I felt awful about him sitting up with no bed around.

"You can go to your cabin now," I said. "I'm okay."

"I won't. I need you around so I can keep guessing sex positions and locations."

"But I'll fall asleep," I mumbled, already half gone.

"That's what I'm counting on. Preferably, you'll have that one recurring dream and I get to watch you as it happens."

"I have a feeling it's less entertaining to watch than you think."

"You have no idea how entertaining you are to watch. Awake or asleep."

A warm glow in my chest, I fell asleep. I might have had a naughty dream or two, but when I woke up, it was the least of my worries.

CHAPTER 16

Trevor

It was amazing how you could tell someone was scandalized, even if you didn't understand a word they said. As we woke up to a group of Germans muttering in the doorway, I picked up on the unmistakably judgmental vibe before my brain caught up to the situation.

I rolled over on the cold, hard floor, my eyes searching for Teresa. There she was, already standing by the cable pole in her wrinkled elf outfit, smiling at them.

"Excuse me?" Our realtor appeared from behind the Germans. "I thought you were coming in later for the second viewing! I have another key, so..."

"I'm sorry!" Teresa's voice was bright and cheery. "I lost Trevor's car key, and we got a bit stuck."

Annalise scanned our little campsite, and her professional smile morphed into shock. "You *slept* here?"

"That's my fault," Teresa continued. "Trevor offered his cabin, but we had no car, and my shoes are not made for walking."

Annalise cocked her head, palpable confusion on her face. "And you're dressed as an elf because…"

"Wardrobe issues."

I was amazed at the way Teresa faced them with a smile, not flinching. It was reassuring to find yourself impressed by someone you'd already fallen for. I would have loved Teresa regardless, but everything I learned about her pulled me in a little deeper.

I scrambled to my feet and gathered our things, heaving the bags onto my shoulders. "I apologize. Here's the key. We'll be out of your hair."

Annalise accepted the key, her mouth still hanging open, and the Germans shifted to let us pass. Once we made it to the sidewalk, we both burst into hysterical laughter.

Teresa pulled herself together first, quickly throwing her overcoat on top of the elf costume. It didn't hide the striped leggings, but she looked a little less like she was headed to a poorly-timed Christmas party.

"I'm so lucky I was already awake when they showed up! I was brushing my teeth when I heard the door," she said.

"That explains why you look way more presentable than me," I replied, desperately trying to straighten my achy back and peel open my eyes. I felt exhausted and beaten, yet almost giddy after last night.

She looked down at her legs. "I look like I've escaped from an institution."

"What do you mean? That could easily be a fashion choice. You don't even have the pointy boots with jingle bells."

"I jingle, though," she said, throwing her purse over her shoulder. "Okay. I don't know about you, but I need coffee. So badly that I don't care what it tastes like."

She headed down the street towards Cozy Confectionery, sounding like the intro to Jingle Bells, playing over and over again without the song ever starting. Insanity-inducing, but she was that to me anyway, so I just rolled with it.

Moments from last night played in my head, making my step feel lighter than it should have.

We received a few sideways looks from other patrons, mostly due to that incessant jingling, but the smell of cinnamon and butter was as heady as ever, and we were both too hungry to care. I bought us protein smoothies and cinnamon rolls and watched Teresa mix four creamers into her coffee.

The morning was cloudy, with muted daylight competing with artificial lighting. The pink decorations still hung everywhere. Softly floating snow behind the window added to the ambiance. Valentine's Day was technically over, but Cozy Creek clearly wasn't done celebrating love.

I checked my phone for messages. Charlie hadn't given any updates, but I knew they were traveling. Even if all went well, he wouldn't make it here before tomorrow. If I wanted to avoid bringing Teresa to my cabin, I had to find her a ride out of here today.

I'd been warned about Cozy Creek not having Uber, and that its alternative, Huber, wasn't necessarily available to outsiders. I wanted to think of myself as an insider, but I'd only just bought the cabin, and was still in the process of selling my place in Denver.

"So, I was thinking we could maybe ask around and pay someone to give you a ride back home? There are tourists stopping here on their way through as well; someone might have room in their car."

She looked up from her smoothie, frowning. "What? Are you staying here?"

"I have Charlie and Bess coming up to bring the car key, so I'll have to stay. But you don't have to."

She pinned me with a look that made my every muscle tense simultaneously. "Why am I not welcome in your cabin? Do you have a secret wife up there, or a dead body?"

I laughed, trying to shake the tension. "No."

"Or are you trying to get rid of me before Charlie and Bess arrive so you guys can make a decision about the company moving without me?"

"No! They wanted to see it, but I'll make sure no decision is made before we're all back in Denver."

She propped an elbow on the table and leaned closer, looking distressed. "Then, what is it? I've tried to explain this to myself and everything I can think of is... bad. It's freaking me out."

"It's nothing," I said quickly. "I thought your shoes weren't good for walking."

The whole point of this was to *not* freak her out. If I couldn't avoid it, I might as well show her the cabin.

"Then let's get me another pair of shoes!"

I bit back a smile. "Aye. Do you want another outfit, too?"

She was being a good sport about it, even removing her coat as the heater blasted next to us.

"You look good in green," I said. "I don't think I've ever seen you wear it."

"I feel like I'm in disguise." She looked relaxed, sitting back in her chair to finish her smoothie.

Did she want to be in disguise? What had she left behind when she'd fled the town? I could barely contain my curiosity, but I knew that pestering her wouldn't work. I had to wait until she was ready to tell me.

The door swung open and a middle-aged man in a puffer jacket stepped in, shaking snow off his shoulders. He headed straight to the counter with a stack of flyers. After a quick exchange with the young woman behind it, he turned to the rest of us, raising his voice. "Good morning, everyone! I'm here to spread the word about the sled contest. We just heard some of our contestants have dropped out to join the search for the missing tourist, so we're a bit short on entries for tomorrow. Please consider joining! We have new prizes that were just donated. It's going to be an amazing event!"

He began handing out the flyers. "All you need to do is turn up with your sled!"

I grabbed one, reading it out loud. "Cardboard Sled Contest, sponsored by Neville Architects."

Teresa stiffened, her face pale.

"What is it?" I asked.

Teresa shook her head. "Nothing... anyway, I don't think we can make it."

The flyer guy stopped at our table, smiling at her like she'd been talking to him. "Well, if things change, we'd love to see you. There's prize for the best dressed, and you, young lady, are well on your way to winning."

When he left, Teresa took the flyer and studied it, her eyebrows drawn. "I'd forgotten about this contest. We never built anything, but it was fun to watch."

"Sounds like all you need is a box with some duct tape on the bottom. And someone to give you a push."

She slid the flyer back to me. "It's way more elaborate than that."

I read the small print. "Warm cider, cinnamon rolls, hot dogs, and you can place bets! I think the spectators are having more fun than contestants."

"Probably why they're short on contestants." Teresa finished her coffee with a grimace.

"If I was into gambling, placing bets on cardboard boxes going down a hill would be my number one choice. Imagine the adrenaline!"

She gave me an eyeroll and a smile. I loved seeing her smile— it soothed my soul. Whatever was on that flyer, or whoever it was that had drained the blood from her face, was momentarily forgotten. Despite my curiosity, I didn't want to dredge it up.

I gathered my courage and asked, "So, how was your Valentine's Day?"

She sunk her fingers into her hair, messing up those adorable curls even more. "Yesterday was insane. I'm still processing it. I keep thinking, if I hadn't caught Richard with Carolyn, I would have gone out with him. He might have told me about her and broken up with me. Or..."

"The 'or' is more likely," I said gently. "Would you rather not know? You could have had a nice date with him. Chocolate soufflé, then going back to his place..."

She shuddered, gripping her hair with both fists. "No! Don't say that. He would have broken up with me. We would have never..."

"I don't know," I said truthfully. "I don't know him."

I didn't want to think about her sleeping with Dick. The last year had been hard enough.

"I'm glad I was here with you," she finally said, releasing her hair and dropping her hands into her lap. "It's been eventful, but I feel like I needed a distraction. I needed an elf costume." She chuckled, shaking her head.

Teresa always had bed hair. Or maybe I saw it that way because I kept imagining her in bed, a dark, curly halo around her face, naked and smiling. If she'd really had sex dreams about me, I had sexy daydreams about her, constantly. Mine didn't involve exciting costumes or locations. I couldn't really focus on anything but her. And now that I'd gotten a taste of her, my imagination was running wild, visualizing things that before had been hazy. She was every bit as sexy and incredible as I'd always thought. Yet, reality trumped fantasy every time. It was messy, scary, and profound.

That deep dimple on her left cheek, the way her eyes lightened to the color of whiskey in the sun and the way she bounced on the balls of her feet when she was excited. That tattoo on her hip. Everything I knew and didn't know fascinated me.

"I'm glad, too," I said, taking her hand across the table. "And I'm not trying to get rid of you, I promise. But I thought you had a lot of work on, so you might want to get back."

Panic flashed behind her eyes, and I regretted bringing it up. "I'm getting behind. I can feel it. There's no deadline today, but I need to send stuff on Monday."

"Sweet. We'll ask Charlie to swing by the office and bring your laptop. Then you can email updates and whatever you need to do before we head back to Denver."

"Yeah. Okay." She relaxed a little.

"Shoe shopping, then?"

"Do you think they sell those pointy elf shoes anywhere?" she asked as we exited the cafe.

"Let's find out."

I grabbed her arm to help her over the slippery steps. To my surprise, she hung onto mine and didn't let go. My heart glowed as we walked down the street, browsing the selection of shops along Main Street. There was a hairdresser, a real estate company, an adorable bookstore, a ski shop… and finally, an old-style shoe shop and repair store with a giant leather boot in their window. At the door, she finally let go of my hand.

"Bingo!" She bounced a little, turning her excited eyes to me.

Emboldened by her move, I slid my hand to her waist, guiding her inside. I never wanted to stop touching her. Her short winter coat showed off her perfect butt, highlighted in red and green stripes, framed by the jingle bells sticking out from underneath the jacket's hem. She was the hottest elf I'd ever seen.

Would she ever go for it again? Did she think last night had been a mistake? I was too scared to ask.

CHAPTER 17

Teresa

We browsed the shelves full of handmade shoes, admiring their detailing. The smell of leather hung in the air and the noises from the back room told us the shopkeeper was on his way.

I tried to pretend I didn't notice how Trevor's hand slid from my waist, grazing my bottom, but it took a lot of effort. My whole body vibrated from that slight touch, sending a very familiar zing into my core. I was hot for him again. I'd thought of last night as scratching an itch—a one-time thing, brought on by wine and circumstances. But I was developing something akin to a fever and my whole body hummed with possibilities I was scared to think about.

I'd been free from these feelings for so long I didn't think I'd have to worry about them ever coming back.

Had I really been free from them? I'd never felt indifferent towards him, but I'd been angry and disappointed. I'd kept him in that too-hard basket, thinking it was the same as getting over him.

I wandered through the shop, browsing the beautiful leather shoes, taking pleasure in the way Trevor followed me, standing so close I felt his body heat and energy. Sensed his gaze on me. I was enjoying myself. That delicious pulsing between my legs was the sweetest distraction he could have offered. If fooling around with Trevor was a mistake, it was still the best thing that had happened during the train wreck that was yesterday. Those moments of pure bliss and that blinding orgasm... I couldn't exactly pretend I was indifferent about it. If I was honest, I wanted more. *Much* more.

But once was a mistake. Twice was a pattern. Or in this case, a relationship, and I'd only just walked out of one. I couldn't start another on the same day. That was doomed to fail.

Could I make it a multi-day mistake? An extended one that included several orgasms? Surely that still fell into the scope of a mistake. It seemed Trevor could wipe Richard from my brain, and that sounded like a win. If the delete-memories-of-your-ex service from *Eternal Sunshine of the Spotless Mind*—incidentally, my favorite film—had been available in real life, I would have instantly booked an appointment.

But if I used a fling with Trevor to sanitize my brain, I had to make sure we wrapped things up before returning to our regular lives. A rebound fling was one thing. A rebound relationship with a guy I had to work with... that would be a disaster.

It didn't have to go that far, though. Trevor was a fun guy, so I could have fun with him.

A pair of footwear on the bottom shelf caught my eye. They were green, looked like they were made of thick felt, and had pointy, upturned ends.

"Oh, my God!" I lifted them up to show Trevor.

"A local lady makes them for us," the gray-haired shopkeeper said. "They're fantastic if you have cold floors. Anti-slip and everything."

Yep, the soles had textured rubber patches.

"It's an improvement, I suppose," Trevor said, taking the boots and turning them in his hands. "She does slip quite a bit. So, they're only for indoor use?"

The old man cocked his head. "I suppose you could use them for snow walking. With thick woolen socks. As long as the weather stays cold."

"I don't even care. I need these. My elf outfit is not complete without them!" I looked pleadingly at Trevor. "I'll pay you back."

He smiled at me, shaking his head. "That's all good, aye. But should we still get you boots that are designed for outdoor use? It's a bit like snow tires. Up here in the mountains you need the proper gear."

"Sure, if I *lived* here."

Our gazes snagged, and we held still, silently finishing those sentences neither of us was ready to speak. He wanted me to think about the future in this town, but he didn't know my past.

I pulled on the elf booties, posing in my full gear. His smile was warm, like he'd decided to push everything else aside. Just me and him, and the perfect moment.

"It's a braw look. Let's hope the weather disnae turn."

"The cold front should hold for a few days," said the shopkeeper helpfully, ringing up the purchase.

I slipped my 'city slicker' leather boots into the bag the shop provided, happily stomping out in my full elf outfit. "Maybe we could find one of those red and green elf hats. Did they have any at the laundromat?"

Trevor laughed. "Do we not have enough elf items?"

I hooked my arm around his. "Are you embarrassed to be seen with me? What if someone thinks you're dating a real elf? Or that you have some kind of elf fetish?"

It was fun to mess with him. I wasn't sure why it didn't bother me more that I was dressed like a cartoon character in my old hometown. Maybe because I'd always felt like a freak here. Now I was just flying the flag. It felt liberating. Also, there was nobody from my real life within a one-hundred-mile radius, which granted its own sweet freedom. I'd needed a break, and it had come at the right time. Here in Cozy Creek, I didn't have a reputation to uphold. At least not a good one.

"Are you okay with carrying all that back to the cabin?" I asked. "I only have a pair of shoes. I can take the other bag."

I tried to grab the overnight bag off his shoulder, but he shrugged me off. "It's too heavy for you."

"I'm stronger than you think."

I wrestled the smaller bag from him until he gave in, and we walked in silence, Trevor leading the way. Main Street turned into a smaller side road, then another one. The fresh snow glowed brightly, making everything look clean and white. Smoke rose from the chimneys, and the houses caked with snow looked like iced muffins.

"This is my road," he said as we turned onto Mountain View Lane.

"Is it a two-mile road? Because we've only walked a few minutes."

"No..." He drew a breath, looking a bit guilty.

"Did you lie to me about the distance?"

I wanted to ask "why", but as he nodded, looking increasingly uncomfortable, I decided to hold back any follow-up questions. The house was probably a ramshackle shed with a roof missing, or something else atrocious. I'd find out soon enough.

The road sloped uphill, the houses fewer and further between than before, with patches of snow-covered spruces in between. And there, at the end of the road, by the small turning bay, stood a huge, beautiful log house with floor-to-ceiling feature windows.

"This is not a little cabin," I said, turning to him. "This is... a chalet, or a lodge?"

He looked almost embarrassed. "Did I say little? Sorry, no. It's... um... not little. I had some money."

"From selling those tokens?"

He nodded. "I cashed out when they peaked. They're not worth that much anymore. It was just good timing."

I felt a pang of jealousy but pushed it aside. "Well, I'm glad you got something out of it."

Was that why he was weird about the house? Because he'd bought it with the money he made from that job?

He opened his mouth a couple of times, but no words came out. Finally, he opened the gate and gestured for me to step in. The path to the door had been cleared of snow at some point, but more had fallen, creating an obstacle course of white stuff. My felt boots sunk in, making that crunching sound that brought back memories.

Trevor unlocked the door, and we dropped our bags on the floor. As I raised my gaze to examine the space, I gasped in shock.

CHAPTER 18

Teresa

Trevor's cabin wasn't just a gorgeous house. It was my dream house—the exact interior I'd planned in my head and on my computer when house hunting. The huge, overstuffed armchairs with button details, the inviting leather couch, the soft throws, and textured cushions. The wall-to-wall bookshelves, the giant candle holders, and overlong velvet curtains. The room was full of things I'd pinned and dreamed of.

It made no sense. He'd stolen my dream job, made a fortune, and then stolen my dream house? I loved my little condo in the city because it was mine, but I'd never had the budget to create all this. I lived amongst mismatched second-hand items and cheap Ikea furniture. And Trevor had *this*?

Was it possible our tastes were this aligned? Was my taste

particularly masculine? My gaze drifted to the coral velvet arm-chair, and I shook my head. "Trevor?" I waited for him to look at me and as soon as he did, I picked up on the worry in his eyes. "Are we the same person?" I asked.

"What? Why?"

"Because this is exactly the house I would have created if I'd had the budget. Apart from maybe that mountain scenery, but honestly, now I'm thinking that was the one thing missing from my plans." I gestured at the tall windows, sighing in awe.

His cheeks reddened. "No. It's for you. It's... what you showed me. Please don't freak out. You told me about your dream board, remember? By the pool. You showed me those pictures, and I re-membered your username. Dragonfly. And later, when I bought this place, I had no idea how to decorate. I don't decorate... I don't have preferences." He let out an exasperated sigh. "So, I hired someone, and gave them your board for reference."

"So, you stole my dream and made it for yourself?" I stared at him in confusion, too many emotions fighting for my attention. Was I supposed to feel flattered or betrayed?

His voice turned frantic. "No! I did it for you. I told you, I don't have preferences. A couch is a couch. But I had to choose some-thin', and I thought if I chose what ye liked, then you'd... feel at home." He wrung his hands, looking at them like he didn't know who they belonged to. "Honestly, you were so hellbent on avoiding me back then that I didn't think you'd ever see it. And in some weird way, it made me feel closer to you. But when I re-alized ye were going to see this, I came to my senses, and I knew it was a really stupid, really creepy idea."

As if claiming defeat, he picked up a picture frame propped up against the wall, turned it around, and hung it up. It was an intricate drawing of a dragonfly and the most beautiful piece of art I'd ever seen.

I stared at it, then at him, lost for words. I felt so torn I could barely form a sentence in my head, let alone speak one. He'd taken my dream, *my* dream, and created it to feel closer to me?

"You do realize that *I* couldn't create this dream, because I wasn't on that team and didn't get those tokens and that payout? My house looks nothing like this. I've never actually seen this in real life, only on my Pinterest board. That first picture—"

"That was the one I asked the designer to run with. I thought it looked amazing."

"So, you *like* this? It's not just for me?"

His eyebrows pulled together. "It's great! The couch is very comfortable. But you know I'm not a designer. I've never worried what my couch should look like, as long as I'm sharing it with people I love. I may not get much out of Pinterest, but I've visualized curling up on that couch with someone I love... and one day having my kids use it as a trampoline."

Trevor exhaled, rubbing his forehead. "And now I'm freaking you out even more."

"No! It's... beautiful." I raised my hands to my face. My cheeks were burning hot.

He took my coat and guided me to the cognac leather couch, adorned with soft throws. It felt surreal, like walking into my favorite Pinterest image come to life around me. I still didn't know what to think, but I had to sit on that couch to confirm it was real. It received me like a cotton candy cloud, and I let out a reverent sigh. "Is this why you didn't want me here? Because of the décor?"

Trevor got busy with the fireplace, facing away from me. "Kind of."

I caught a whiff of lighter fluid, then the smell of woodsmoke as the logs were licked by flames. I'd forgotten how soothing the sound of a crackling fire was on a cold day.

With the fire going, he joined me on the couch, which startled me so much that I jumped up. "I'll just take a look around, okay?" I said breathlessly, wandering over to the window.

The tall, paneled feature windows offered a vast mountain view, including a glimpse of the snowcapped Rockies. We were still very close to town. Beyond the strip of snow-dusted forest, I could see a glimpse of the town center, with a hint of pink on the lamp posts.

I wasn't sure what I'd expected from Trevor's house, but it wasn't this. Walking around the room felt surreal, yet I couldn't help it: I loved this place. He'd created the haven I'd always dreamed about. It was perfect.

I walked across the room to the open-plan kitchen, studying its tasteful details. It wasn't directly lifted from my dream board, but perfectly matched the look of the living area. If I'd come across a picture of it somewhere, I would have pinned it. I ran my fingers along the cool stone countertops, imagining how nice it could be to cook with this much space. No need to stack countertop shelves onto every available square inch. There was ample space, a giant pantry, and overhead cabinets to hold everything you needed.

My city mortgage was huge, yet my apartment was tiny. Even if I saved for years, I couldn't create this look in such a small space. It'd always look boxy and crammed.

Driven by curiosity, I kept walking, heading towards the doorway leading to the bedroom. It turned out to be a door to another, smaller living area that led to three bedrooms. Two were empty, but the master had a king-sized bed and a dresser. The Pinterest stalking didn't extend to the décor around here. The bed seemed high quality, but the room had nothing else. No cushions, chairs, rugs, or art. Not even curtains. Just white sheets, white walls and a lot of floor space.

Trever appeared behind me.

"You still working on these?" I asked.

"The designer said she needs direction, and I didn't have enough visuals to go on."

"I didn't have any bedrooms on my Pinterest board?"

It was almost too absurd to say out loud, but he nodded. I took a breath and stepped in, looking at the stark white walls surrounding the huge bed. White on white. Even the scenery outside was white.

"Your bed needs a headboard," I said. "And you need some kind of curtains."

"I know."

"A rug."

"Uhuh."

"And a chair, maybe—"

"I know what normally goes in a bedroom, Teresa. I just didn't know which ones to choose."

He looked so stressed that my heart lurched. I stepped closer, placing my hands on his huge chest. "Would you like me to put something on a board for you?"

His gaze darted around the room, as if searching for an escape. "I know I messed up. And I promise I'll list all that crap on eBay and replace it with random stuff ye'd never look twice at on Pinterest. I'll get fifty beanbag chairs and cover the walls with posters and—"

I covered his mouth, horrified. "Shh. Stop talking. The gorgeous couch will hear you!"

"I promise I'm not this creep," he said as soon as I removed my hand. "I was going through something, but it's over now. I will get rid of it. I—"

I grabbed him by the arms. "Chill, Trevor. What you did here is super weird, but it's also sweet. I think it's one of those things that is simultaneously both. If I'd seen this last week, before we spent the night together, I would have thought it was some kind of sick power play." He stiffened under my touch, but I held on. "But I feel like I know you a little better now, and maybe it's still odd, but not that creepy. I know you didn't do this to gloat."

"Of course not! What would I gloat about? Being a dick to you? Being possessive? I didn't want ye to work with Gavin, but

I had no right to influence the outcome."

"You really didn't want me around, Gavin, huh?" I thought back to our earlier conversations, trying to make sense of it. I'd never believed those arguments. It had sounded like something he'd cooked up after the fact to make himself sound like a hero.

"I've had that feeling about a couple of other guys before, and they both turned out to be rotten eggs, so I thought I had some sort of psychic ability. Turns oot I was just a jealous idiot."

"What kind of rotten eggs?"

"A scam artist who worked on my nan, a long time ago. I remember telling my parents there was something off about him and they finally decided to look him up. And then this high school teacher I had, who was having affairs with students. He'd been going for years without getting caught."

"Did you catch him?"

He shrugged. "I like to think I helped. I followed him a couple of times and picked up on some hints. I was a young lad, so it took me a while to make sense of it. But I was friends with the girl he was seeing, and she told me some stuff. I finally convinced her to talk to the guidance counselor, and the guy got caught. It took forever, though. I'm patient, but I still remember the frustration."

A shiver ran through me as I thought about my own youth. I'd been fighting for justice and run out of patience. "I'm glad they caught him."

"Me, too."

"I'm not as patient as you," I confessed, leading us back to the living room. "I wish I was. Revenge is a hollow victory."

I sat on the couch, pulling my striped legs against my chest. He remained standing, his tall frame hovering over me. "Are you hungry? I could fix us some lunch."

"Sure. Do you need help?" I was about to get up, but he waved me off and continued into the kitchen.

I sank into the plush cushions, listening to the sounds of cooking. Faucet running, pots clanging, the fridge door smacking open... Trevor was out to impress me, and I still couldn't decide how I felt about it. For one, I couldn't remember ever listening to anyone cook for me, not since childhood. Suze cooked for us sometimes, but I usually joined in.

I had to admit, it felt nice to be taken care of. My whole life, I'd been the capable one. The independent one. At work, I'd looked out for Bess. But she didn't need my help anymore, not like she'd used to. I was happy for her and grateful that they'd saved my ass after I lost my job at Wilde. Yet I was still getting used to the shift in dynamics. We had an exciting little business, I had a good salary and interesting work, but I was the odd one out. Not a shareholder. No skin in the game. Even Lee had some shares, and he only worked part time.

I was also the only one with no access to any wealth. Trevor with his crypto money, Lee with a bit less crypto money, Charlie with his grandmother's backing, and Bess now married to him. I was the one who looked after herself with no lucky breaks. Trevor had stolen the only lucky break I'd ever been gunning for.

So, what the hell was I supposed to think of him?

"Bon appetite!" He set an impressive egg salad sandwich on the coffee table. "Coffee?"

"Is your coffee better than Cozy Creek Confectionery's?" I asked.

"About a hundred times better."

He left to make them, and after a few minutes, returned with two steaming cups.

"Here you go." He set the perfectly cocoa-dusted macchiato in front of me and took his black coffee to the adjacent armchair.

I shouldn't have been too surprised that he knew my coffee order. It had come up enough times in the office, with one of us fetching drinks for everyone else. Still, I couldn't have named anyone else's drink preference, not with any confidence. Bess ordered a different drink every time now that she felt financially secure enough to even order anything. Charlie was usually the one who ordered and paid, and Trevor... what did Trevor drink? I should have known, and my cheeks warmed from shame as I thought of all the ways I'd been ignoring him.

He hadn't hated me like I'd hated him, and that made my insides churn so hard I didn't know which organ was where. Trevor had *never* hated me.

"This is perfect," I said between sips, my voice thick and scratchy. "You must have an amazing memory. I don't think we've had coffees together in a long time."

He laughed. "My memory is both shit and selective, but I pay attention to what matters to me. Sometimes, I write it down."

I tried to make sense of it. "I understand writing about that night at the pool ... but mundane stuff like coffee orders?"

He took a sip of his coffee. "Remember the designer pub quiz?"

I nodded, thinking of my victorious night. I'd won the main prize—a brand-new pack of Pantone color swatches.

"You were naming all those weird colors, and then you got to Tyrian and said, 'my personal favorite.'"

"Did I?"

"Well, I wrote it down right after."

"Why?"

"I just wanted to know things about you."

I thought back to that time. "But it was after that night. After... it all went to hell."

He shrugged. "I still wanted to know about you. That never changed."

"I was practically freezing you out that night."

He set down his cup, smiling. "It was impressive."

I shook my head, sinking back into the couch. "How do you not lose hope? If someone acted like that towards me, I'd file them away and move on."

He watched me intensely. "Maybe I have a masochistic streak."

I didn't buy it. "No. You believe. You kept believing... How?"

He was quiet for a long moment, staring into his cup. When he spoke again, his words brimmed with raw honesty. "I had hope. As long as you hated me, you had feelings for me. Even when you were dating Rich the Dick, you had enough energy to actively avoid me. And you talked to me, every day."

"It's our work chat!" I argued, but the truth sat heavy on my chest.

I relied on our private chat more than I wanted to admit. Trevor was always there. He never left my messages on 'read'. He knew how to diffuse the tension when clients got on my nerves. He knew how to cheer me up. With him, the work felt different. Lighter.

"I know," he said. "But it was my lifeline. As long as we had that private chat, I had a little hope."

I thought about it. I sometimes chatted with Bess, but I didn't have a private chat with Charlie. There was the group chat, and then there was us. Me and Trevor. The job that had prompted us to start that chat was long gone. Either of us could have closed the channel. It would have made sense, given we all worked together on most jobs.

"You apologized, and I forgave you. So, of course I was talking to you."

"And every time we were in the same room, you acted like I didn't exist. It takes a lot of effort to ghost someone in person."

I grimaced. "I didn't want to think about it. I didn't want to dredge up anything." I took a bite of my sandwich. It was so delicious tears rose to my eyes.

"I figured," he said. "And that tells me we have something, even if it's buried under... I didn't know if ye'd ever want to look under that rock, but I knew ye weren't indifferent towards me."

I swallowed my perfect mouthful, washing it down with a sip of perfect coffee. "That's quite the rose-tinted, half-full glass you're holding there."

"Well. Answer me this. If I died, how would you feel? Happy? Indifferent?"

My chest pinched so hard that it was difficult to breathe. In that moment, I felt it—the raw affection I'd buried under all the hurt and anger. I felt the need and desperation, and the black hole he would leave behind. Had it been there all this time?

I couldn't form words, so I simply shook my head.

CHAPTER 19

Trevor

I held my breath, watching the transformation on her face. I hadn't imagined it. Teresa cared about me. Maybe she'd always cared. Whether she had any stronger feelings, or could one day develop them, I didn't know. But I had to go forth in my blind faith. What else could I do?

It would have been so much easier to move on. Any sane person walked away when they weren't wanted. Why did I hang around, hoping? I knew guilt had played a part, at least in the beginning, but after so many months, it was mostly stubbornness.

"Ye'd miss me." I couldn't help smiling. "If I died, you'd cry."

She rolled her eyes affectionately, and I saw the film of tears on them. "Death is generally considered sad."

She took a huge bite of her sandwich, focusing on chewing.

"That's true. But you work more closely with me than anyone else. You comment on every word I produce. You suggest new headings and edits all the time."

She swallowed, considering this for a moment. "Sometimes, there's a font I want to use, and a certain letter has a beautiful glyph, so I want to make sure that letter is in the heading."

I nodded. I'd figured that out a long time ago. "But it's not just that. You comment on everything I do. You don't comment on everything Charlie does because you're indifferent to him. But me..."

I set down my coffee cup and leaned so close I could have reached across the table and touched her. She swallowed another piece of sandwich and leaned forward, too. "You're special, Trevor. Happy now?"

"You have no idea."

She leaned back, feigning disinterest, but her cheeks had an adorable color to them. "You make a pretty good sandwich, too."

We polished our plates, watching the crackling fire. Outside, it was snowing again, heavier this time. I'd chosen the house for its view and its location right outside town. As much as I liked to imagine myself in the middle of nowhere, hunting and fishing, Teresa liked living around the corner from her favorite deli. Cozy Creek was small, but at least it was right there, outside the window. I knew I was unhinged to dream of her ever living here, with me, especially now that I knew she'd grown up here. But I had to dream.

When she finished eating, I collected our plates and loaded

them into the dishwasher. Teresa followed me into the kitchen, observing me. She looked deep in thought, a little crease between her eyes.

"Are you okay?" I asked.

"You load from back to front."

I looked up, confused. "Never thought about it. Why?"

"Just something Richard always ranted about. How his ex used to load from front to back."

"The ex he was snogging yesterday?"

She nodded.

"He complained to you about his ex?"

It sounded odd.

"Quite a lot, to be honest. I didn't think too much of it." She shrugged.

"Did *you* talk about your exes?" I asked.

She looked surprised. "No."

"Not even me?"

She gave me a reproaching look. "You're not my ex."

"But I am a man you could have complained about if you'd wanted to match his stride."

She blew a frustrated breath, grabbed a cloth, and began wiping the counter. "That's the thing! I don't talk about my exes because I don't think about them. Even when he went on and on about Carolyn, I just remember thinking, 'Oh, I'd better not do that thing he hated.' Now I don't know if he really hated it, or if he just wanted to keep talking about her."

"He was probably trying to convince himself that he'd made a good choice, being there with you. Which tells me he's a douche."

The guy was a cheating piece of shit, but that was not why I wanted to punch him. I wanted to punch him for taking her for granted. Never realizing what he had.

She froze, the cloth dangling from her fingers. "I *did* complain about you," she said in a small voice. "I talked too much about you and all the reasons I hated you."

"Really? That's great!"

She frowned at me. "Why?"

"Well, Lil' Dick complained about his ex and look where he ended up!"

"On her face?"

I flashed her a victorious grin. "Probably in her pants, too."

"You're a dick!" She huffed, throwing the wet cloth at me.

I caught it in midair. She was so cute with her cheeks burning, eyes like two flames swallowed by black coals. Was she turned on or furious? Probably just furious.

"I *have* a dick. There's a slight difference," I corrected.

"Is there, though? Whenever there's a dick involved, I seem to end up betrayed." She spat out the words, looking at me with a mix of hurt and something else.

I swallowed. The energy in the room shifted, like a cold breeze had snuck in through a crack. I'd been feeling so hopeful, reading into her every word, every expression... But if she couldn't see any difference between me and her cheating ex, I was doomed.

Maybe I'd been depleting my hope, gradually using up the stores, until it was all gone. Like a car that ran out of gas, suddenly sputtering to a stop.

"Fair enough," I said. "If you think I'm the same as him, you should definitely stay away from me." I turned on the dishwasher, even though it was barely half full, grabbed my phone and headed for the bedroom. "I'll see if I can organize you a ride out of here, so you don't have to wait for those car keys with me."

I didn't mean to storm out, but I might have closed the door with more force than was necessary. My heart pounded as I browsed my phone, unable to focus on the screen or whatever I was supposed to do. I didn't want to find her a ride and send her away, but I couldn't be this delusional. She might have taken me out of the shit basket, but she'd just put me in the same basket as her ex.

Last night had been a fluke, brought on by wine and some sense of danger. Now, she'd seen what a nutcase I was, decorating my house to match her vision board. She was being nice about it, but that was probably a survival instinct. She was stuck here with me, relying on me, trying to keep me happy until she got back home.

She'd never give me another chance.

I leaned on the door, letting the pain dig its way through me. Allowing it. Because there was no other choice. I'd made a pact with myself that I'd risk the hurt. I had to be man enough to take it.

CHAPTER 20

Teresa

I stared at the door, my limbs frozen, mind spinning. What had I done? I'd seen the pain in his eyes, almost like a substance that swallowed the calming blue-green. He'd been so buoyant, so full of faith. He'd had enough faith in us to create an entire house and keep track of each interaction we had, finding hope in signs of hate. Who had *that* kind of faith?

I'd thrown my fresh sense of betrayal at him without thinking. I'd lumped him in with Richard. He was the one I wanted to be yelling at right now, not Trevor.

And now he was calling me a ride, getting me away from this house I never wanted to leave. I was still unsure about my feelings for him, but if I wasn't honest now, I was going to lose him for good. Neither of us could cross that bridge again if I let us get there.

I knocked on the door, then tried opening it, but it didn't budge.

"Trevor? I need to talk to you."

After a moment, the door opened. His eyes looked a little red, but he met my gaze squarely, leaning his shoulder against the doorframe. "Yes?"

"I'm sorry I put you in the same category as Richard... Dick. You're not. And I've already told you I've forgiven you, so I shouldn't bring it up. Not anymore."

"You're still angry," he stated, watching me carefully.

"Yes. But only like twenty percent. There are a lot of other emotions in the mix. And the anger is mostly for Richard. I think I'm taking it out on you because you're here, and I haven't had any closure with him."

"Sounds like you need that."

"I think I do," I admitted.

"Good. You can go talk to him when the driver takes you back to Denver."

My stomach dropped. "You want me to leave?"

"I won't keep you against your will. I can't keep up this one-sided thing between us. I thought I could, and for months, I did. I had hope. And now I feel like I've run out. I can't anymore. I won't chase you, Teresa. I'm done."

"You're... done?" My heart felt like a swelling ball bursting out of my chest. "You liked me and now you don't like me anymore?"

He looked sad, shaking his head. "I can't turn off how I feel, but I'm done trying. I can't take it anymore. Not with ye right here."

I took a step forward, stepping into that close range where air vibrated between us. "Am I allowed to try? Or is this just your game?"

He held perfectly still, watching me. "What do ye mean?"

I ran my hands up his chest, curling my fingers around the collar of his Henley. "Am I allowed to try... us? I haven't been thinking about this and Pinterest-stalking you. I'm still catching up. But I enjoy having such a non-threatening stalker who is so incredibly considerate. It's flattering. It's building me up when everything else around me is tearing me down. You're the only good thing that's happened to me in months."

"Good? Not creepy?" He glanced at the living room behind me, looking so mortified that I couldn't help myself—I hugged him.

He didn't react at first, but I kept hugging, breathing in his shirt, my eyes stinging from the realization that I already recognized his scent. This was Trevor. Not like the Trevor I remembered from way back, since I didn't remember much at all. This was Trevor now. And despite all the warnings still lingering in my mind, he felt like a safe place.

After a moment, I felt his arms around me and his breath in my ear. "Are you hugging me because you feel sorry for me? Is this a comfort hug?"

I lifted my head to look him in the eye. "Are you too comfortable? Do you want me to punch you?"

He allowed a faint smile. "I just don't want pity. I know I've done pathetic things, but—"

"No, you haven't! You're being brave and romantic. It feels like a lot," I confessed, "and I'm not used to it. But don't give up on me yet. Please."

Hope lit up behind his eyes, and he leaned in to kiss me. I met him halfway, brushing my fingers across his beard, then wrapping my arms around his neck. The kiss deepened and an avalanche of need rushed through me, settling between my legs. He held my waist, his thumbs stroking my sides, deliciously dipping into the hollows beneath my hip bone, firing another connection down there. I wanted to fall in love. I wanted to be as sure as he was. But I was scared.

"I don't want you to be a rebound," I said breathlessly as I pushed him backwards toward the bed. "I feel like I'm using you to get over... him."

He stopped us, picked me up by the waist and gently threw me on the bed, landing on top of me, locking me in between his arms. "I always thought *he* was the rebound. You used him to make me jealous, right? It worked."

I'd never admitted it, not even to myself, but there must have been a grain of truth because I felt a zing through my middle. Maybe I'd been using Richard. I wasn't mad about the thought. It felt a lot better than being betrayed and powerless.

"You were jealous?" I asked, a small smile breaking through.

"Of course. I plotted his murder." He smiled, placing a kiss on my collarbone. "Several murders." Another kiss, lingering on my skin until everything tingled. "I hated seeing ye with him. He never looked like he even saw you. A self-centered, blind man. That awards dinner we went to... He kept ogling the waitress and I wanted to beat him up so badly."

"You went home early."

"Aye. I couldn't watch it. I was *this* close to taking him behind the building..." He pulled his fingers a hair's width apart, a vein in his neck bulging.

"I had no idea."

"You're the sexiest, most incredible woman in any room. If he doesn't see that, he doesn't deserve to be with ye."

My heart swelled, along with the other body parts that had already given up on any resistance. I wanted him so desperately, I hardly cared if this was right or wrong, doomed or fated. In that moment, I only wanted more words, more touches, more of him.

I'd felt his eyes on me that night, months ago. I'd been wearing a low-cut dress and my favorite heels. For myself. That was my favorite lie because I never dressed up for myself. I'd known he'd be there, and I'd known he wasn't seeing anyone. I'd known he was always looking at me, and I had enjoyed taunting him, showing him what he'd lost by being an asshole. None of that had been about Richard, who'd been my official date, my driver, and the perfectly acceptable guy I could hang out with when I felt lonely, which wasn't even that often. I'd kept my distance and protected my independence, only giving away a small slice of who I was. But with Trevor, I wanted to give it all, and it terrified me.

His hand grazed my hip, nudging the edge of my elf leggings, and the thought of undressing brought me back to reality. "Actually, I wouldn't mind taking a shower," I said.

He pulled away, as if sobering up. "Aye, you're right. That's a great idea. How about I run you a bath, and you get to test my clawfoot bathtub?"

I clambered up. "No, you didn't!"

"I did." He nodded, looking a little sheepish. "There was such a great reference pic."

I was up in seconds, heading for the ensuite. *Holy shit!* It was my favorite picture with almost an identical dragonfly wallpaper framing the most inviting bath I'd ever seen, with candles and luxurious bath products lined up on a shelf. I stepped closer, reverently running my hand across the wall. "Dragonflies." My voice cracked.

He stepped past me to plug the tub and turn on the faucet. "I don't know how to use these," he said apologetically, gesturing at the products. "The designer just left them here."

I browsed the selection and chose a jasmine-scented bubble bath. We both watched as the tub began to fill with foam and the smell lingered in the air. "It's perfect," I said, so moved by everything, I found it hard to speak.

"Great." His voice caught in his throat in a similar way. "I'll leave you to—"

"Stay."

He held at the doorway, frozen like a statue, as I pulled the elf top over my head, then unhooked my bra. I heard his sharp intake of breath. Keeping my back to him, I peeled off the leggings and my panties and stood there, naked. I could feel his eyes on me like thermal lights burning my skin.

I finally turned around to face him, holding my breath. I'd never seen his eyes so clouded.

"Fuck. Teresa. Fuck," he muttered, adjusting the crotch of his jeans. "I hope you know what you're doing."

"And I hope you have condoms in your house, because I'm going to need you later."

His laugh echoed off the walls. "I'm a hopeless romantic, but I'm not that hopeless. Top drawer."

I opened the drawer, noting the packet of condoms, and smiled. "It's a big tub if you want to join me."

He undressed in seconds, reaching the bathtub by the time I was standing in it, easing myself into the hot water. It wasn't scalding hot, but my limbs were still cold from the walk outside and my skin screamed from the adjustment, gradually settling into the blissful warmth. I sat down and pulled my knees to my chest, risking a glance at Trevor.

My gaze traveled down his chest, following the trail of dark, curling hair, and I gasped. I'd expected him to be a little turned on, but the erection I came eye-to-eye with was huge and almost purple. Gravity had nothing on it.

He glanced down at it. "Yeah, it's all your fault." He stroked himself briefly, bringing up a droplet of precum I couldn't tear my eyes off.

I'd slept with Richard maybe a grand total of ten times in eight months. We'd never been that crazy about each other. I couldn't even imagine staring at him naked like this. But then again, he was a pasty, average-sized guy and Trevor was some sort of Scottish warrior with a solid, muscular upper body, bulging thighs and king-sized cock. He wasn't soft in the middle, either.

"Have you lost weight?" I asked as he lowered himself into the tub, raising the water level so high it nearly spilled over.

"I've been working on myself. I told you."

"Good work," I said thickly. "It's really showing."

"Good."

"I don't mind a dad bod, to be honest. But you look great. Solid. Amazing." One more adjective, and I was officially unhinged.

"Sweet. Make me a dad and I'm sure you'll get your wish." He grinned.

I inhaled my own saliva and ended up coughing so hard the water did spill over.

"Don't worry," he assured me. "It's all tiled and there's a drain underneath."

"Okay. That's not what I'm worried about, though."

"What? You told me ye wanted kids one day."

I blushed, my mind rushing back to that night by the pool. I *had* told him that, and I'd meant it. But with Richard, I'd been so adamant to keep my independence I'd changed my tune. Had I changed my mind? How did I not know myself better than this? I'd changed so many things after that night. My work schedule, my cafe of choice (to make sure I didn't run into Trevor), my smoking habit... I'd also adjusted how much of myself I was willing to share with someone. How far into the future I was willing to look.

"I think I sabotaged my relationship with Richard," I said. "He went back to her because she needed him. She probably wanted a future with him, and I just wanted someone to hang out with on my terms."

"It doesn't make him any less a cheater, but I get that. You were protecting yerself, and falling in love is the biggest risk you'll ever take."

"How can you risk it?" I asked. "How can you look at me like that when you don't know me? You don't even know if I'm capable of falling in love. Maybe I'm too messed up to do it."

He smiled affectionately. "You're capable."

"But how do you know?" I insisted.

"Because falling in love is not for the healthy and well-balanced. It's part hormones, part madness. It defies logic."

I raised an eyebrow. "So… I'm mad enough?"

His eyes glinted in the low light. "If you have enough passion to hate me for a year and a half, you have enough passion to love me."

"You keep surprising me," I said. "I love that."

I could surprise him, too, I thought, rising to my knees, and wading through to his end of the tub, straddling him. His hard-on nuzzled against my stomach like a warm metal pole, but I was a dancer. I rocked against it, enjoying the sparks that erupted and shot through my body. It would have been so easy to raise my hips a little higher and fill myself with him, let that erection stretch me to absolute capacity. Find out if I could take him. I'd never had anyone that big.

"Oh, my God, Teresa," Trevor growled, grabbing my ass underwater, helping me move up and down. "You know I can't resist you..."

Our mouths crashed together, and our tongues followed. More delectable pressure built in my core. I wanted him inside me right now.

"You can't put a condom on underwater, can you?" I asked, breaking the contact. Our breaths mingled as I stared at him through hooded, unfocused eyes. I could hardly believe how he made me feel. I needed more.

"Probably not safe," he said.

I reached out to the other end of the tub and pulled the plug, then climbed back on his lap, rocking even more shamelessly against that erection. It felt amazing. The water coursed between us, creating a strong current between my thighs, rushing against my swollen flesh. I held still, nearly undone by the sensation. We looked at each other, waiting for the tub to drain. When that final gurgle faded, he grabbed a towel and handed me one.

"Wannae take this to the bed?" he asked.

I shook my head and reached for the condom drawer. I gave him one, and he rolled it on, sitting down in the empty tub. We were both still slightly damp, and my skin felt hot against the cool air. A layer of bubbles lingered on the bottom and my knees sunk into it as I approached him the same way I'd done in the water.

"Your bedroom doesn't have curtains," I said. "And I've never done it in a bathtub."

"Never have I ever," he rasped, leaning in to catch my nipple in his mouth.

A bolt of lightning shot through me, gathering its energy between my thighs. I leaned closer to feel him against me. The hottest pole I'd ever danced. He grabbed my hips, grunting every time I moved against him.

"Let me see you," he pleaded between the more primal noises.

I moved back until I was leaning on my elbows, my knees open. Bared. Sexy. Waiting. I felt his gaze on me as he shifted onto his knees, all the way to the moment his lips touched my inner thigh, trailing closer. He took his time, circling and teasing my clit with his tongue. My entire core throbbed like it was on fire, desperate for more. When he pulled away, I whimpered in frustration.

I heard his soft laugh. "Patience, Dragonfly."

When I couldn't take it anymore, he took my arms and helped me back up. "Ready?" he asked, sitting back so I could straddle him like before.

I couldn't speak. I raised my hips and gently lowered myself onto him. I felt the pressure everywhere. My back and chest, hips and stomach, everything was expanding to make room for him as I sat there, willingly captured. I could barely breathe, but I didn't care.

There was a quiet stillness about that moment I hadn't expected. This wasn't a race to the finish line. The need I felt was deeper. It sat somewhere further back, building up behind my ribcage, cascading down in waves. I felt his hands cupping my buttocks, holding me there. I was locked onto him, but I didn't want to escape. I wanted to stay there forever, right on the cusp of unraveling.

"What do you need?" he asked. "You feel too good. I can't hold on for... I can't."

"I'm so close," I gasped as I tilted my hips for a little more friction.

He tightened his grip on me. I was so incredibly charged, a feather could have sent me over the edge. I was done. I was finished. The orgasm ripped through me, making my hips move on their own, my muscles spasming out of control. He followed with a deep growl, pumping his release inside of me.

I collapsed against him as we panted in unison. "That was insane."

"Did you... come?" The concern in his voice sent a ripple of laughter through me.

"You're funny," I said, wiping my eyes, then hugged him. "Don't worry, Trevor. You took very good care of me."

"Okay, good."

The air was starting to feel cold against my skin, so I reluctantly peeled myself off him. We got out of the tub, wrapped ourselves in towels, then collapsed on the bed. He pulled me to his side, and I nuzzled into his warm skin. There was no going back. I'd slept with him, *really* slept with him, and it had been too good. Too good to ignore. I was supposed to be scratching an itch, but now I knew how he could make me feel, I wanted him even more. This was not a slippery slope. It was a scary, arm-flailing free fall.

Trevor pulled a blanket over us, and I relaxed even further, letting the incredible warmth lull me to the brink of sleep. Last night had been a struggle, with sore muscles and discomfort. Trevor had slept on the cold, hard floor. He must have been exhausted.

It wasn't long before I noticed his breathing deepen and slow down. He was asleep.

I raised to my elbows, gazing at him. He was a beautiful man, under all that scruff. Solid and strong. My heart clenched as I looked at him, the countless eyelashes resting against his cheekbones, faint creases in the corners of his eyes. He still looked young, but with a hint of wear and tear. Had he really changed? Had I changed? Did we really have a chance to make this work?

The bedroom felt exposed with no curtains, but the snowfall behind the window acted like a privacy screen, offering little visibility, and dimming the daylight. I imagined us floating inside a white cloud, hiding from the world below. How I wanted to keep hiding.

When I heard the knock, I first thought it was the wind throwing something against the wall. But then I heard it again, and my heart jumped up to my throat. Someone was at the door!

Was it the driver taking me back to the city?

"Trevor!" I nudged him, then jumped off the bed to frantically gather my clothes and pull them on.

He lifted his head as I hobbled across the floor, tugging up my elf leggings. Why hadn't I brought our bags to the bedroom? I wanted my own clothes!

Someone banged on the door again. I was dressed now. "Get dressed!" I hissed at Trevor on my way out.

CHAPTER 21

Teresa

I opened the door to two snow-covered individuals, smiling with excitement. Bess and Charlie!

"That's some weather," Charlie huffed, as they shook off the excess snow and came inside. "Made for a slow drive, but here we are."

"You haven't killed each other yet?" Bess gave me an unsure smile, looking over my shoulder.

"He's... um, taking a shower. We had a bit of a rough night at the office last night."

She raised her brow. "A rough night?"

"An indoor camping experience."

"Sounds great." Charlie laughed. "How's the office?"

"Pretty good for camping," I said. "Probably better as an office, though. And will be infinitely more comfortable with furniture."

"You coming around to Cozy Creek?" Bess shot me a hopeful smile, and I smiled back.

"It's cute," I said noncommittally.

"Speaking of cute, what are you wearing?" Bess scanned my elf outfit.

"Yeah… I didn't have anything comfortable for the night, so Trevor found this at a laundromat."

Bess stared at me, blinking. "He brought you an elf costume, and you put it on voluntarily?"

I stretched the waistband of my leggings, amused by her shocked expression. "These are way more comfortable than my jeans, and Cozy Creek is hardly the Mecca of fashion."

"You're my fashion icon, so I first thought this was a trend. Like, an ironic after-Christmas elf style."

I laughed. "Pretty sure it's not. But anything goes in Cozy Creek. I think I saw someone dressed as Cupid earlier."

"I know! We saw the pink decorations and stopped to buy some themed sugar cookies from one of the Cupids. They were advertising a sled contest."

"They must be desperate for entries. How were the cookies?"

"Very sweet. A bit nauseating, but only because I'm nauseated most of the time." She touched her stomach, wincing.

She'd been looking pretty green for her first trimester, patiently waiting for February.

"Is it getting any better?"

"A little." She pulled a face. "But I guess I expected everything to change overnight, and it wasn't that clear cut."

"Where's Celia?" I asked.

She peeled off her jacket, and I helped her hang it on the rack. "With my mom. She thought we could use this opportunity for a little getaway. We had a fun trip, but traveling with a six-year-old is full-on. I miss adult interaction!"

I nodded in understanding, watching as they shed their winter layers and took in Trevor's living room. *My* living room.

"Wow." Bess whipped around to look at Charlie, then me. "Trevor told us he bought a cabin up here, but I never imagined..."

Charlie studied the room, turning to me with a guilty look. "He told you, didn't he?"

"Told me what?"

"I mean... he didn't have to tell you. You're a designer, with eyes."

"Having eyes is a great advantage to a designer." I used mine to bombard him with a look of absolute innocence.

Charlie was starting to look red, which gave me a modicum of satisfaction. If he'd known about this, he might as well come clean right now.

"Don't play dumb!" he said. "This is straight out of your Pinterest board. He told me."

I pinned him with a questioning look. "And you encouraged him?"

"No! He showed me the pics, and I told him not to make a fucking replica." He browsed the room. "Fuck me. This is..."

"I swear I didn't know!" Bess cut in, casting a panicked look in my direction, then a fierce one at Charlie. "I can't believe this."

Charlie sighed, glancing apologetically at his wife before he turned to me, his voice level. "Are you okay? I know he's a bit much and I know you hate him—"

"For good reason!" Bess inserted.

"For good reason," Charlie repeated dutifully. "I'm sure this feels creepy as hell, but I swear he's a good guy. He's just a bit lost. He needs to move on, and he will. We've been talking about this. He's seeing someone..."

"Seeing someone?" I swallowed.

"A therapist," Charlie clarified. "And I know he's working on it. For the record, I told him to check out the office space *alone*. I said we could talk to you later if it was any good. I don't even know how he managed to drag you along, but I'm so sorry. I really hope he hasn't crossed any boundaries."

He looked at me expectantly, eyebrows drawn in concern. It took me a moment to catch up to the real meaning behind his words, and I shuddered. If only he knew.

"He's been fine," I replied curtly.

Bess observed me with caution. "You two getting along?"

"Like a house on fire!" Trevor announced, emerging from the bedroom. "Sorry, I was in the shower." He hugged Charlie, then Bess. "I wasn't expecting you today at all. How did you get here so fast?"

His hair looked damp. Had he wet it in the sink or something? Mine had dried into awkward curls.

"We just thought we'd better not leave you two alone for too long," Bess said, her gaze darting between the two of us.

I clenched, glancing at Trevor. I didn't want to lie, but I wasn't ready to publicize our fledgling relationship. I wasn't even sure what we were to each other. Enemies? Lovers? Enemies to lovers? The Pinterest stalker and his stalk-ee? Was that even a word?

"We're cool," Trevor said, placing his hand on my shoulder, giving me a wink.

I must have looked particularly uncomfortable, since Bess pulled me away from him, her eyes filled with concern. "You don't have to pretend for us! Come on, let's go find something to eat. Do you have any snacks? I'm ravenous."

"Please! Help yourself!" Trevor called behind us.

I wasn't particularly hungry, but I followed Bess to the kitchen, helping her open cupboards until we found a bag of chips and some pistachios. She filled some bowls and started eating. "God, I wish I could have just one glass of wine right now."

"I promise I won't drink either," I said. "We can be awkward and sober together."

I had to keep a clear head, or at least avoid getting any more emotionally overwhelmed.

"I can't believe you got stuck here with him on Valentine's Day! How did Richard take it? I know you guys had plans."

I cringed at the thought. I'd gushed about those plans with Bess before she'd left for her trip. Harmless office chatter, which now made me feel sick.

"He... um... we're not together anymore."

"What? Since when? What happened?"

I took a breath and gave her a quick rundown of recent events, leaving out the little detail of me having sex with Trevor. That part sounded insane, and very much like a crazy rebound tryst. I didn't regret it but couldn't say it out loud. Not yet.

Bess stared at me, dumbfounded. "That's quite the Valentine's Day. Are you *sure* you're okay? I don't think I'd be."

I glanced over my shoulder, checking the men were out of earshot. Trevor gave me an upward nod across the room, throwing another log into the fire. Charlie sat on the ottoman next to him, warming his hands by the flames.

"Trevor's been a good distraction." A smile crept up my lips despite my best efforts.

"You're not giving him false hope, are you?" Bess's words yanked my gaze away from him. There was a pained look in her eyes. "I know what he did was deplorable and you're over him, but he's so in love with you, it's painful to watch. I can't help it... He's Charlie's best friend, and I'd hate to see him get hurt." Bess filled her mouth with chips.

So in love with you? My throat closed up, making it impossible to swallow the chewed-up pistachio in my mouth. I'd only just learned Trevor was still attracted to me and wanted me to give him a chance. Sure, there were signs... like this living room, but I'd refused to see anything else.

"You never told me he was in love with me," I whispered, forcefully swallowing the nuts. "Nobody said anything."

Bess looked confused. "I thought it was obvious. You guys had a thing... He never got over it and you did." She shrugged as if to say this kind of thing happened all the time. "And we thought he *was* getting over it, slowly. He made a lot of progress over Christmas, and I honestly thought he'd be dating someone else by now. But..."

"What?"

Bess winced. "The way he's looking at you now." She shook her head, taking a crunchy bite of another chip. "It's like he's back to where we started, mooning over you. And this house..." She looked around the room. "It's insane! What if he meets someone else? What is she going to think when she finds out that he did all this for you? Best-case scenario, she'll change every little detail or force him to sell."

"And the worst case?" I asked, my voice sticking to my throat.

Bess looked at me like I was playing dumb. "She'll run. I wouldn't touch this kind of crazy with a barge pole."

I felt all the blood drain from my face. She was right. Trevor might have been crazy about me, but to anyone else, he was just crazy. The only thing that could make this okay was me. If I loved him back with all I had, he wasn't crazy anymore—he was passionate. But how could I ever match this level of devotion? Trevor wasn't just maybe sort of into me. He was obsessed. And I'd been crazy enough to sleep with him. I'd fueled the fire. I'd led him on so hard, I was one hundred percent responsible.

He'd been on his way to getting over me, and I'd ruined it.

I felt like throwing up, but instead stuffed my mouth with chips until the salt burned my lips. What was even worse, I still craved him. My body was insatiable, already pulsing in anticipation of the next time I could be alone with him. Maybe we were both crazy.

I had to be kind and cut him off before I hurt him even more. But that meant cutting myself off. I huffed in frustration.

"How's it going?" Trevor asked, appearing behind me. "We were just talking about the sleeping arrangements. I don't think anyone should be driving back tonight. There's one bedroom, two empty rooms with no beds that I'm still... um... decorating, and then there's the couch."

"Bess and Charlie will take the bedroom, obviously," I said. "You can take the couch and I'll take an empty room and that camping bed I had last night. I'm already used to it."

"Great!" Charlie said. "Really appreciate it."

"You can have the couch. I'll camp on the floor," Trevor corrected.

I shrugged. "I'm easy."

At that moment, our gazes caught, and Trevor's mouth quirked. "Debatable," he said.

"No, I mean it. A nice meal and a glass of wine and I'm good to go." I rolled my eyes, and everyone laughed.

I didn't miss the hungry look in Trevor's eyes. If I truly wanted to cut him off, I had to ease up on the stupid jokes and innuendo.

"Anyway, it's not bedtime yet." Bess raised her hand. "And we planned some stuff on the way."

"Work stuff?" I asked hopefully.

"Yes!" Bess announced.

"No! Not like *work* work," Charlie corrected. "We were looking up team-building exercises. I mean, we appreciate you both. You're amazing at what you do. But there's been a lot of tension at the office."

"We thought this could be an opportunity to work on all that," Bess continued, beaming at us with hopeful eyes.

Oh, fuck.

CHAPTER 22

Trevor

Charlie was my best friend. I would have walked through fire for him, but right then I wanted to send him packing. Teresa and I needed team-building exercises like we needed a hole in the head. What we needed was to sit down and talk about us. I loved her. She... liked me enough to stick around. I couldn't be entirely sure where she was at, and I desperately wanted more time with her.

For months, I'd been hoping and dreaming and buying overpriced furniture, listening to my friend's concerned commentary. Nobody believed I had a chance with Teresa, but I couldn't let it go. And now she'd finally returned my affection. A fraction of it, maybe, but still.

I felt vindicated. I felt invincible. And I was dying to tell Charlie. But I'd seen the look of terror in Teresa's eyes. She wasn't ready for them to know. I'd already waited for eighteen months. I could wait a little longer.

I sighed. "Fine. Let's team-build. What did ye have in mind?"

♥ ♥ ♥

Ten minutes later, I was tied to Teresa, trying to coordinate my left hand with her right to tie a piece of string into a bow. We were not making progress.

"Do we really need this?" she whined, tugging against the cargo strap holding our sides together. "We could just both agree to use one hand."

"It's the rules!" Bess laughed, resting her head on Charlie's shoulder.

They'd already tied three bows, working perfectly in sync. Me and my feisty elf had only managed one knot that looked nothing like theirs.

"We're both right-handed," I pointed out. "Charlie is left-handed. They have an advantage."

After we painstakingly managed one lopsided bow, Teresa cheered. "Done!"

She stretched her arms overhead as soon as we were freed from one another. "So, what's the plan for the rest of the day?"

Charlie grinned. "You think we're done with team building? That's adorable. There's a whole list." He picked up his phone and browsed. "There's the staring into each other's eyes one, and one where you build a statue out of wet toilet paper…"

"For crying out loud!" Trevor huffed. "I have actual building work to finish in this house. Why don't we get some sugar soap, putty and sandpaper and prep some walls for painting?"

Bess lifted her head. "That could work! Makes way more sense than wasting toilet paper."

"So, have you chosen a color for those walls?" Teresa asked. "Or are we just prepping?"

I blew a sigh, leaning back on the couch. "I'm no' saying you should sand my walls. Just… making a point."

"The point being that you don't want to work on team spirit with me?" Teresa's smile was a little cheeky.

"My point being that I don't want to do some pointless activity."

Bess's eyes widened as she raised her hand. "What about that sled competition? It's tomorrow, right?"

"Yes!" Charlie pulled a folded flyer from his pocket and threw it on the table. "This is perfect! Let's make a cardboard sled and join the race!" He turned to me. "You bought all this furniture. You must have some cardboard stashed away."

"Plenty," I said, jerking a thumb over my shoulder. "Most of it is still stacked in the shed outside."

Teresa raised her hand. "Do you even understand what you're up against? People work for weeks on their sleds. And the cardboard they use is thick stuff and they glue it together. They saw pieces and use gallons of glue and duct tape, then spend hours painting."

"We don't have to win the prize for the prettiest cardboard box. We just need to build something that holds our weight and slides down the slope," Charlie argued back.

"I do have duct tape and glue," I said. "I did some light renovations before I let the designer loose."

Charlie gave me a weighted look as if to say, "you didn't let her that loose."

Bess clasped her hands together. "Great! I'm on board. Let's bring in everything we have and see what we can build!"

I felt her excitement gradually transferring to my body, maybe even to Teresa. She was suddenly smiling.

"I can show you what's in the shed," I said to Charlie, gesturing to the front door.

He followed me, and we dressed up in full winter gear before braving the outside weather. The cold hit me at the door, but I felt relieved to be alone with my friend. I needed to talk to him.

Once we made it to the shed, I found the switch for the dim lightbulb hanging off the ceiling. It swayed gently, making the cramped space feel creepy. We rummaged through the stacks of flattened boxes.

"I wish I'd known! I had so many boxes back home," Charlie mused.

"Have you been ordering stuff again?"

Charlie peered at me innocently. "Well, yeah. Baby stuff."

"Can I ask you something?" I held still, waiting for him to detect my tone.

"Sure." He dropped the cardboard and leaned on the carpenter's desk.

"What's with all this team building stuff?" I asked. "What are ye getting at?"

Charlie looked at me like it was obvious. "I can't have you two at odds and not able to work in the same office. It's been going on for too long."

"You know I'd happily share an office with her. I'd share my chair with her! But there's a history... Ye can't solve this with trust falls and toilet paper statues."

He pinned me with a serious look, lowering his voice. "I can see she's warming up to you. All you need to do is get over your crush. If you see her as a colleague and stop mooning like a fool, she'll relax and feel okay working with you."

"Is that *all* I need to do?" I rolled my eyes. "Why didn't I think of that?"

"I know it's hard to let go, but think of the company. If we want to move the business here, we either have to let her go or find a way to work together without this tension between you two. I read that it's best to spend time together to find some level of normal, whatever it looks like going forward. We can't let her avoid you forever, and you pining after her from afar is even worse. I'm sure you've built her up in your head to some sort of goddess level by now. None of this gets us any closer to having a functional team."

"Are we no' doing the work? Are we failin' at somethin'?" I asked, folding my arms.

Charlie sighed, looking out the tiny window covered in frost flowers. "No. That's not what I mean. But if you're never in the same room, we're not reaching our full potential. We need to work *together*."

"Agreed."

"So, you'll work with me here?"

I drew a deep breath, weighing my words. "You should know though, that we slept together."

Charlie stared at me, his jaw hanging slack. "What? When?"

"Just before ye arrived with yer team-building exercises."

"*She* slept with *you*?"

I held my breath, counting to five. "Yes. Willingly. With consent."

Charlie's face reddened. "No, I didn't mean—"

"I know I've acted a bit crazy when it comes to her, but only because I still think she's the one."

"The one, huh?"

"The only one."

Charlie's expression softened, gradually melting into a smile. "My boy's in love."

I nodded. "It's very early, and she's not quite where I am. But I think she could be. Maybe. Unless I'm so hideously unlovable that it's just not in the cards."

Charlie shook his head, still smiling. "No. You're the best. And I'm thrilled if she's finally seeing it."

"You're not worried about us working together and… dating?"

"No! I love working with Bess. It means I see more of her, and we always know what's going on with each other. I suppose it's not for everyone, but it works for us."

"I really hope we find something that works for us, too."

"Okay. Okay." Charlie took a deep breath, glancing around the tiny space as if regrouping. "That… changes things. I guess we can leave the sledding contest, then."

I suddenly felt colder, like someone had taken off my jacket. "No, wait. I don't know if she wants anyone to know about us. We haven't talked about it. Maybe I shouldn't have told you." I looked at my friend with slight desperation. "What should I do?"

Charlie took a moment to think. "I hear you. Okay. I won't say anything and we'll… carry on." He picked up the pile of cardboard. "Let's build a sled."

CHAPTER 23

Teresa

As soon as Charlie and Trevor disappeared out the front door, Bess turned to me, her eyes huge. "Oh, my God! This must be torture for him. I didn't even think." She buried her face in her hands.

"What are you talking about?"

"Trevor," she whisper-shouted. "He's trying to get over you, and we're literally tying you together. Charlie convinced me it would help... that if you spent enough time together, he'd start to see you as a normal person and not as this mythical creature he's built you up to be in his head."

"Mythical? No... that's ridiculous," I protested, but a niggle of doubt made my voice waver.

What if Trevor had put me on some kind of pedestal I was

bound to fall from? He didn't know my flaws. He didn't know my history. How quickly would this relationship crash and burn when he found out?

Bess wandered over to the kitchen to search for more snacks. "Oh, you have no idea. To him, you're the perfect woman who got away."

I followed at her heels, feeling increasingly uncomfortable. "Maybe we do need to spend more time together doing some godawful team-building exercises so that he gets over that idea. There's nothing perfect about me."

Bess found a block of cheese and some crackers. "I guess that's part of any relationship. You gradually find out more about each other, good and bad. And hopefully, the good outweighs the bad."

"Like you and Charlie?"

She smiled, cutting the cheese into smaller cubes. "You find out a lot living and working together."

"I don't know how you do it! I've never had the urge to live with a guy." As I said it, my gaze wandered across the beautiful space.

I had a strong urge to live in this house, but that was just Trevor messing with my mind by creating my dream room. Surely, that didn't count as an urge to live with a man. I could live here all by myself.

"You will, when it's the right guy," Bess said soothingly, presenting me with her simple cheese platter. "I'm so sorry about Richard. That's awful."

She looked at me with such genuine compassion my insides

twisted. I needed a friend and if I wanted her support, I had to be honest.

I piled cheese on a cracker and ate it to give myself a moment. Fumbling my way around the fancy water cooler on his fridge door, I filled a glass with ice chips and water. I could do this. I could tell her and get this off my chest.

I turned around to face her, drawing a breath. "I slept with Trevor," I blurted, my eyes on the front door, watching for signs of it opening.

Bess's eyes widened. "What? When?"

"Just before you arrived."

She let out a strange noise of excitement, or maybe alarm. "What does this mean? Do you… like him?" Her gaze turned from concerned to hopeful.

I grimaced. "I don't know what I feel! It was amazing and obviously I'm attracted to him, but now I'm freaking out because you said he idolizes me. I should not be idolized. That will not end well."

She blinked, confused. "Why not?"

"Because he'll eventually find out that I'm just a normal person, or something worse. You just said that yourself!"

"I didn't say 'something worse'!" She gave me a reproaching look. "And I didn't know you had feelings for him. I thought you hated him."

"Hate *is* a feeling. It's love's first cousin."

"What about how he ruined your career?"

I sighed. I'd been so hurt I might have exaggerated. "I still have a career, don't I? I don't love what he did and I'm still a bit mad, but he's also done great things. That's why I don't know what to feel! I need to figure this out before we both get hurt. Before I do something really stupid…"

"Like sleep with him?"

"Ha!"

She was right. The 'really stupid' ship had already sailed.

Bess leaned on the counter; her tone soft. "Don't take this the wrong way, but maybe it's too early to figure it out. You only just broke up with Richard, and you haven't even talked to him. You said you just drove away… As much as I'd love to see you and Trevor happy together, I'm afraid this is some kind of whirlwind affair brought on by a traumatic experience."

It made so much sense I could only nod, breathing forcefully through the heaviness in my chest. I'd jumped in with both feet. Why had I done this to myself?

Bess took the cheese platter and guided us back to the couch. I hugged one of Trevor's cushions—a creamy white one with a chunky weave cover. It was perfect.

"Trevor thinks it's the other way around," I said. "That we were always meant to be, ever since that night, and Richard was the rebound." My voice sounded a little petulant.

"Did you hook up with Richard within hours of that night?"

"It was about eight months later," I admitted, sinking deeper into the couch, groaning. "I've fallen for Trevor's funhouse of mirrors and warped logic."

Bess smiled a little sadly. "I'm sure it makes sense to him. He never acknowledged you with Richard. But you were together for months. He must have meant something to you."

"It was the safe choice, I guess. It felt like the safe choice, at least. Not some crazy passion that can turn at any moment, but something nice and solid. It was... pleasant."

Bess bit back a smile. "It sounds like you're describing a chair."

"No! If I was describing a chair, I'd use much more passionate language! Like this couch... it's heavenly." I rolled onto my back, stretching out for emphasis. "It receives me like a hug. I always loved that Pinterest photo, but I had no idea how amazing this felt. It molds to my body like I'm floating on air."

Bess laughed. "You're right. That's a lot more passion. I guess Trevor knew the way to your heart."

I rolled to my side, anxiety fluttering in my chest. "Is that a bad thing? He wanted to create a space I'd feel at home in."

Bess tilted her head, considering this. "I guess it's one of those things that is either creepy or cute, depending on how it's received. So, it's up to you."

"Huh." I flopped onto my back.

That's what I'd told Trevor, but hearing someone else say it made it real. Like anything in life, I could choose to frame this either way. I didn't have to accept anyone else's interpretation. If I wanted to be happy with Trevor, I could write that version of the story. I just had to figure out what was really between us.

I heard the front door and hubbub of Charlie and Trevor handling a lot of cardboard. I should have gotten up to help, but I was so blissfully relaxed, floating on that cloud-like couch, that I decided to give myself a minute. Just one minute.

"I do love this couch," I said dreamily, closing my eyes on a smile.

When I opened them, Trevor stood right above me, looking down with a smile wider than mine. "Wasn't sure it was worth the cash, but aye, I'm convinced now."

Snowflakes launched from the shoulders of his jacket, floating down on me. I felt one land on my face—a pinprick of cold that instantly turned into a droplet.

I scrambled up to sitting. "How did it go? Did you find stuff?"

Trevor pointed at a pile of flattened cardboard by the front door. "Charlie's bringing the last bit in. It's the box my telly came in, so it's big."

I looked around me. "You don't even have a TV."

"Yeah, I realized it wasn't part of your... vision, so I hid it in the spare room."

I had to laugh. "I'm not against TVs. But the picture I pinned was basically a home library. I have to ask... where did you get all the books?" I nodded at the bookshelves behind me, full of leather-bound classics.

Trevor busied himself with taking off his jacket. "I've been frequenting garage sales and book fairs."

"Really?"

He flung his jacket across an armchair and ran a hand across his face. "I mean... I love books and I read all the time. I had a decent collection to begin with, but not that many old ones that looked like those in the photo. So, I guess that gave me an excuse to shop. It's been fun. I've found some interesting reads."

I stared at the bookshelves in awe. So, he hadn't outsourced this part of the decoration. Trevor loved book shopping. I'd already known he was an avid reader—which made sense for a wordsmith—but for some reason, I hadn't expected him to buy and collect books. I wasn't sure why it made me so happy. Maybe because books were heavy and impractical. They came with a sense of permanence.

The front door opened again, and Charlie hauled in a huge, flat box with a picture of a flatscreen TV on it. "Where are we going to do this?" he asked.

Trevor met him at the door and grabbed the other end. "Let's build in the spare room, there's more space."

Bess and I followed them, helping them drag all the cardboard and a banged-up toolbox into our temporary workshop. Trevor showed us to the tape, glue, screws, and everything else he'd managed to find.

"Are we even allowed to use screws?" Bess asked. "The rules said cardboard, duct tape and glue."

"I'm pretty sure some people use screws," I said. "It's not like they inspect your sled that closely. That might have changed, though, since the last time I..." I swallowed the rest of the sentence. Too late.

Charlie narrowed his eyes at me. "Wait... you've done this before?"

Oh, shit! They didn't know about my history with Cozy Creek. Ever since they'd come up with this ridiculous 'let's move the office to Cozy Creek' idea, I'd been gathering the courage to tell them. But I knew it would open the door to an avalanche of questions I wasn't ready for.

Now, I couldn't put it off any longer. Trevor already knew.

"I grew up here," I said carefully. "I haven't been back in a long time, but I guess some things don't change. The cardboard sled contest has been around for years. My mom stays in touch with her friends here. She told me it's gotten bigger."

Bess stared at me like I'd just told them I worked for the CIA. "So, you *know* Cozy Creek?"

"Cozy Creek knows me," I muttered.

"Why do you say it like that?"

I swallowed. "Because... I was a teenager and... anyway, the point of the sled contest is to crash so that your sled totally falls apart. I mean, of course you try not to, but nearly everyone does, and that's why it's so much fun for the audience."

Bess looked like she had further questions, but Trevor saw my discomfort and jumped in. "We shouldn't have any problems crashin' and falling apart. Turns out the glue's dried out and the cardboard is not thick enough for the screws." He dropped the useless tube of glue and picked up a roll of duct tape. "Let's hope this holds."

"As long as the temperature stays below freezing," I said. "One year, I remember the weather turned weirdly warm. It started drizzling and everyone's sleds got soaked."

"It should be fine," Charlie said, looking out the window. "Why don't you get started and I'll go order us some dinner?"

CHAPTER 24

Trevor

We worked on our sled design for the rest of the day, taking frequent breaks for pizza, coffees, and drinks.

I was happy I'd stocked the cabin for emergencies. This didn't exactly qualify as one, but it meant the cupboards were full of snacks and the fridge held a variety of drinks. Living in the middle of nowhere meant I needed to plan ahead and buy in bulk—something I wasn't natural at but was gradually learning.

Teresa had clammed up when Bess inquired about her past, and hadn't since volunteered anything else, which was only amping up my curiosity. What did she mean about Cozy Creek knowing her? What could she have possibly done to earn a reputation she had to worry about fourteen years later? A fresh crop of teenagers emerged every year to do new stupid shit. Surely whatever it was had been outdone many times since then.

After entertaining some wild guesses from public urination to robbing a liquor store, I concluded it was probably something that felt big to her but wasn't anything major. Our minds did such a great job of amplifying our own mistakes.

"Do you have a big tarp we could use for painting?" Bess asked me as I returned to our spare room workshop after cleaning up our dinner mess.

The sled was starting to look a little more like an intentional shape than an abandoned box. We'd settled on a simple shape of a cartoon car, which did look rather drab in its original cardboard color.

"Charlie said he saw some paint in your shed we could use," Bess continued, "and if we open the windows in the spare room, maybe we could paint there." She glanced at Teresa. "Oh, no! But then you can't sleep here. It'll get too cold and the fumes..."

She grinned. "It's okay. I'll be too high on fumes to notice I'm cold."

"Wait, what paint are you talking about?" I asked. "I thought we agreed the white doesn't stand out against snow."

I'd told them I only had some off-white base coat, which had been rejected by all.

There was a telling silence as Bess glanced at Charlie. "We found a can of purple paint at the back. It's unopened, so maybe you were saving it for something, but it would look amazing!"

She fetched the can from the pile of supplies by the door, and Teresa grabbed it off her. "Tyrian!"

"It's gorgeous!" Bess agreed.

"This would go really well in your bedroom," Teresa mused, lifting the can, turning the color swatch against the light.

I held my breath, waiting for her to connect the dots.

"Wait." She turned to me. "Did you...?" She peered at me, head tilted, and I nodded.

It's your favorite color.

"Did he what?" Bess asked.

Teresa blushed a little, shaking her head. "Nothing." She lifted her eyes to me. "You bought this for your house. We shouldn't waste it on some cardboard."

"Let's!" I said quickly. "I can buy more if I need it. And if the spare room is too cold or full of fumes, we can both sleep in the living room."

Her gaze flicked to the couch, and she bit her lip. "Sure. It's not a problem."

Bess and Charlie exchanged another look, this one far more knowing.

Teresa's head whipped from side to side as she took in the situation. I saw the moment something snapped, then words spilled out of her mouth. "Stop it! We all know what's going on, right? Do we have to keep pretending?"

Her gaze pierced me, and I stopped breathing altogether. I wasn't trying to keep secrets between us. I didn't even believe there were any. But saying it out loud felt like an invisible barrier I didn't know how to cross. What if I made things worse again?

"Pretending?" Bess shot an alarmed look at Teresa, who

straightened her spine.

"You both know we slept together," she said, pausing for a moment until they nodded. "And you know it's complicated and we don't know what we are to each other."

My chest squeezed, but I couldn't dispute her words.

"We'll figure it out," she continued. "And it won't affect us working together, I promise."

"No, it won't," I echoed.

I wouldn't let it. I would never again be the reason her career went sideways. I'd sacrifice mine a hundred times over before I let that happen.

We stood still, eyeing each other. The silence felt loud. Finally, Charlie threw his arm around me and grinned at Teresa. "If you want to get with my man, you're gonna need to do better than that. He's the best thing to ever come out of Scotland."

I swallowed hard but plastered on a smile. "Better than whiskey."

"Or Braveheart," Charlie chorused. "I'd trust him with my life. This guy always comes through. You don't even know what he's done for—"

"Okay. No more beer for you!" I cut him off, sensing this would not play out well.

I gave Teresa an apologetic smile, but to my surprise, she looked close to tears.

"I know," she said, meeting Charlie's eyes. "I know."

Seemingly satisfied with her response, Charlie let me go and turned his attention to our cardboard car. I noticed Bess giving him a concerned glance, but she held her tongue.

We covered the spare room floor with a tarp and got to work painting our funky cardboard car. After a few minutes, Bess, who'd insisted on doing her part, looked like she was about to either throw up or fall asleep, so we sent her back into the living room.

"Are you okay here if I go with her?" Charlie asked, casting a worried look over his shoulder. "I have a feeling she's not happy with me... for whatever reason, and I need to make amends."

"Go!" Teresa urged, closing the door behind him.

The spare room felt like an ice box, with two windows creating a cross breeze, and odd snowflakes floating inside, melting against the floor. We painted quickly, dressed in our winter coats, fingers stiff from the cold.

"I'm dreaming of that bathtub of yours," Teresa confessed as she set down her paintbrush to blow into her hands. "I could spend the night there if we're divvying up rooms."

"In a hot bath that cools down within twenty minutes or an empty tub?" I teased.

"In a hot bath that stays hot because... right now, in my imagination, there's no room for that kind of negativity."

"Okay. Just keep in mind that it's right next to the newlyweds. Apparently, pregnancy makes you extra horny."

She gave me a warning look. "Dude!"

"What? It's true. Charlie said—"

"Stop it!" she hissed, threatening me with a dirty paintbrush.

I wasn't going to say anything, but winding up Teresa was now my favorite thing. I loved seeing her relax and look at me a little differently. Like I was her disgusting friend, not just the poor sod desperately in love with her. Both could be true, after all.

"Sometimes, I look at them and I can't believe Charlie is married," I said.

"And about to become a dad," Teresa added, matching my bewildered tone. "He never seemed the type."

"But they're so…"

"Perfect together?" she finished, now looking at me straight in the eye.

"Yeah."

Teresa turned back to her paintbrush, circling the cardboard car to help me finish the other side. "They didn't have to hate each other for eighteen months. They just fell in love."

"I never hated you, and you know that."

She sighed. "Fine. But you have to admit, it's not been that easy for us. And it should be easier, right? If it's meant to be."

"Why's that, then? Is there a rule for it? Some kind o' hardship quota?"

She looked at me over her shoulder, her nose rosy, dark curls wet from the snowflakes blowing in. "Sounds legit."

"And how was yer relationship with Richard the Dick? Easy or hard?"

"What do you mean?"

"How did you get together? Just fell in love, did you?"

I braced myself as she shook her head, an incredulous look in her eyes. "My friend played matchmaker and set me up with her colleague. I should have known since her work stories are dreadfully boring." Her mouth twisted. "And we didn't fall in love. We dated... We enjoyed ourselves. Or so I thought."

The way she emphasized "fall in love" felt like air quotes.

"Do ye think it's ridiculous to fall in love?" I asked.

Teresa looked surprised. "Oh... I didn't mean that. But I've never been in love, I don't think.

"Never?"

She looked a little embarrassed, shaking her head. "I know that's weird. And I've had crushes... Maybe it's the same thing. How do you even know?"

"How do you feel when you're crushing on someone?"

She blushed, looking at the ceiling. "You know how it feels! You think about them way too much and wonder what it would be like... Wonder if they like you. You dream about all kinds of stuff."

Teresa finished the last spot of painting, dropped the brush into the tray and picked it up. "I wasn't in love with Richard."

"Okay," I said, standing up with her.

We left one of the windows ajar and closed the door, leaving our strange, purple cardboard sled to dry.

It was late and pitch-black outside. Charlie and Bess must have moved to the bedroom.

"Oh, my God!" Teresa hissed as she spotted the sock on the doorknob.

"That *is* cheeky," I admitted. "Even from Charlie."

"Do you think they're really..." She looked at me, eyes wide.

"Apparently, pregnancy really increases the blood flow down—"

"How on earth do you know this stuff?" she hissed back.

I shrugged. "People tell me stuff and I listen."

I'd been called a human sponge for all I heard and absorbed, and I'd never felt like I had to limit my interests to my own gender or age group. I often had to write copy from a female perspective or communicate to women, elderly people, or teenagers. Each target group was fascinating.

I grabbed a chair and propped it under the bedroom door. "There. Now we both have privacy.

She smiled, stepping so close her coat was brushing mine. It was warm here, with the fire still on, red-hot embers glowing behind the glass doors. Charlie must have kept it going.

"I'm going to lose my jacket," I said. "Before I sweat through it. Can I take yours?"

She shook her head. "I'm still freezing. The cold got through all my layers in there and I can't shake this chill."

"The only bathtub is in that ensuite, sorry. But maybe we can get you warm by the fire."

I brought her in front of the fireplace and threw a few more logs in. She sat on the sheepskin rug in her jacket, holding her hands to the heat. I made her a cup of tea and brought it over.

"I'm sorry. I should have shut down that painting project before it got too cold," I said.

"It's okay. I'm used to freezing myself. It's part of the Cozy Creek experience." She smiled. "I used to go without a hat all the time to not mess up my hair and would freeze my ears off."

I sat next to her and gently pushed a strand of hair behind her ear. "Oh, good. Just checking..." She angled her head, and I inspected her other ear. "Great. Still there."

She giggled quietly, and I snuck a quick kiss on her cheek, almost reaching the ear. To my surprise, she grabbed hold of my face and pulled me closer, bringing our lips together. Gradually, my disbelief melted into a flood of sensations.

She's kissing me.

I tried to slow down my breathing, to stay in control. I wanted her in every way, with every cell of my body, and that was a recipe for disaster. She didn't really want to be with me. She'd never been in love, and she wasn't in love with me.

But it was hard to engage my higher functioning brain when the rest of me pounded with one thought, blood humming in my ears on its way downtown. Only one thing was clear.

I could never resist her.

CHAPTER 25

Teresa

I shouldn't have kissed him. He deserved better than my tangled, conflicted emotions.

But I couldn't stop myself. My lips reached for his again, craving more. This time, the kiss deepened immediately, turning breathless. His tongue swept to meet mine and responded with more intensity. This was our dance. This insatiable push and pull. Give and take.

And I was taking more than I was giving.

I pulled away, my lips raw, lungs gasping for air. His pupils had turned into magic eight balls with no numbers, only magic. I loved how I could dissolve every shred of his willpower and resistance. I shouldn't have abused my power, but it was such a heady feeling, having that effect on someone. Being their first choice, not someone filling a gap, ready to be cast aside for something better.

Richard had been agreeable, but he'd never looked at me like this, like I held his heart in my hands.

The heat of the fire made my skin glow, and I finally removed my jacket. I didn't want to let go of him. I needed his weight on me, grounding me.

"Please," I rasped, gripping his Henley as I laid my back against the sheepskin rug.

He shifted on top of me, his weight carefully balanced on one arm as his thumb stroked my cheek.

"Crush me," I said, yanking on his shirt again.

He lowered his hips on mine, and I gasped as the steely erection lodged between my legs. But his arms were still holding him up, leaving room for my lungs.

"Closer." I tugged him again.

"Ye won't be able tae breathe, mind."

"I don't want to breathe. It makes me think."

"And ye don't want to think?" He gave me a sad smile.

I shook my head, smiling a little. "It's all too complicated."

He dipped his chin and kissed my lips, lowering his weight on me a little more, locking me against the fluffy rug and the hard floor underneath. My thoughts quieted, turning into a low background chatter.

"I need you," I rasped as he raised his head to look at me.

I needed him to fill me until every confusing, vacant space in me disappeared. Until he owned every inch, and I didn't have to make decisions. I was tired of arguing with myself.

"This is not a good idea," he said. "But I can't say no to you."

"So, if I ask you to..."

"Anything, Teresa. Anything for you."

I caught a flash of sadness in his eyes, and shame shot through my heart. He was trying to hold back, to protect himself. I was leading him on. I just didn't know where.

"You think this is a bad idea?" My fingers still held onto his shirt. I didn't want to let go.

"My therapist would likely tell me I'm daft for this." A muscle twitched in his cheek before a smile broke through.

I swallowed. "Did you really go to therapy to get over me?"

He rolled off me and propped himself on one arm, running a hand over his face. "Aye."

"And...?"

"And..." He dropped the hand, meeting my eyes. "I should ask for my money back because it's been eight months and all I want is you."

Tears sprang to my eyes. "I want you, too... But I feel like I'm using you."

"How would you be using me? I choose to be right here."

I scrambled to sit up. "But what if it doesn't work out? What if I can't fall in love, no matter how much I want to? What if it's like a... defect?"

He pushed up to lean on the ottoman. "What? You mean like how Bess can't burp? That she'll just sit there making frog sounds when the rest of us belch the alphabet."

A laugh bubbled out of me. That had been one hilarious night at the pub, right after I'd signed the contract to work with them. I still remembered how weird it had felt to sit next to Trevor with all the unsaid things hanging between us.

"That night at the pub, were you trying to tell me something?" I asked.

"I thought it was obvious. I even followed you, thinking you were going out for a smoke..."

"And then I told you I quit smoking," I finished for him.

"You made a comment about how disgusting it was," he added. "And I went home thinking I had to quit. Otherwise, you wouldn't let me stand next to you." He gave me a rueful smile.

I felt the warmth of the fire on one side, the warmth of his body on the other. I wasn't cold anymore, and I felt safe. Safe enough to ask him almost anything.

"So, what were you trying to tell me?"

"I wanted to ask you about working together. If you were cool with it."

My shoulders dropped. "That's all?"

"I had a feeling you didn't want to take that job."

"I didn't."

"And I wanted to see if I could tease a smile out of you. Or even a blush. Anything, really."

"And I basically told you that you smelled disgusting." My hand flew to my mouth. He'd teased a blush out of me now.

"I still walked away thinking ye gave me hope. I'm that delusional, aye?" He smiled that self-effacing smile that made me feel fluttery inside. "It sounded like a promise, that if I pulled myself together, you'd give me another chance."

I couldn't remember what exactly I'd told him, but the truth of it hit me hard. I'd been finding reasons to hate him, to stick to my opinion, because nothing was more painful than changing your mind. But I could hear it now like he'd heard it, as a challenge to be better. To be worth my time.

"I'm sorry, Trevor. I didn't mean to imply you weren't good enough. I was just angry with you."

"I know. But I had to change, and ye gave me the push I needed. You challenged me to really look at myself and ask who I wanted to be, how I wanted to live. And for how long," he added with a rueful half-smile. "I didn't want to be a flabby, spineless weasel with fucked up lungs. I wanted to be better, even if I never had a chance with you."

"You were never—"

"I was." He cut me off, and I sighed.

"Were you really making progress in therapy, before... you know... yesterday?" I winced.

He tilted his head, blowing out a breath. "Yes, and no. That's not why I started therapy, but my therapist did caution me about going after you. And Charlie agreed, obviously. Nobody thought I had a chance. They still don't."

"Why? They know we're sleeping together."

"No. You told them we slept together. Past tense."

I shifted on the rug, trying to shake my discomfort.

"I don't know why I said it like that," I admitted. "I didn't mean it was a mistake or anything. Twice is a pattern, right?"

"No. Once is by chance. Twice is a coincidence. Three times is a pattern." He smiled his lopsided smile, his warm eyes studying me.

"Well, I see a pattern!" I insisted, my cheeks hot. "But maybe we have to sleep together one more time, so you see it, too."

"Maybe." His eyes sparkled.

"I mean, it keeps happening. Against my better judgment, or yours. And even if I don't know about our future, I hate all that talk about you pining for me, like you're pathetic for…"

"Falling in love with you?" he finished.

My heart squeezed so hard I almost clutched my chest. There they were—the words I'd been dancing around. I turned my head, too overwhelmed to look at him. "You don't know me that well. I'm not perfect. I need to change, too."

"You're perfect to me."

My face flushed with heat, and I laughed a little desperately. "Oh, shut up!" I aimlessly swung my arm at him, and he dodged, grinning.

"Make me." He backed away and stretched out on the sheepskin rug, arms behind his head, smiling like the invincible fool he was.

I didn't like distance between us. I didn't like it at all. I climbed on top of him, sitting down so he couldn't escape. I leaned forward, slipping my fingers under the waistband of his jeans. "See? We keep sleeping together. In present tense."

"It seems so."

"I don't want to overthink this." I popped the button.

"Okay."

I paused, narrowing my eyes. "You're not supposed to go along with this. This is not what you want, remember?"

My heart hammered in my chest. I felt like a scammer who'd been made, yet somehow evaded punishment. But I was also touching him, my crotch pressing against his, my forehead brushing his shoulder. I never wanted this contact to end.

"How do you know this is not exactly what I want?" His voice was soft, eyes half-closed.

"I thought you wanted more." I swallowed past the twinge in my throat. "And I just want to sleep with you."

He laughed. It was a gentle, rolling sound that made his body rock against mine. "No, you don't."

"Excuse me?"

He grabbed my hips and tossed me on my back, landing on me like he'd been before, but with more weight. Overwhelming and solid. "Maybe you don't know how you feel, but I do. And I'm happy to wait for the moment you connect the dots, Teresa."

"You're very sure of yourself for someone I've rejected multiple times."

"Rejected?" He murmured into my ear, slipping a hand between my legs. "I'd like to see you try."

I was so wet he could feel it through my leggings. He dragged two fingers across the soaked fabric, and I gasped out loud. I'd already discarded my underwear after the last time, and now I'd have to throw away this elf costume as well.

I could have proved my point by rejecting him right there. But I was too far gone. In that moment, I was willing to pay any price, and he knew it. Maybe he knew something I didn't.

"You"—he kissed my nose—"are lying to yourself, but I'm going to let it slide." He kissed my neck and slipped his fingers under my waistband, sliding down almost to where I needed him. "Falling in love is scary. Falling for someone you're supposed to hate is confusing. But you're doing great."

"I—"

He shut me up with his lips, then his tongue. My whole body was on fire, skin hot and clammy, chest falling and rising in the tight space under his, hips bucking against his hand. "Ask me, and I'll give you anything."

"I'll take your cock. And your couch," I said, giving him a bullish look. "I'll take this room."

"It's yours."

I heard the sound of foil ripping and he tugged down his jeans and underwear to roll a condom on. When his fingers slid between my legs, I shivered from head to toe. He stroked me, slowly and deliberately, circling my center, watching my face like it had instructions written on it.

As my mouth opened on a gasp and my hips lifted to meet him, he stroked one finger across my clit, so softly I nearly screamed.

Then he lowered his lips to mine just in time to keep me quiet, holding my tongue against his. I throbbed, overcome by the beautiful ache, on the edge of unraveling. He stroked me again and again, keeping a steady pace, drawing the feelings out.

I shuddered, on the brink of release, before he pulled away, smiling.

"More," I pleaded.

"Soon." He cupped me in his hand as I pulsed against his palm, so frustrated I wanted to squirm.

I'd never felt more ready, more carved out for someone.

He took his time, teasing my opening with the head of his cock, until I stifled a moan. He lowered down to whisper into my ear. "I built this place for you, Teresa. It's yours. I'm yours. Do you want me?"

"Yes. Please!" I lifted my pelvis, desperate for him.

"Are you sure? I've never been this hard."

Looking into my eyes, he pushed into me, slowly and gradually. My body stretched and morphed, expanding to take him in, to join with his, until I saw stars. They burst behind my eyelids like fireworks as he invaded every inch of me. I was locked between him and the floorboards, so perfectly tight and full I could have floated off like a helium balloon, had I not been trapped under his weight.

He held still for a moment, waiting for me to adjust. To relax into this perfect invasion.

After a moment, he shifted against me. It was not enough and too much, all at the same time. I whimpered something, trying to move with him. I was used to being in charge and chasing my pleasure. But here, trapped under him, I was at his mercy, my body overcome by the building sensation, like a vessel receiving a message from another dimension. He rocked, tiny micro movements that built up more and more tension. After a moment, he paused, holding half-way back, smiling. My clit ached in sync with my heartbeat, and I held my breath.

Finally, he filled me again, squeezing my lungs flat.

"I love you," he whispered.

My release was almost instant. Pure physics. The uncoiling of something tight that couldn't be held back any longer. A force of nature that sought to restore balance where pressure had built for too long. I muffled my cries with his shirt, riding the long downhill, sweeter than anything I'd experienced before.

To my surprise, tears followed right after. My chest heaved as if the orgasm had moved up there, still sweet and satisfying, yet slightly embarrassing.

I raised a hand to my face to hide from his gaze.

"Are you okay?" he asked. "Did I hurt you?"

I shook my head. He pulled away, discarding the condom—evidence of his own release. I hadn't even noticed, and it made me feel ashamed. But as soon as he rolled off me, I felt worse. Adrift.

"Don't go," I pleaded, grasping for his shirt.

He returned on top of me and gently kissed my neck, his arm draped around my waist. "I'm not going anywhere."

I'd hated him for so long and so passionately. I'd made up my mind, and those opinions had become part of my world—one of those immovable truths I lived by. I'd told myself Trevor was a spineless coward, not worth my time. If it wasn't true, what was?

Trevor was the best lover, with the world's sexiest accent.

Trevor was surprisingly fun to be around.

Trevor was my... boyfriend?

I couldn't think that far. It was way too soon, and we worked together. He was obsessed with me. Our pairing had all the ingredients of a disaster. Maybe that's why my emotions were all over the place. I wiped my eyes, and we lay still, his body tight against mine, until our breathing synchronized.

"I didn't mean to make you cry," he said, placing a soothing hand on my stomach.

"You didn't. I don't know why I'm crying. I'm not sad or upset. I'm just... emotional."

I finally sat up and gingerly pulled my leggings back on. I felt awkward and exposed. "All my clothes are dirty and yuck." I grimaced.

He sat up, too. "Do you want a T-shirt to sleep in?"

I glanced over my shoulder. "But we can't go into your bedroom."

"I have one in my bag." He pointed at the overnight bag we'd left by the door and got up to fetch it for me.

It was huge and had a picture of a bear on it. I did a double take. It was my bear—the one I'd designed for the crypto game. The one Boris had modified and used.

Trevor winced. "That's all I have, I'm sorry."

"This is why you went to buy an elf costume? To avoid giving me this?"

He averted his eyes. "I didn't want to rub your face in it."

"Boris made the ears too big," I said, staring at the picture. "Bears don't have big ears. It looks like a teddy bear."

He still wouldn't look at me. "I know. They wanted it to be more of a meme coin."

I huffed, shaking my head. "I thought this was supposed to be the one that went to the moon." I couldn't help the sarcasm in my voice. I knew the stock had crashed and never recovered. I took a deep breath and yanked off my elf top, changing into Trevor's XL shirt, then peeled off the leggings.

"It looks great on you," he said mildly, throwing another log on the fire before he went to the kitchen to get a glass of water. His phone buzzed on the counter, and he picked it up, staring at it with a deep frown.

"What is it?" I asked.

He shook his head. "Nothing."

He filled another glass for me, sliding it across the marble island. I sat on a barstool to down it. "How did you get your money out?"

He shook his head, like coming out of a trance, still a million miles away. "You mean... from..." He slowly lifted one finger off the glass to point at my shirt.

"The tokens... coins! Whatever they are. You must have gotten out before the rug pull... to pay for all this." I glanced across the room.

Trevor's voice was thick, like it didn't want to emerge from his throat. "I... I was with Gavin and overheard something, figured oot it was time." He drained his water. "I'm sure I was half the reason it crashed. We got in so early and I bought more, so I was holding a lot of coins when it went parabolic. Made me one of the whales, I guess."

"You bought more?"

He gave a solemn nod. "I put in my savings, thinking I'd cash in early. But Gavin was keeping everyone in line, telling us it was going to go ten-X. No one was supposed to pull out. But of course, he did."

"So, you tipped the others? Charlie, Boris..."

"Yes, but they weren't fast enough. The stock was already half-way to zero. I mean, they made a profit, but not like..."

"You?"

He nodded. "And Gavin."

I stared at him, trying to get my head around it. I'd seen the charts. I didn't know how many tokens he'd held, or how much they'd been worth, but I'd seen the green spike they called a 'God candle'. A meteoric rise, followed by an immediate crash. Kind of like our relationship. "How much did you make?"

He set down his water glass, pinning me with a careful look. "About a million."

"And Boris?"

"Maybe half of that. Charlie got even less. He was busy with Bess, had his phone off."

I couldn't argue Boris's share was mine. There were too many variables. But it didn't sting any less—being left out. Overlooked. Taking on a crippling mortgage for the rest of my life when he bought a house with cash.

"It should have been you," he said softly, leaning over the counter.

His fingers reached for mine but didn't touch.

"Maybe. But it's a game of chance, isn't it? Change one thing, and you wouldn't have been in the right place at the right time. If I hadn't been replaced by Boris, we might have got together. We might have dated, right?"

"I wanted to."

"Me, too," I admitted. "And then you might have been with me, instead of wherever you were when you cashed out." My eyes scanned the beautiful mahogany cabinets. "You might have missed out on all this."

His voice cracked with pain. "I missed out on you. I didn't want a house. I wanted you. I still do."

His index finger brushed my thumb, and I froze. "I have a thirty-year mortgage. I'm paying nothing but interest," I said.

He took my hand, his eyes glossy. "Sell it! Move in here with me. I'll put this house in your name."

"What?"

A deep crease appeared between his eyes. "I know I shouldn't say this. It's too early. But we're so good together."

I swallowed a mouthful of air, panic stirring in my chest. I'd worked so hard to buy my condo. It was my independence, with a side dose of loneliness, but it was all mine. I couldn't live in Cozy Creek. He had no idea how badly I'd messed up in my youth. He had no idea how much I didn't fit into this place.

"Trevor," I managed to croak out, at a loss for words.

"What are you feeling?"

"I don't know. I can't name a single feeling!" I wailed. Why did he keep asking?

"Last week, you wrote a passionate essay about office snacks. I don't think you have any trouble recognizing or describing your emotions."

I smiled, thinking of my defense of the humble yogurt raisins over some fancy chocolate truffles Charlie wanted to order from a local startup. Trevor had given me a thumbs-up, agreeing with my points. I'd ignored him.

I couldn't ignore him anymore. I had to meet his eyes. I had to be honest.

"I don't know how I feel about you. About us."

"You don't know?" He gave a slow nod, disappointment spreading across his features like an invisible cold shower.

I wrung my hands, desperate for the right words. "I don't fall in love. It doesn't happen to me in that way. I'm not like you!"

"Of course not," Trevor huffed. "*I* fall in love every Thursday!" He sounded like a gameshow host on steroids.

I rolled my eyes to acknowledge the skit, but he sighed deeply, dropping the sarcasm. "Nae. I fell in love with you. That's it."

"That's it? But you proposed—"

"I loved her, but it wasn't like this. And maybe you'll never feel what I feel, but trust me, when it hits you this hard, once is enough."

I felt a strange pressure in my chest, like my heart was too big for my rib cage. "How do you know you're in love?"

He shrugged. "Ye just know."

"You look at someone and... just know?"

"You look at them and... either you see a poor sod you like

enough to sleep with, or someone you don't want to live without."

He looked at me, his brow slightly raised as if to ask, "which is it?"

My chest felt even more uncomfortable. I couldn't imagine living with anyone, merging with another person like that. It sounded like living without oxygen. Delirious for a moment, then dead.

He read the conflict on my face and nodded. "It's okay."

"I only just broke up with Richard. It's too early."

"You're right." His voice was thick with hurt as he took our glasses and loaded them into the dishwasher.

I'd shot him down again. I'd stomped on his heart. I'd done exactly what Bess had warned me about. I felt shitty and cornered. But most of all, I felt sad. Whatever was brewing between us was burdened by too much, right from the start. Maybe we'd never had a chance.

"You must be a bit sore from sleeping on the floor last night," I said. "Take the couch. I'll get the camping mattress." A persistent yawn stretched my jaw, reminding me of how poorly I'd slept last night. "Also, we should probably take that chair off the bedroom door. It's a fire hazard."

Trevor took care of the chair as I fetched the mattress and set it up by the fire. I chose one of the many cushions and grabbed a soft throw from the couch, thinking it was a good thing my Pinterest dream came with so much bedding.

We took turns using the second bathroom. Trevor was done in five minutes, avoiding my eyes as he stepped out in a towel, leaving the door open for me. My belly flipped at the sight. He looked so beaten, like a wrestler after a losing match, his muscles rippling under dewy skin. I shut the bathroom door, steadying myself against the sink. I wanted so badly to fix everything. I wanted him to be my friend. I wanted him to be okay. But I couldn't fix myself.

Taking a deep breath, I faced the mirror. Mascara flakes decorated my cheekbones like a fallout of soot. My cheeks burned ruddy red, and my hair was a frizzy mess, ears peeking from between rogue curls. I looked like an insomniac elf, even without the costume.

I missed my hair-smoothing spray and face cream. To be honest, I missed my entire bathroom shelf and my evening rituals, but at least I had the toothbrush. I hadn't worn any makeup all day, apart from that little mascara I'd managed to apply in the cafe bathroom, which I must have rubbed off at some point.

I always made an effort before I left my apartment. That night by the pool, I'd spent two hours getting ready. Although, jumping into the pool might have canceled out most of that effort. And Trevor had kissed me after, before I'd fixed my hair or re-applied makeup. On this trip, he'd seen me at my barest.

Richard had joked about how the face-washing at the end of the day ruined the illusion. He'd wanted me in my party gear, face painted to perfection. And I'd played along, making sure he only saw me in flawless makeup. Okay, maybe not flawless, but better than this. He'd never said he'd kick me out of bed, but I'd picked up on those hints and adjusted to his expectations.

Because I wanted to be loved and admired. Everyone did.

With Trevor, I hadn't once thought about my appearance or doubted the attraction between us. It was as obvious as the trees surrounding the cabin. There was an ease with him my soul craved. Knowing that he adored me, and me alone. I didn't deserve it, but it drew me in, making me buzz like a stupid little fly above a jar of honey.

My legs a little shaky, I returned to the living room and found him on the camping mattress by the fire.

"Get up!" I told him. "We agreed you'd take the couch."

"No." He gestured at the couch, then rolled over, facing away from me. "It's yer couch. You should have it."

I huffed, folding my arms. I couldn't fight him. The man was built like a tree. "Only if you share it with me."

He jerked a little, turning to peer at me over his shoulder. "What?"

"You heard me. I'll take the couch if you sleep there with me. It's a very deep couch."

He sat up, frowning at me. "You trying to torture me or something?"

"No. I like you, Trevor. I *really* like you. And I could use a friend."

He got up and sat on the couch, eyeing me from under drawn brows. "I can't spoon you all night without getting hard."

"That's fine," I assured, climbing in next to him. "I didn't mean a platonic friend."

"That ship has sailed, aye?" He laid down, and I curled up next to his warm body. Maybe it wasn't fair to him, but I needed his body next to mine.

Everything about him soothed me.

I liked his voice. I liked the heavy hand that landed on my hip, securing me against the couch. I liked the smell of leather, cinnamon, and something woodsy that seemed to surround him. There was so much I liked, and I wished with my whole being I could feel what he felt. That certainty and conviction. Maybe then we'd have a chance.

CHAPTER 26

Trevor

"Aww, you guys are adorable!"

Charlie's words, followed by a laugh, cut through my sleep and I jerked upright, nearly launching Teresa off the couch.

She cracked open her eyelids, peering at me through dark lashes. "Is it morning?"

"Yes!" Bess announced. "Good morning! We have two hours until the competition. I was thinking we could grab breakfast at that cute cafe in town before we head out to Grandview Hill."

Charlie wrapped his arm around her, and they smiled at us, looking every bit the perfect couple, ready for brunch.

"Can't we just eat here?" Teresa muttered sleepily.

"You go," I told Bess and Charlie. "Take the sled. We'll walk to my car and meet you wherever Grandview Hill is."

"It's not far," Teresa supplied, burying her face in the pillow, clearly not ready to get up.

Bess cast Charlie a coy look. "Maybe we should give them some privacy."

"Yes, please," Teresa said. "I told you guys, we're... sleeping together. In the present tense." She flashed us an adorably wicked, sleepy smile.

Yes, I thought. I needed time with her. Waking next to Teresa felt like Christmas morning as a kid, full of wonder and uncertainty. I lay back on the couch, letting my head sink into the pillow, stretching my arms overhead so I didn't accidentally snuggle her. I'd wait for her move.

The door slammed as Bess and Charlie left, sending a cool blast of air our way. Teresa sat up, rubbing her eyes. "How did you sleep?"

"Surprisingly well," I said, forcing myself upright. "You?"

The couch beat the floor I'd laid on the night before, but I missed my bed. Teresa got to her feet and rummaged through the bags we'd left by the door, pulling out her earlier work clothes. "I'm okay, but I really need some fresh underwear." She grimaced, taking the clothes to the bedroom.

I got up and made my way to the kitchen, listening to the sound of the shower. What was she thinking? Did she regret last night? Stupid, bullish optimism had gotten the better of me, again. I'd forged ahead in blind faith, then crashed into a wall.

She wasn't sure about us. She'd never been in love.

The heavy thoughts circled my brain on relentless repeat as I paced the kitchen, pulling random items onto the breakfast bar. A packet of waffle mix caught my eye. That I could do. That, and coffee.

A bit later, Teresa emerged in her purple sweater and jeans, a literal skip in her step, hair still damp but curling behind her ears.

The waffle iron sizzled, melted butter dripping onto the counter.

"It smells amazing in here," she said. "What are you making?"

"Waffles."

"Oh." She inhaled deeply; her eyes closed. "I could get used to this."

My heart leaped, but I held my tongue. She took the macchiato I offered and looked at me over the rim of her cup, eyes sparkling. "Good thing I own your couch now. Can I keep it here? So, it's like a consulate in a foreign country."

"Sure. I'll check your passport every time you visit." I took a fortifying gulp of my own coffee.

I wanted to ask how she was feeling, but I'd learned my lesson. My phone buzzed on the counter, and I picked it up. It was a text message from Boris.

Did you hear about Gavin?

Underneath, he'd added a link to a news article. When I saw the headline, my heart lodged in my throat.

Billionaire Gavin Hellsten Questioned About Missing Tourist

I browsed the article, which contained little information other than that a female tourist was missing in Cozy Creek. A search was underway, as well as an investigation. She'd disappeared right outside her cabin, which sounded suspicious.

"What is it?" Teresa asked.

I closed the message and dropped the phone on the counter, contemplating my choices. Was it possible Gavin had something to do with this? The article alluded to the possibility of a crime, but there was no hard evidence, not even a body.

"It's... an article about the missing tourist. Boris sent a link."

She smiled. "Is he concerned you'll be captured by the evil lurking in Cozy Creek?"

I bit my lip. If I said something about Gavin, I'd open a can of worms. And she looked so relaxed right now, sitting by the window as faint morning light flooded into the room.

She sighed. "This place is so gorgeous."

Just as we finished our coffees and waffles, there was a knock on the door and Charlie barged in. "Somewhat dressed," he informed Bess, who stepped in from behind him, holding a bag of pink, heart-shaped biscuits.

"Thank God." She smiled. "We thought you might be... you know."

Teresa glanced at me, and pink blotches appeared on her cheeks. That's all my imagination needed to run through every intimate moment we'd spent together. I took a breath, trying to keep my partial under control.

Bess placed the cookies on the counter. "Look, fifty percent off! But you were right about the coffee, so we decided to take everything to go."

"There's another cafe down the road," Teresa piped up. "Cozy Coffee. My mom says their coffee is great."

"Well, too late. Can you make us coffees?" Charlie pleaded. "I hear yours are amazing."

I nodded and got to work as they peeled off their winter gear, shaking snow everywhere.

Before she made it back to the kitchen, Teresa grabbed Bess's arm, pulling her towards the bedroom. "I need to borrow her for a sec, sorry."

"What was that about?" Charlie asked me, taking a seat across the kitchen island.

"I don't know," I said, although I suspected it was about underwear.

I worked on the coffees, my mind on Teresa's naked body, until my phone pinged again, reminding me of the news article. My neck twitched.

"Are you okay?" Charlie asked. "You look pale."

"I'm Scottish and it's winter."

He fixed his sharp stare on me. "Something's up."

He knew my subtle tells. I took a breath, grateful for the opportunity to unload my conflicted thoughts. I picked up my phone and opened the article, this time reading all the way to the end. It was worse than I'd thought.

I handed Charlie the phone and watched his face also turn white. "Gavin? They're questioning *Gavin* about a missing tourist? Seriously?"

"I always had a bad feeling about him. There was a reason I didn't want him working with Teresa. And now…"

He nodded at the bedroom door. "Does she know? Did you tell her?"

"No."

"Why not? She needs to know! This is relevant information."

"She'll find out. It's in the news. But if I bring it up, it'll sound like I'm trying to justify my actions. I never had any proof, only a feeling. I could still be wrong."

Charlie frowned, staring at my phone. "This sounds suspicious."

"Even so, I should have never tried to control who she works with. I should have been there, keeping an eye on that guy. Protecting her."

"But what if he killed this lady? What if he's killed before? That missing tourist… it could have been Teresa!"

A shiver ran through me. I picked up the milk jug and turned on the steamer, letting my fingers rest on the warming metal.

"I don't care about being right. I want to be right for *her*."

"You are! If she doesn't see it, it's her loss."

"In which case… Let me guess… Ye want me to move on?" I gave him a wry smile.

Charlie smiled apologetically. "Disagreeing with your therapist seems like a stupid move."

I handed him the coffee and offered him the remaining waffle. "Thanks. I'll save it for Bess," he said.

Along with the discounted Valentine's Day cookies, they'd

picked up smoothies and sandwiches, spreading them across the counter.

"She doesn't love me," I said quietly, starting another coffee. "She's never been in love."

Charlie frowned. "Does she even know what it's like?"

"I don't know, and now I'm wondering if I know that either. I thought it was this horrible feeling I have... like nothing makes sense without her. That I'd rather have her angry wi' me than not have her in my life. I don't want to imagine my life without her. Maybe I shouldn't have told her that."

Charlie hung his head. "No! You didn't really say that to her, did you?"

I grimaced. "Well, kind of."

He groaned. "You've been obsessing over her for months. She's not going to be on the same page. She needs time to catch up."

"I know! I'm not expecting her to be where I am. Maybe she thinks I am, but I'm not. But it's hard to not feel disappointed when, you know..."

Charlie let out a long sigh. "I know."

"She wanted to sleep next to me, maybe not totally out of pity. Wasnae about sex, either." I pushed the button and watched coffee drip. "The sex is amazing, though."

Charlie nodded. "The way she was looking at you... she's warmed up a lot. Give her time. And she needs to know about Gavin. You could have saved her from getting murdered. If it was me, I'd love you for that."

"Aw, cheers, pal." I rolled my eyes. "They've no' even found a body yet. I don't want to jump to conclusions."

Charlie gave me a long, appraising look. "You used to trust your instincts, man. What happened?"

My instincts led me to lose the love of my life, that's what happened, I thought with painful clarity. If Charlie was right and I had another chance with her, I wouldn't let any gut reactions ruin it.

It was time to take deep breaths and chill the fuck out. I'd be so chill she'd think she was dating a snowman.

CHAPTER 27

Teresa

I'd never seen that many people in Cozy Creek. In my youth, the sled contest had been a small event with a handful of dedicated spectators drinking lukewarm cider and freezing their toes off, waiting to witness one entertaining crash.

The waiting was still very much part of the deal, but the organizers had bagged some major sponsors. Large logos decorated the gazebos set up to serve not just hot drinks but hotdogs and pizza rolls. With a stage built of pallets and "Eye of the Tiger" blasting from wardrobe-sized loudspeakers, there was now a sports event vibe. Progress, I guess.

Trevor grabbed my hand. "There!" He pointed to the top of the hill, where our purple cardboard car stood by a flagpole.

I spotted Charlie and Bess next to it, waving madly. I waved back with a purple mitten. They'd gone ahead of us, transporting the sled, which took up the backseat of Charlie's car.

We'd taken a detour via Trevor's car, where I'd finally been reunited with my phone and wallet, as well as kitted from head to toe with Trevor's knitting efforts. He'd been underselling his progress and had revealed an entire bag of socks, wool hats, and mittens.

I wasn't hugely surprised. He'd been not smoking for months and had evidently replaced one addiction with another. I'd seen the relief in his eyes when he'd grabbed the needles and yarn from the car, shoving them into his backpack.

It was a bit weird, but I wasn't complaining. It was as cold as a corpse's balls, so we'd divvied up his knitted items to ensure our collective survival. I was currently sporting purple mittens, a deep blue hat and the purple scarf that still had the needles attached to it. Trevor had wrapped some yarn around the ends to keep it together, but I held it in place with one hand, worried that the whole thing would snag on something and unravel.

I was out of the elf costume, feeling far more human in a fresh pair of underwear I'd borrowed from Bess, but it seemed looking even borderline normal in Cozy Creek was not an option for me.

"Teresa!"

I turned and found Peony smiling on the side of the slope, holding a thermos and a giant tote bag.

"Hi!"

I told Trevor I'd catch up with him and stepped off the path to talk to my old friend. "I just got my phone back!" I picked it out of my purse, waving it around for emphasis. "Now I can call you."

"Wonderful!" Her smile was so warm it was like going back in time.

I wondered if we could go back far enough to not remember any of the crap that had come between us. I missed her. She was a friend from an era where friendship meant something. Sleepovers. Confessions. Round-the-clock emotional support. Everything I had in Denver felt mild and lame in comparison. We'd been so close, always physically together. My emotional support was mostly remote these days—text messages and phone calls.

I looked around. "Remember when this event was just three families and a handful of cardboard boxes?"

She laughed. "It's grown quite a bit. And I heard we have a record number of tourists this year."

"Because of the ski resort?"

"Yeah. And Cozy Creek's been in the news. You know that missing skier?"

"Ah, yes. I've heard something."

"She's been missing for a few days now, and we've had all these volunteers running around the mountain."

"It sounds like a morbid form of tourism."

"That's what I said!" Peony's eyes widened. "But I swear some people draw sick enjoyment from that. Trekking around the forest, looking for human remains."

"And then what? Brunch in town and a spa treatment?"

"Yeah, probably!" She held onto my arm, giggling.

"They're not suspecting anything... sinister, are they? I mean, people get lost in the mountains all the time."

"It's a bit of a weird case. She vanished from the cabin she was staying at with her boyfriend, and he swears he's innocent, of course."

"So, she wasn't skiing or hiking or...?"

"No. I think they were meant to go, but she wasn't even fully dressed yet. She just popped outside to take a picture and never came back."

"What? That's bizarre!"

"Yeah. That's why it's getting so much publicity, I think. It's like this mystery every Sherlock out there wants to solve."

"Wow. That sounds crazy. I should look that up."

"You should! Just don't get freaked out." She lifted her Thermos. "Sorry! Where are my manners? Would you like some coffee?"

"I'm fine. We just had coffees."

She nodded, dropping the Thermos into her bag, and pulled out a packet of cookies. She was dressed sensibly in a puffer jacket and ski pants, ready to spend the day outside. I took a cookie, fighting the welling emotion that threatened to close my throat. She'd been the one baking and feeding me, looking after everyone. She was the one who always understood and never made a fuss, even when she should have.

"I... I'm sorry I didn't call back then. I'm sorry I just left."

It felt like an overdue apology, given at the wrong time, in the wrong place. But she still deserved to hear it.

Peony's smile had a sad tint, but she nodded. "It's okay. I'm sorry, too."

I knew what she meant. We'd both run away in our own ways, desperate to leave it all behind. And that had meant running away from each other.

I glanced up and saw Trevor on top of the hill, gesturing at me. The race was about to start.

"I have to go," I said.

"We'll talk soon." She put away the cookies to free up her arms.

I gave her a quick hug and climbed up the hill, slipping and sliding in my felt slippers, stuffed nice and warm with purple wool socks, courtesy of Trevor.

As I got closer, I counted at least six different cardboard sleds lined up on the peak. Behind them, another dozen, including our Tyrian-shaded beauty, waited in the wings.

"We're in the second heat," Bess announced. "After these guys." She gestured at the creative selection.

Three local firemen stood around a cardboard-made firetruck with 'Cozy Creek Fire Brigade' hand-painted on its side. There was also a sled shaped like an oil drum, a cardboard hamburger, a cardboard house and one that looked like a heart-shaped chocolate box.

"How's that going to work?" Trevor pointed at the house. "The center of gravity is at the top."

"It'll crash gloriously," I told him. "That's the whole point."

Charlie frowned. "I thought the point was to reach those hay bales down there and do it in record time. The race marshal just explained the rules. They checked our sled and said it's fine."

"Fine just means we didn't use any forbidden materials. But we built this thing yesterday," I reminded him. "If it holds together all the way down, that's pretty good."

"And if it doesn't...?" Bess wondered as we watched the first contestants getting into their sleds, their team members poised to give them a push.

I didn't have to answer. The loudspeaker crackled as the marshal counted down from three and the sleds launched down the slope. The tall house sled demonstrated the concept of crashing by toppling over and splitting into pieces. A teenager in well-padded overalls tumbled out and rolled down the slope, landing on top of a rogue cardboard piece. He got up and pumped his fist in the air before limping towards the side fence.

Moments later, the hamburger met its fate, bumping into another sled and splitting open. The child and adult inside it kept sliding until the sled came to a stop. Only the firetruck made it all the way to the hay bales with two guys onboard.

"I'm starting to understand why they recommended helmets," Bess mused. "Too bad we don't have any."

"Congratulations, Cozy Creek Fire Brigade!" The voice in the loudspeaker blasted. "You go onto round two! And now it's time for the second heat. Contestants, please line up."

I helped the others to push our sled to the starting line. We were up against two groups of kids with colorful, decorated boxes, one with a tail made of empty toilet rolls, the other with an incredible cardboard airplane. There was another sled shaped like a sprawling house that made me think of an architectural model.

"Please note that the house on the left is by our sponsor, Neville Architects, and is not part of the official competition. They are here to... actually, I'll hand over the microphone so they can say a few words..."

I froze. Neville Architects. Julian's dad's company.

The mic rattled and then a vaguely familiar voice came on, laughing self-deprecatingly as he spoke. "Hi! I'm Julian Neville and we're so proud to sponsor this event. The models we build in the office are usually smaller, and we don't use as much duct tape..."—someone laughed in the background—"but it's been a fun side project."

He went on about what an incredible community event this was. With every word, my stomach wound itself into a tighter knot. Of all the ways I'd imagined running into him and his family, this was not one I could have ever pictured: sliding downhill in a cardboard box and potentially crashing right in front of them. Best-case scenario, I'd puncture my lungs with the knitting needles hanging off my scarf and quickly lose consciousness.

"Where's the race marshal?" I asked. In other words, where was Julian?

"I think they're at that gazebo, by the stage." Charlie gestured down the slope.

Right by the finish line. Of course.

"Are you sure you don't want to ride?" I asked Bess, who lifted an eyebrow.

"Well, I'm not supposed to go on rollercoasters or have hot baths. I'd rather play it safe."

Charlie gave me a questioning look. "You said you were happy to."

"Are you okay?" Trevor leaned in to talk straight into my ear, over the noise around us. "You look like you saw a ghost."

"I'm fine. I just... I know that guy." I glanced at the loudspeakers, where Julian's self-important speech went on and on.

"The architect who loves his own voice?"

I nodded.

"And I suppose you have a history?"

He'd probably find out soon enough. All my dirty secrets were about to be exposed. I wanted to tell him. I wanted him to hear it from me. The whole story, with context. But there was no time. My insides churned, and I grabbed his hand, my eyes stinging. "I set his car on fire. And burned a bit of the school building."

"What?"

"It's... a long story. I didn't mean to burn the building."

"Please prepare for take-off!" Julian bellowed.

"They're not rocket ships," Charlie muttered, herding us into the sled.

I lowered myself into position at the front of it, holding onto the flabby sides.

"We can talk later," Trevor whispered into my ear as he sat behind me, extending his legs on either side of me.

I had to sit against him, feeling the confusing warmth of his body and those strong arms tightening around me. I removed the scarf, tucking it inside the sled, away from our bodies. I couldn't let myself be impaled before I explained myself. Trevor needed the whole story.

The countdown blasted through the sound system and Charlie got ready to push us.

Three—two—one—we were off. The cold breeze hit my face, my eyes watering so much I struggled to see ahead. But it didn't matter. There was no way to steer this thing. All we could do was to hold on, hoping it held together through the steepest part of the slope, over the two slight bumps.

The first one sent us airborne and delivered a painful landing that might have bruised my tailbone. The second one was much lower, almost at the finish line. For a second, I thought we might avoid it, but no. Our sled veered straight to the highest part of the bump.

This time, I didn't notice any lift-off, only the pain in my already bruised bottom. And suddenly, there was no sled. The sides of it were torn off by the impact, pieces of cardboard scattering in the wind as we continued riding down on the bottom piece, then slid off it, rolling down and finally hitting the first hay bale.

Somehow, the unfinished scarf landed on top of me, the knitting needles grazing my cheek, as if to remind me of my mortality.

"Are you okay?" Trevor hoisted me upright, untangling the scarf.

I stood, tentatively stretching my arms and legs. My ass was sore, but nothing seemed broken. I straightened my back to look ahead, and that was when I saw him.

Julian.

He was as strapping as he'd ever been. The quarterback. The hottest guy in high school. In Hollywood justice, he would have turned into the washed-out loser who never moved out of his hometown, but no. Julian might have left, but now he was back—now the hottest architect in town. He was surrounded by a group of older, well-dressed men, one of whom I recognized as his father.

He took one look at me, and his face fell. "Teresa?"

"Hi, Julian."

"Teresa Shaw?" His father echoed, his voice rising in alarm. "You have some nerve showing your face here."

I was suddenly sixteen years old, cowering in a doorway as Julian's father and the school principal shouted at me. The crazy girl who couldn't be trusted, the one who was too dangerous and unpredictable. An absolute hazard. A liar.

I hadn't been lying, though. I'd been telling inconvenient truths. No one believed me. I'd been too scared then, but I wasn't scared now.

"I have every right to take part in town events," I replied, my voice hoarse.

Julian's smile was condescending. "I don't think you do." He cast a cursory glance at Trevor, then turned his icy gaze back at me. "I'm pretty sure you're permanently banned from Cozy Creek, all things considered."

I stared at him, stunned. "Banned? Are you the mayor now?"

Trevor appeared by my side, gently squeezing my hand. I appreciated his presence, but this was my fight. He had a house here. Associating with me wasn't going to help him settle into this town. I took a step to the side to create distance between us.

"I didn't think you'd even consider coming back," Julian's father said, stepping so close I had to raise my chin to look at him. "But if you do, we can make things difficult."

Julian shifted closer too, lowering his voice. "We can make your life hell."

"What's happening here? Ye can't ban someone from the town they grew up in," Trevor said, reaching for my hand again. "Or any town, for that matter."

I sidestepped his touch, my throat so tight I couldn't swallow, let alone breathe. More people had gathered around us, drawn by the threatening tones and general commotion. Somewhere behind me, the sled contest went on, with the haybales shaking as another cardboard creation hit the barriers. People were everywhere, adding a layer of cacophony that made my brain hurt. I spotted Peony from the corner of my eye, looking like she'd turned into a pillar of salt. Next to her, the realtor stared at me with her mouth open. I recognized two other people from high school but couldn't recall their names.

I couldn't do this. I couldn't face all of them and stand my ground. I couldn't drag Trevor into this. I had to get away.

Tears blurring my eyes, I retreated through the crowd, bumping into random bystanders, and ran down the hill toward the parking lot, past Trevor's car and down the road leading to town. I had no direction, only a burning desire to put as much distance between me and Julian as I could. The man who'd broken my heart and my trust. Was he the reason I couldn't take the leap and fall in love? The reason I could never let go of my independence? I'd tried so hard not to think about him, because as soon as I did, I lost my new sense of self. I wobbled. I became weak and lost and powerless, and I hated it.

Coming back here had been a mistake. A huge mistake. A sharp pain in my lungs told me I was running too fast. I slowed to a jog until I reached the next intersection and leaned on a road sign to catch my breath and wipe my eyes.

"Teresa?"

I didn't recognize the voice behind me, but as soon as I turned, I recognized a familiar face. He smiled at me through the rolled-down window of a shiny Tesla, dressed in a blue ski outfit, complete with goggles on his forehead.

"Yeah?" I stared at him, trying to connect a name to that face.

"It's Kyle. We met at Gavin's party," he said, offering a gloveless hand through the window.

That's right! The guy Trevor had dragged me away from at that party. I took off my snow-crusted mitten and shook his hand.

"What are you doing here?" I asked, trying to smile just enough to not make it seem like an accusation.

My neck felt cold without Trevor's scarf, and I pulled at the collar of my coat to shield myself.

"Just coming back from the sled competition. That was fun."

"Is it over already?" I asked.

"Yeah. The fire department won." He glanced around as

if to check I was alone. "Are you... okay? Can I give you a ride somewhere?"

I shook my head. "No, it's fine. I needed a walk."

"One of those days?" He cast me a compassionate look.

I nodded. Even if he hadn't heard the Nevilles banning me from the town, it was probably all over my face.

"You look like you could use a drink," he said. "Maybe in a remote location overlooking the town. From a distance."

I huffed. "How much distance?"

"Enough to make everyone look like ants, I promise."

"So, you heard?" I cringed.

"I have no idea what those guys were harassing you about, but it didn't look pleasant."

"It was... old stuff." I said evasively. "I grew up here."

"Really? I'm just a seasonal resident. I've got a ski cabin up there, not far." He gestured at the mountains rising behind me. "It's not as big as Gavin's but it has a nice view and a nice liquor cabinet."

He smiled the same disarming smile I remembered from the party, moments before Trevor had dragged me away.

"I'm not looking for—"

"No hidden agenda, I promise! You just look like you could use a moment to catch your breath. And it's cold out here."

It was freezing, and I missed Trevor's scarf more every minute. I missed him, too, but that feeling was more complicated. He knew about my past now, at least the worst of it in bullet point format, and he'd heard the Nevilles. I wanted to tell my side of the story, but I wasn't ready. I needed time.

"Okay," I said, circling the car and collapsing into the passenger seat. "Take me away from here."

CHAPTER 28

Trevor

"Where is she?" I demanded of Charlie. "She can't have gotten this far!"

We'd driven all the way back to town, me following Charlie and Bess in my car, scouring the roads leading away from the slopes, but Teresa had vanished.

"Has she messaged you?" I asked Bess.

She removed her gloves to check on her phone again.

"Nothing yet. I don't think she's seen any of our messages. She's offline."

Gentle snowflakes floated down, hitting our phone screens. We'd parked right outside the cafe, which still sported some pink decorations. The ones hanging from lampposts looked a little wilted, but there was nothing sinister about this winter wonderland scene. The terror existed purely in my mind.

"Was her phone out of battery? It must have drained while it was locked inside your car," Charlie suggested.

"It was working when she picked it up. She messaged her sister."

"Did she say it was running low?" Bess injected.

"No. But maybe it was. It must have been." I was trying to calm myself down, but nothing was working.

Teresa had run off, upset, into the cold. I'd forced myself to not follow, to give her space. To *not* suffocate her. I'd expected her to head for the car and wait for us there. I'd even unlocked the car from a distance. But she must have run right past it, either down the road or into the forest. There were no tracks leading off the road, though. We'd checked. The thick layer of snow made you sink in. She would have taken ages to trudge through, easy enough to track.

At one p.m. it was still light outside, but it was winter, and days were short, the temperature just below freezing. If Teresa was lost somewhere, we'd have to find her quickly. Yet there was the possibility she'd turned off her phone on purpose. On top of that, there was a potential murderer on the loose, already responsible for another missing tourist.

Was I jumping to conclusions again? Thinking I was protecting her when I was acting out of fear, having knee-jerk reactions?

But, as much as I tried to be the chill guy who gave her space, I couldn't shake the ill feeling. Something was wrong and I had to get to her.

"Maybe she just needs a minute?" Bess suggested. "That whole thing with those douchey guys was awful. Who do they think they are, banning someone from town? I'm so glad you said something!"

What had I even said? I remembered how I'd raised my voice and how it had cracked from emotion. I couldn't let those pricks have the last word. Maybe it was best Teresa hadn't been there to see it. This was not the new, snowman-level of chill I was supposed to exude. If anything, I was getting more intense.

"For what it's worth, I don't think it was about Teresa burning down a building," Charlie mused. "They're architects and developers. They tear down and build new stuff all the time, and they've obviously done very well. It's not like she burned down the entire town and it's still a pile of ashes... so what am I missing?" He scanned the buildings around us as if looking for evidence of fire damage.

"I'm not sure," I said. "But you're right, it seemed personal."

"Why did she do it?" Bess wondered. "She's never mentioned anything. She didn't even tell us she grew up here when we talked about the office move. She was just against it."

"It's making more sense now," Charlie agreed. "I mean... she's a fiery person." He couldn't hide his grin.

I threw him a dirty look. "She was sixteen and I'm sure she had a reason. It doesn't even have to be a good reason. Everyone's allowed a teenage blunder."

"Totally," Bess echoed. "Nobody is perfect."

"I'm just worried she'll never want to live here," I said. "It's not like the town has welcomed her with open arms."

Charlie gave me a pointed look. "The town? That was two people and their two buddies, and to be honest, the other guys looked uncomfortable. I know we arrived a bit late, but I saw the tail end of it."

"I looked them up," I confessed. "The Nevilles own a lot of real estate around here. They support the local events and the school. I'm sure they're well connected."

"Doesn't mean they rule the world," Bess muttered.

Charlie glanced at the cafe, then at our cars. "Where to? Should we grab some lunch?"

"I'm so hungry," Bess added apologetically, gazing at the cafe.

"Go eat!" I urged them. "I'll head back to the hill. There might still be people around. Someone might have seen her."

I was running out of ideas, but I couldn't imagine sitting down to relax or even swallow food.

I drove back, scanning the roadside so intently I spotted a deer behind some trees. The sledding competition was in full packing-up mode, the stage pallets and broken cardboard pieces being hauled onto trailers in the empty parking lot. When I made it to the competition site, I saw the PA equipment had already disappeared and only a handful of kids remained on the slope, sliding down on toboggans.

The Nevilles were gone, but I spotted two parents grasping Thermoses and instantly recognized the lady Teresa had run into earlier. What was her name? My brain flipped through a Rolodex of flowers until I hit a familiar one—Peony.

"Peony, right?" I approached her with a tentative smile.

"Yes! You're Teresa's friend. Sorry, I forgot your name." She smiled apologetically.

"Trevor," I supplied.

"Hi, Trevor! Would you like some coffee?" She raised her Thermos. "I have an extra cup."

Before I could refuse, she'd rummaged through her giant tote bag and discovered a plastic cup that looked like the cap of her Thermos. I accepted a cup of steaming coffee, suddenly grateful for the sense of normalcy it brought.

"Thank you. So, did you take part in the race?" I asked, to be polite.

"Oh, no! The kids don't have patience for building those things. They just want to slide—"

"Actually, I need to ask ye something." It seemed I had no patience either, with panic gnawing my gut. "Did you happen to see which way Teresa went? She ran off when those guys cornered her."

"Julian and his dad? They're the devil! I hope she didn't take it to heart. The Nevilles like running their mouths but they wouldn't do anything."

"Are you sure?"

She shrugged. "They like being seen as benefactors of the town. They wouldn't do anything to hurt their reputation." The look in her eyes belied the light tone she applied to her words.

"Are ye scared of them?" I asked without thinking.

Peony tried to laugh. "Oh, no! Not anymore. I just keep out of their way. It's... mutual."

She was scared, but I couldn't figure out why.

"So... any chance ye saw which way Teresa went?"

She shook her head. "No, sorry. I think she ran towards the parking lot, but I didn't see anything beyond that."

"Me neither. To tell you the truth, I'm worried." I took a sip of the coffee. It was black and so strong my eyes watered.

"I can ask my friend Kerry. She already left, but she was on parking duty so she would have seen more of what was happening on that side."

"That'd be great. I'm probably overreacting, but she's not answering her phone. I mean... her phone is not on."

"Maybe she's out of range? You don't have to go far up Mountain View Road and you lose the signal. People who live that way are always complaining."

"She was on foot, though. Could she have walked that far?"

Peony glanced over her shoulder, maybe to check on her children, then tilted her head. "No, you're right. But maybe she got a ride with someone."

The possibility had already crossed my mind, and now it wouldn't leave me alone. "Did you spot any of her old friends? Anyone she might have known well enough?"

Peony thought of this for a moment, her head still tilted. "Only myself and the Nevilles. I didn't see anybody else from our class. Most of us don't live here anymore. I didn't recognize that many people today, but we get quite a few vacationers this time of year and they love these events."

I sighed, forcing down the rest of the coffee. Maybe it'd kick-start my brain and give me ideas. After a moment, one thought surfaced.

"What happened with the Nevilles? Do you know the details?"

Peony bit her lip, eyes wide. "She... didn't tell you?"

"She said she burned a car and a building, but I don't understand why. What does that have to do with the Nevilles?"

She looked conflicted. "It's really not my story to tell."

"I'm only asking in case it has something to do with where she is right now and whether she's in danger." I hated even saying it.

Peony whipped her head left and right. The only other human within a hundred-foot radius was the stocky guy right behind her—presumably her husband. He gave me a subtle nod.

"I don't know if it has anything to do with that," Peony said. "I don't think the Nevilles would offer her a ride. And I don't think she'd get in the car with them. Do you?"

"Probably not."

We stood in silence, watching the kids climb up the slope with their sleds and toboggans in tow. I'd all but given up hope when she finally spoke. "Julian had this car... it sounds lame now, but back in high school, it was the coolest ride. He'd pick up girls in it and take them to the lookout. You know—the make out spot? Every girl had a crush on him. I mean, everybody." She shifted a little further from her husband, who was pretending with great effort that he wasn't listening. "And when I made it onto the cheerleading squad, he noticed me. It was right after the summer when I got my boobs, so it shouldn't have been such a surprise."

I nodded, keeping my gaze firmly on her eye level.

"I should have believed Teresa when she told me to stay away from him. That he was the kind of guy who wouldn't hear the word 'no'. I wanted so badly to think I was special. I heard he wasn't really into her; he just had a bet going on with the guys over who could pop her cherry."

"What?"

Peony winced. "Teresa could be a bit scary. She had a sharp tongue and I guess they saw it as a challenge. But she's the sweetest soul and the best girlfriend you could ever have. Fiercely loyal." She wiped a tear from her eye, her voice thick with regret. "That's probably why it all happened. She felt like she needed to avenge all of us. Every girl who'd been picked up in that stupid Mustang."

"So, she burned the car?"

"She didn't mean for the shed to catch on fire. Or the school! And the fire department was there so fast there wasn't too much damage. It was late. She knew he parked by the shed when they had evening practice. It wasn't even a proper parking space. It was just convenient and since their family had donated the money to build the shed and the stadium…"

"He felt entitled," I finished. "I know the type."

"Yeah, well. Teresa didn't tell us. She didn't want to implicate anyone else. She just said he'd pay. But I think she struggled with the heavy canister of gasoline and left a trail, so the fire spread."

"To the shed?" I held my breath.

Peony nodded. "The shed and the school building. It was May

and warm and dry. She called 911, then ran away. But of course, they tracked her down. I'm not sure what exactly happened, but I know she didn't go to jail. She saw a shrink for a while and did some community service. Maybe because she was underage and had no priors."

"So, justice was served? What do the Nevilles have to complain about?"

She shrugged. "She destroyed their property."

"If they donated the shed, it's not their property. That's not how donating works!"

"The car was, although I'm pretty sure she paid them back. Or her mom did."

"Then what's the issue? Why are they being such colossal pricks?"

Peony took a deep breath. "She accused him of sexual assault, so I guess they freaked out. Attack is the best form of defense."

I swallowed, looking for the right words. There probably weren't any, but I had to know. "What happened in that car? Did he... pop her cherry?" I cringed at the words. Why couldn't I think of any other phrase?

Peony shook her head, looking away. There were tears in her eyes. "Not quite, she fought him off and ran away. I wasn't strong enough."

Teresa

Fear was a strange thing, like a switch in my head I couldn't un-flick. I'd been picking up clues all the way to the cabin, thinking nothing of it, but then suddenly, opening a bathroom cabinet sent me over the edge and I found myself in a grip of terror.

In my relief to escape the judgment of Cozy Creek town roy-als, I'd accepted that Kyle's cabin was twenty minutes outside of town. I'd shrugged at the fact that there was no cell phone coverage. I'd even smiled at the joke he'd made about it being so secluded that nothing worked—no phone, no internet. When he'd told me his closest neighbor had been found months after his death, partially mummified, I'd stared at him in shock, rather entertained, but I'd felt no fear.

Once we'd arrived, he'd given me a tour of the beautiful

property, skipping over a basement door with a heavy padlock, joking, "this is where I bury the bodies". I'd laughed. We'd even discussed the missing tourist, exchanging theories on what might have happened, from alien abduction to a lying scumbag boyfriend.

After we'd settled into his living room, I'd accepted his offer to mix me a Cuba Libre and excused myself to use the bathroom. And now, I'd opened the bottom cabinet, not even sure why. Why was I poking around in a stranger's bathroom? And, more importantly, why did this man have a four-gallon container of bleach? What would anyone need that much bleach for, unless they were in the business of breaking down human remains?

I couldn't answer my own question and was beginning to work up a real panic. This was crazy, I told myself. I had to calm down. This guy was a client. I knew him. Charlie and Trevor knew him even better.

What could I do? If Kyle was up to anything at all, I couldn't let him know I suspected him. That would probably get me killed faster. I took a deep breath, trying to expel the terror running through my veins. These thoughts were absolutely unhinged, yet I couldn't seem to be able to stop them.

Why hadn't I notified anyone the moment I sat in his car? By the time I'd pulled out my phone, we'd been well on our way and out of range. Kyle had sounded genuinely apologetic about it, putting me at ease. After all, it wasn't a dark and stormy night. The world was bathed in soft, white daylight with a dusting of snowfall making everything around us look new and fresh. A perfect winter's day. Covering car tracks and footsteps... I shivered.

I closed the cabinet as quietly as possible and checked my face in the mirror, adjusting my expression to a relaxed half smile that hopefully raised no suspicions.

Kyle waited for me by the drink cabinet—Yes, he had an actual, old-timey drink cabinet—and handed me the cocktail. I thanked him and smiled, raising my glass to toast him.

But when I brought the rim to my lips, my brain screamed "Danger!" What if he'd spiked it? Drinking this thing could be the last thing I ever did. He was watching me, holding up his own, seemingly identical drink. I tilted the glass until my lips touched the liquid, inhaling the smell of coke and something stronger. There was no way to tell. I couldn't pretend to drink it, not with him watching me.

"Wait!" I said, lowering the glass. "You promised I'd get to see Cozy Creek from a distance!"

Kyle laughed. "Of course. This way."

He led me to the doors opening to a wide, snow-covered balcony.

"The view is nicer from out there, but it's pretty cold and snow boots are recommended."

There also seemed to be a huge drop down to the ground below, so I nodded in understanding. "Happy to stay inside. I can still see the town, I think. It's over there, right?"

I pointed down the mountain range at an area where the blanket of snow-covered trees gave way to some dwellings. It was too far to make out any detail, but if wishful thinking could have activated teleportation, I would have been there. I would have been in Trevor's cabin on the couch I'd already claimed. Safe.

Kyle raised his glass again, and I mirrored his movement, forcing myself to take a sip. It didn't taste odd, but as I swallowed, my mouth felt numb, and my fingertips tingled. I felt lightheaded.

"Are you okay?" he asked, guiding me to an armchair.

I collapsed into it, trying to control my breathing. I had to stop gulping air. "I... I think I'm still a bit out of sorts after that..."

He sat next to me, his eyes full of concern. "What happened out there?"

He sounded so genuine, but it must have been an act. This was how he lured the girls and gained their trust.

"Just... old things. Ghosts from my past." The word ghost made me shiver, even though I'd said it myself. I was pathetic.

I set the drink on the table, too lightheaded and upset to finish it. I could only hope that the amount I'd ingested wasn't enough to knock me out or kill me. Did he kill his victims with a poisoned drink, or merely drugged them so he could then chop them up with a chainsaw? That was what he needed bleach for, right? Chopping up was messy.

My vision was starting to blacken around the edges. The numbness and tingling intensified. Was this how it all ended?

♥ ♥ ♥

I woke up to Trevor's face, and an overwhelming sense of relief.

"Teresa? Teresa?" He tapped my cheek, hovering over me.

"Trevor?"

"You passed out."

I felt strong arms lifting me off the floor, onto a couch I didn't recognize. It took me several beats to make sense of it. I was still in Kyle's cabin, but Trevor was here. Either I was safe, or we were both in danger. My mouth felt dry, and I scanned the room. Kyle stood back; his arms folded. He looked concerned. Or maybe a little annoyed.

"Do you have your car?" I whispered. "Take me out of here. Now."

Trevor nodded, a quizzical look in his eyes. "Why are you whispering?" He turned to Kyle. "Did she hit her head on the way down?"

"No, I don't think so." He scratched his head, frowning. "Look, I'm not trained in first aid. I didn't know what to do. One minute she was fine and then... bam."

"Please," I pleaded with Trevor.

He scooped me up and planted me on my feet, walking me to the door.

"I'll drive her home," he told Kyle. "Maybe via the hospital."

"Keep me posted."

Outside, the damp smell of evergreens hit my nostrils. I'd never felt more grateful to smell something. To be alive.

I sank into Trevor's passenger seat like it was my final destination. "Thank you. Thank you." Tears blurred my vision as I waited for Trevor to start the car and drive down the winding road. Every yard we put between us and Kyle relaxed me further.

My head felt light and woozy, but I could breathe, and all senses seemed to work. Whatever I'd swallowed hadn't killed me.

"How did you know where I was?" I asked.

"Peony's friend Kerry said she saw a blue Tesla leave right after you. That's when I remembered Kyle's cabin."

"Have you been here?"

"No. But when I was buying mine, we exchanged notes. He was really helpful. Lovely guy. I think he… likes you." Trevor threw me a resigned look. "I would have left you two to it. I mean, it's none of my business if you want to…" His jaw twitched, his expression hard.

"What?" I demanded, confused.

"I was just going to double-check you're okay and leave, but he dragged me in, scared shitless."

"Scared?" I blinked, trying to catch up. "Of what?"

"Of ye fainting."

"But… he gave me the drink. I thought he drugged me."

He shook his head. "I dinnae think so."

"How do you know?"

Trevor cast me a concerned look. "Because we checked the drink. He showed me the bottles and swore there wasn't anything unsavory in them. He knew it looked bad, with ye passed out on the floor. He was freaking out."

"He could have slipped in something—"

"He drank it, Teresa. He was so desperate to show me he hadn't drugged you that he downed your drink in front of me."

"What?" My mind spun like a film on fast forward. Or maybe it was backward. "The drink on the table..."

"Cuba Libre."

I hung my head. It was still spinning. What was wrong with me? How had I misjudged Kyle that badly? I'd been sure that I was going to die. Had I made myself faint by the power of suggestion? Your mind could play tricks on you. I knew that. We were all biased. I'd once built an entire beer campaign around biases. I'd studied them. How had I missed this prime example of confirmation bias? Of course. When you were looking for clues, you saw them everywhere.

I felt so stupid I hardly wanted to talk, so we drove in silence. When we got to town, Trevor pulled over and called Charlie, explaining to him that I'd been at Kyle's, just like he'd suspected, and that he'd take me home.

The call was short, his tone clipped.

"I'm sorry," I said, when we made it to the highway.

"For what?"

"For not texting you my whereabouts. I tried to, but we were already out of range."

"It's okay."

"No, it's not. I can see from your face that it's not. I should have asked Kyle to turn around, but I felt like I needed a moment to cool off and organize my thoughts. Julian... I haven't seen him in years. Not since—"

"He sexually assaulted you and you set his car on fire."

"Wait. How do you know that?"

"Peony told me. I freaked out when I couldn't find ye and went to talk to her."

"Did she tell you that she and Julian—"

"That he raped her? Yes. And it doesn't sound like she told the police. What am I missing?" He sounded angry now, his fist squeezing the steering wheel.

"She didn't want to talk about it or think about it. And I promised I wouldn't say anything. We were young. It was a difficult time."

"So, she let you take the punishment?"

"I'm the one who burned the car. It *was* my punishment."

"But she could have outed him! She could have given context. It sounds like that guy really struggles with consent and she wasn't the only victim. Don't tell me you haven't thought about that."

Of course, I'd thought about it, but a promise was a promise. "I warned her about him, but she was so in love she wouldn't listen. We had a horrible fight. She made up all these excuses for him. That I'd misread the situation and elbowed him in the nuts when he was just reaching for the door handle."

"Holy shit."

"Yeah. It threw me and I started doubting myself. But I remember him touching me. I remember his hand between my legs..."

"No door handle there."

"No." I attempted to laugh, but it sounded like a cough. "I don't think she meant to gaslight me. She just wanted so badly to believe his version of it. Because the hottest guy at school had noticed her. So, she went out with him. Later, I found out what happened to her, and I don't know... I was just relieved that she even told me. She came to see me, and we talked all night and she cried and cried. She made me swear not to tell, and I didn't want to pressure her. I was so scared of losing a friend."

"I thought you lost touch, anyway."

I sighed. "Yeah. Because I'm stupid and didn't do what she asked. I couldn't leave it alone. I went back with gasoline and a packet of matches. She wanted to stay far away from all the drama and after that, I was roped into all of it."

"She could have given a statement. She could have said something."

"She kept saying it wasn't really rape because she didn't fight him that hard. That maybe she wanted it on some level."

"That's bullshit, and she's changed her tune since then."

My heart ached for Peony. "That's good, I guess. I hope she found the courage to tell her story, even if it was later."

"Did you tell your story?"

"I did, during the arson trial, but it didn't help. It was my word against Julian's. He said he broke up with me and I flipped out. I had no evidence, and they all believed him. Everyone but my mom and my sister. And Peony. I guess I'm lucky I had no evidence," I concluded. "I got away."

"It doesn't mean he didn't hurt you," he said quietly.

We stared out the windows at the endless trees flicking past. I felt a sense of sadness, but also calm. Like I'd taken the first step by letting light into a dusty basement to see the damage.

It wasn't as bad as I'd feared. The memories felt shrunken and lifeless. They held no power to hurt me.

"I couldn't believe he was interested in me," I said. "I wasn't a cheerleader. I wasn't one of those blondes. But I fell for it all the same. The gifts and compliments and car rides. And when he decided it was time for us to… you know, he sort of implied it was unreasonable for me to say no or even ask for him to wait. Because he'd put in all that effort. Ticked all the boxes. I'm so glad I ran off." I filled my lungs, the memories swelling inside me like I'd eaten something spoiled. "Because later, I found out he and his friends had a bet going on. That's why he was asking for my underwear, trying to rip it off. It was supposed to be his trophy."

"Fucking hell!" Trevor's jaw muscle worked overtime, his knuckles popping as he squeezed the steering wheel. "If I ever get my hands on that guy—"

"You'll remember me telling you they have great lawyers. I already tried vigilante justice, and I paid the price. That's not how you get these guys."

To my relief, his hand relaxed, and he nodded. "You're right. We want to take him down, for good. Peony could still come forward. She and anyone else he might have hurt."

"I think it's past the statute of limitations now."

"It needs to be public knowledge, for everyone's protection. That guy got away, and I bet anything that he's still doing what he did. You can't let him rule your life and tell you where you can and can't live."

I shrugged. "I never wanted to live in Cozy Creek, so it was never an issue."

"And now?"

"Now... it's complicated."

I turned on the radio, channel surfing until I found a familiar song. I didn't have the bandwidth to discuss the future. Rehashing the past was so exhausting I was still fighting to shake the lingering nausea brought on by those memories. Trevor probably understood, since he held back any further questions, humming along to the 90s tunes on the radio.

It was getting dark, and the city lights were flicking on, glowing in the distance. We were nearly back home.

"So, what did you think of the office space we went to see?" he asked in a lighter tone when we reached the first traffic light in Denver, crawling to a stop.

A tried to smile. "You mean the one you said we'd quickly check out in one afternoon?"

He grinned back. "That's the one. Did it have enough power points?"

"More than any other campsite I've ever used." I hoisted my elbow onto the edge of the cool window and leaned on my arm.

"Thinking of this Julian... I didn't cross any boundaries with you, right?"

I almost smiled at the concern in his voice. "You'd still be feeling it if you had."

"Oh, right. Elbow to the nuts. Got it."

I turned to him, wishing I could lose the weird, shaky mood and slip back into that connection we'd shared back in his cabin.

It had felt so effortless, almost like we'd been bouncing on a diving board, ready to fall. But that was before all my baggage had been dragged into daylight. "Thank you for the distraction," I finally said. "I needed it, and I loved your cabin. I love the couch."

"So, you'll be back to visit?" he asked. "Don't forget your passport."

I heard the neediness in his voice, cloaked in light humor. I couldn't blame him. I was giving him nothing, no matter how much I wanted to close this chasm between us and make it all okay. I laughed a little. "I won't."

We turned onto my street. I could almost smell my own bed. My clothes. My shower. The familiar coffee made with my own coffeemaker. I needed those things to regulate my nervous system. To feel I was back on the ground and no longer on a roller coaster. Maybe I was too set in my own ways.

Trevor pulled over in front of my house and turned to me, about to ask something, but I cut him off.

"I can't wait to take a shower and get changed."

"Of course."

I still felt my heartbeat in my throat, like an echo of the events that had unfolded. I had to get home, out of these dirty clothes and back to my normal life. I had to get my head straight and figure out what it all meant. I needed some perspective.

CHAPTER 30

Trevor

Harry Styles crooned on the radio as I peered over Teresa's shoulder at her home. It was one of the new complexes—six units crammed onto a lot that previously might have accommodated one medium-sized house. The units were so narrow I wondered how they'd managed to fit stairs in them. The windows faced a busy road which led to a large intersection, the one with the corner deli I knew she liked.

I'd never been invited here, but I knew the approximate location. My latest rental was close by—not totally by accident—and I'd walked past many times, trying to imagine which ones of the identical three-paneled windows belonged to her. I'd only been able to narrow it down by a process of elimination, concluding that her tiny strip of lawn was the one that didn't have kids' toys lying around. It was cute in that factory-made way that always made me think of Lego.

"Handy location," I commented.

"You can say it looks boring," she shot back. "And before you ask, it feels exactly as narrow on the inside. You'd bruise your shoulders."

Was this her way of saying I wasn't invited?

"I better drop ye off here, then. Don't think I can take any more bruising."

She turned to look at me, holding still, her teeth skating along her bottom lip, her eyes conflicted. "I need time, Trevor. I need to clear my head."

"Okay," I replied. What else could I say?

"Thank you. For everything," she finally uttered, opening the car door. "I'll talk to you later."

And then she was gone, leaving behind an empty seat that mocked me. I'd freaked her out. I'd driven her away. And I still wasn't over her.

Would I ever be?

♥ ♥ ♥

"Meet me for a beer," I said as soon as Charlie picked up.

I'd arrived home to my stale and dusty apartment with one wilted house plant, but I couldn't be alone with my thoughts.

"Hang on a sec," Charlie said. "I'll check with Bess."

I dodged a pile of moving boxes to throw myself on the bricklike couch. Next week, I'd have to give up this place and move to my cabin in Cozy Creek. I would either work remotely, or the company would move closer. Either option didn't worry me. I'd taken this gamble for a reason. I couldn't keep living in the same town, two streets over, hoping to run into her at the deli. It was probably best I put some distance between us and start over. Besides, with my current income, I couldn't keep both places.

I waited for a moment, listening to the muffled conversation between Charlie and Bess, with Celia's young voice in the mix. She must have missed her parents during their little getaway. I heard Bess say something about me needing a friend, and Charlie agreed. I did, too.

"O'Malley's in half an hour?" Charlie finally replied.

"Perfect."

It was the Irish pub around the corner that had at least two happy hours every night, possibly more. We'd never been able to avoid one.

Ten minutes later, I pushed open the door, taking in the sticky floors, cracked vinyl seats and bowls of beer nuts you usually ate, by accident, after a couple of beers, and ended up ordering vodka after to disinfect your mouth. Not that I was planning on getting wasted.

Charlie appeared thirty minutes later, his jacket hanging open and cheeks red from the cold. I'd already ordered for us, snatching a private booth at the back.

"Sorry if it's gone flat." I nodded at his beer. "I got here a bit early."

"All good." Charlie took a sip and winced. "So, what's going on?"

Normally, we would have wasted a good half hour with idle chitchat, talking about work or sports or movies. But today, it seemed pointless.

"So, I'm not over Teresa," I said.

"No, you're not," he confirmed.

"But she... I don't know if she feels anything for me. What should I do?"

"Nothing."

"Nothing?"

"I think, in general, you've done... enough. More than any man should ever do. I mean, you make the rest of us look lazy." Charlie took a sip of beer and grimaced.

"And sane."

"That, too. But also, a bit lame. Bess asked me yesterday if I was obsessed with her before we got together. I mean, I had a crush on her, but I didn't know her last name. I didn't know where she lived. I didn't know what she did outside of work."

"We work pretty closely together," I argued. "We have a private chat, and we talk every day. It's different."

Charlie straightened in his seat. "You have a private chat? She talks to you... in private?"

"Yeah."

"You mean, before this trip, when she was avoiding you in these super-creative ways?"

"Like when she suddenly had covid with no symptoms when

I was coming to the office?" I let out a sad chuckle, finishing my beer.

"Or when she had huge bunions and couldn't walk?"

I laughed a little less sadly. "She definitely doesn't have bunions."

Charlie's laugh fizzled out and he gave me a serious look. "You're saying, she was talking to you all that time? In private?"

I nodded, not sure what he was getting at. "It started as a work chat. I had to send her all these alternate headings, and she ripped them apart and I needed to be there to rewrite and rewrite… It made sense."

"For the culinary school campaign? That was months ago!"

"Why is this news? We all work together. Of course, we talk."

"But… privately. Is it all about work?"

"No. We talk about anything. I try to make her feel better when she's stressed out. She sends me memes…"

"She was dating that other guy. Did she talk about him?"

"No." I hadn't asked, either. "Sometimes, she said she'd had a late night, or something like that, so I figured she'd been out with him." I thought back to our chats. "Sometimes, she messaged me on the weekend. Once when she was babysitting Celia and was nervous about bedtime."

"She talked to *you* about it? You don't even have kids."

"I have nieces and nephews. She doesn't. And I'm sure she was talking to her sister, too. Maybe other friends. I was probably way down the list."

"I don't think you are," he said. "I don't think you realize how much she's leaning on you."

I shrugged. She could lean on me as much as she liked.

"Has she messaged you since you dropped her off?" Charlie asked.

I picked up my phone and there it was—a chat message from Teresa. The first one she'd ever sent me with a photo of herself. She sat on an unmade bed, wearing a white tank top, her hair shower fresh, smiling.

Teresa: Shower + fresh clothes = magical combo!

I showed it to Charlie, who shook his head, looking almost angry. "You need to cut her off."

"Cut her off, how?"

"Close the chat, man! She's friend-zoned you in that chat box and you need to get out."

"She's never sent me a selfie before," I argued, my eyes lingering on that smile, heart aching over how much I wanted to touch her.

"She's stringing you along."

I released a heavy sigh, turning the phone face down on the table. "Okay. I'll think about it."

Charlie huffed at my hesitation but changed the subject. "You still moving house? Because I'm not sure we can move the office just yet. They discovered a leaky pipe and there's some water damage that needs to be fixed first. The agent just called me."

"Okay. That's fine. I'm moving on Wednesday. I can't keep paying rent."

"We can raise your salary."

I shook my head. I knew what he was talking about, and it wasn't an option.

"Suit yourself," he finally said. "Did Teresa say what she's going to do if we move? Is she leaving?"

"We barely spoke on the way back. She was rather shaken when I picked her up from Kyle's."

Charlie's chin lifted in curiosity. "What the hell happened there?"

I gave him a rundown of what I knew. His frown deepened with every word. "She thought Kyle was going to *murder* her?"

"I know. It's a bit wild."

"There isn't even a murderer loose or anything. They found the missing tourist. It had nothing to do with Gavin *or* Kyle. She just ran off with her ski instructor and finally emerged from her sex-cation. It was just in the news."

"So, she didn't know everyone was looking for her with dogs and helicopters?"

"Apparently, there's no cell phone coverage around there and they were... busy." Charlie raised his brows.

"Bloody hell." I let out a long sigh.

"So, is there something going on between Kyle and Teresa?" Charlie asked.

"Other than one thinking the other is a serial killer? I don't know. I think Kyle likes her. He was hitting on her at that Fourth of July party."

"Wow." Charlie took a drag of his beer, staring out the window.

"She's got two guys with cabins in Cozy Creek after her."

"So, what do I do?" I asked again, part of me still hoping for a different answer.

"About what?"

"Teresa." I hated how desperate my voice sounded. "I love her. I'm an idiot, but I do. All that stuff we found out about her past, I want to fix it. I want to take down that jerk who threatened her. But she didn't sound that keen. She told me she needed time. So, what do I do?"

Charlie looked at me like I was playing dumb. "I already told you. Nothing. If she needs time, you give her time."

My stomach twisted. "How much time?"

"As much time as she needs. And stop talking to her. Delete that chat."

We sat in silence, slowly draining our beers, as I digested Charlie's advice. He was right. I couldn't insert myself into any of it. All I could do was wait.

CHAPTER 31

Teresa

It took me a week to catch up with all the work I'd missed on our Cozy Creek excursion, and another to get back to a work-life balance as I knew it, with occasional lunchtime walks and my mid-week pole dancing class. All in all, it was business as usual, which somehow felt wrong.

Trevor was still online, supplying me with copy and headlines. He did it through the official channels, though. No more private chat. I'd sent him one message after he dropped me off, desperate to hang onto that connection we'd shared, but he'd never replied. Not even with a thumbs-up. It had stung, but I knew I deserved it.

I hadn't gathered my nerve to try again. Not yet. We both needed time. I'd promised myself that once the dust settled, I'd be able to process what had happened between us and what it meant. Clarity would come to me eventually, like it did with each tricky design job. I kept tweaking and testing ideas until everything made sense. I wasn't sure what would bring clarity to this scenario, but it probably wasn't me harassing Trevor online.

At night I lay in bed, feeling sad and lonely and confused. But it didn't mean I loved Trevor, did it? I couldn't even tell if I missed him or simply missed having someone in my life. I'd only just broken up with Richard, who—angry that he couldn't contact me in any other way—had slipped seven notes under my door. The content ranged from apologies to accusations and possibly something else. I'd stopped reading after the first two and enjoyed burning them all over the sink. I'd set off the fire alarm with the first one, angering my neighbors.

Maybe I really was a pyromaniac. They'd called me that at school after I'd torched Julian's car. There was something cleansing and final about fire. Not that I planned to destroy any more property. I'd put the batteries back into my fire alarm like a responsible citizen and aired out the room.

Neither Charlie nor Bess had mentioned anything about the office move, or Trevor. We were all busy trying to get on top of the workload, but I wondered if they were speaking behind my back. Maybe it was already a done deal, and I'd be the last one to hear about it. Probably after Lee, who was now working closely with Charlie on a new website.

I felt so emotionally exhausted that I couldn't even bring myself to raise the question. I had no real say about it, anyway.

It was Friday morning when I finally showed my face in our shared office and found Bess there, plucking away at the latest campaign. This, too, was business as usual, which meant Trevor wasn't taking the opportunity to catch me in person. He didn't want to bump into me.

"Morning!" I hung my jacket by the door and connected my laptop to the external screens.

"Great to see you!" She beamed at me, reaching for a pretzel. "I was worried I'd have to sit here all alone today. Sorry, I'm snacking all day. I was feeling yuck this morning, skipped breakfast and now I'm starving."

"Pregnancy sounds like fun."

"It really is!" She rolled her eyes. "Do you want to ditch work and go get coffees?"

"Where? Outside?"

We usually made a cup of instant in the tiny kitchenette, too busy to fetch coffees.

She bit her lip. "I need to talk to you."

I was instantly tense but forced a smile. "Sounds serious."

"It is." She put on a smile. "But don't worry. It's good, serious."

What did that mean? I glanced at my laptop, weighing the most urgent items on my to-do list. If I was honest, there wasn't too much there. I'd worked so hard for two weeks that we were ahead of schedule. I should have been relieved, but instead felt hollow and lost, like I had nothing to hold onto.

We pulled on our jackets, and I followed Bess down the road to the nearest coffee shop. It was busy, mostly catering to the takeaway crowd, but offered a couple of tables and long bars with barstools by the window. We hopped onto the stools with our takeaway cups, as if ready to leave at a moment's notice.

I missed the pace in Cozy Creek. Not feeling like the weirdo if you chose to sit down and spend some time eating, drinking and digesting what you bought.

"So, how're you feeling?" Bess asked.

I chuckled softly, taking a sip of coffee. "Can we start with an easier question?"

"Okay... what happened with Kyle? I wanted to ask you earlier, but we were so busy, and I felt like you needed a bit of time."

"I did," I admitted. "Thank you."

"Can you tell me now? I'm worried. About you, about Trevor, about the company. Everything."

"Why? We're okay. We're on schedule. Ahead of schedule. I just sent the first drafts to—"

"I'm not talking about work! You can't just pretend nothing happened."

To be honest, that's exactly what I was pretending, at least to myself. I didn't want to think about my past and how much certain individuals in Cozy Creek hated me, or how I'd watched my boyfriend making out with someone else, or what an idiot I'd been at Kyle's. Or how Trevor now knew my dirty secrets, and no longer wanted to see me or talk to me.

"Things happened," I said tentatively. "I'm trying to put them behind me."

"I thought you liked Trevor?"

"He's great. He's... amazing." I smiled, despite myself, thinking of our time together.

I thought about the Scot every day, every night, every morning when I woke up.

"He's been in love with you for a long time," Bess said quietly.

"He didn't even know me."

"I bet he knows you a little now."

I gave her a wry smile. "And he hasn't called or messaged me outside of work once. He left me on 'read'."

"There's only so much rejection a man can take. Even Trevor."

"He has this lumberjack dream... of hunting and fishing and splitting logs. That's why he bought the cabin. And now he knows I'm not welcome at Cozy Creek. He knows—"

"Did you hear what he said to those guys after the sledding contest? After you ran off? I got part of it on camera."

I held my breath as she pulled out her phone and brought up a video clip. Trevor's booming voice shot an instant arrow into my heart. "She's with me, and if you mess with her, you mess with me!" he shouted. "If you start any trouble, I'll make sure your dirty laundry gets aired very publicly!"

I heard Julian's irritated voice in the background, but Bess closed the video. "You don't need to hear that," she said apologetically.

I stared at her silent phone, Trevor's words still ringing in my ears. "Dirty laundry? He didn't even know what happened. Not until later."

I'd since told Bess the whole saga and told her to tell Charlie.

It was better that they all knew.

Bess shrugged. "He took a wild guess. Guys like that always have dirty laundry. And he was right on the money."

I sighed, shaking my head. "I can't believe he stood up for me. I'd only just told him what I did, and he didn't even know why."

Bess smiled. "Love is blind. The only question is, how do you feel about *him*?"

I shook my head, feeling the familiar confusion and panic. "I don't know! I've never been in love, and I've been waiting for that thing to hit me. It's supposed to feel like a freight train, right?"

Bess wrinkled her nose. "A freight train? That doesn't sound pleasant."

"You know, big! Heavy. Not subtle."

"Why not subtle?"

"Because I'm not a subtle person. I feel strongly about many things. But when it comes to men, I've never felt like I wanted to give up my independence, my freedom... and *merge* with another person." I shuddered. "I see people doing that. Changing every-thing about themselves and blending together."

Bess gave me a reproachful look. "You say it like we exist in liquid form. You don't lose your essence by falling in love. You discover it. You get to see yourself through the other person's eyes."

I thought of the way Trevor had looked at me, like I'd hung the moon and the stars and half the galaxy. But that was before he knew my past.

"I feel like I can't live up to this image he has of me. Or had. I don't know what he's thinking now."

"He loves you, plain and simple."

I sat with the uncomfortable truth, drinking my coffee with its mildly burned flavor, watching the people outside the window. A blur of dark winter coats. That's what other people were. A blur of coats. Unless I stopped and focused on someone and truly connected. Unless I let someone in to see the mess.

I'd start with Bess.

"That day in Kyle's cabin, I was convinced he was going to murder me."

She spat her coffee. "What?"

I cringed. "Yeah. He joked about dead bodies in his basement and then I found a four-gallon container of bleach under his sink. Is that suspicious?"

Bess lifted a shoulder. "I don't know. People who live remotely tend to buy in bulk."

"Anyway, it turned out I misread the whole thing. I heard the story of the missing tourist, and my imagination ran with it. My whole life, I've been waiting for the freight train of love to hit me, and I always thought I could at least trust my instincts to tell me when it happened. But now I feel like I can't trust myself. I freaked out so badly that I fainted. I fucking fainted, thinking I was going to die." Shame pulsed through me, coloring my cheeks.

"That's horrible!"

"But it was all in my head. So, even if I was in love with Trevor, how would I know? My brain is misfiring!" I fought tears, trying to turn so that nobody else in the cafe saw me, but we were sitting at the window. On display.

Bess placed her hand over mine. "I get how awful that was. I might have freaked out as well. But it doesn't mean your instincts are broken. It just means you let the fear take the wheel. It's hard to tell the difference sometimes."

I thought about what Trevor had told me about his premonitions, and how he'd been convinced Gavin was bad news. That was why he'd wanted me off the project—to protect me from a threat he had perceived, one that I couldn't sense at all. It had been real for him. Just as real as what I'd experienced in Kyle's cabin. Real enough to knock you out.

"He's been trying to protect me. All this time," I said quietly to no one in particular. "Trevor's never wanted to hurt me."

"No, he didn't," Bess said, relief in her voice. "I'm glad you can see it now."

"But how can I know if I'm in love with him? I miss him. I have this awful, hollow feeling, like I'm not okay. Like I don't know how to 'be' when I'm alone. I used to be okay alone. I loved being alone. Something's changed, but I don't know what it is. And I feel like Trevor deserves better than that. He deserves someone who's just as passionate. Someone who's sure about him and all of it."

Bess grabbed my hands, forcing me to look at her. Green eyes burning with conviction. "I'll try to help you, okay? But you just have to go with it, like an improv exercise. Are you ready?"

"Ready for what?"

"Just... ready?" She nodded in confirmation, her eyebrows raised, that intense look in her eyes.

I nodded. "Okay..."

"Close your eyes."

I did.

"Now... if you have great news, who would you share it with? Who'd be the most excited for you?"

The faces of Bess and my sister flickered behind my eyelids. But I couldn't help seeing Trevor, too. And when I imagined his face, I felt the warmth and intensity of his attention. No one else could match it. "I don't know," I said. My face felt hot.

"If you're feeling lonely, late at night, who do you wish was there?"

"Trevor," I whispered.

"And if you're scared, who do you want?"

I saw Trevor's face again, just like I'd seen it at Kyle's house, first in my imagination before I passed out, then for real.

"Trevor," I said again, a little louder.

"And who do you love?"

Trevor, I thought, but I couldn't get the word out.

Bess sighed. "So... what's wrong? What did he do wrong? I mean, I get that it was too soon and too much, but is there something else? Do you hate beards? Scottish accents? Tall guys? Knitting?"

I opened my eyes, blinking away tears. "No! He didn't do anything wrong. He just picked the wrong woman."

Bess frowned, cocking her head. "Wrong? How're you wrong

for him?"

"For one, I can't live in Cozy Creek, and he's setting up his whole life there. He bought a house. He—"

"He's selling it. He listed it on Monday."

"What?"

Bess gave me a pained look. "Charlie said he already has two offers."

"Really?"

I had no right to feel angry. I had no claim on that house, or even the couch we'd joked about. I didn't own anything there, and I had no say in Trevor's affairs. Yet I found my hand shaking as I reached for my takeaway cup. How could he sell that house? *My* dream house. The most beautiful house I'd ever seen.

"Well, I hope the new owner appreciates it." I was going for a neutral tone, but it came out spiteful.

"I'm sure they will. It's gorgeous."

I took a breath, weighing my words. She was friends with both of us, but I really needed an ally. "Do you know... why? Is the office not moving?"

Bess shook her head. "Not at this stage. I think we'll fit into our current space just fine for a while, with Trevor moving back to Scotland and all." She held still, studying me with concern, waiting for her words to hit home.

"What?"

"I'm sorry to be the one to tell you. He asked me to pass on the message."

I hung my head. It felt so heavy I wished I could have dropped it on the table. "When is he leaving?"

"This weekend."

Cold sweat prickled on my neck. There were so many things I wanted to ask, but none of them felt appropriate. "What about the company? What are we going to do?"

"He asked us to give his shares to you. We'll struggle, but we'll survive. You know he's been on a very low salary? That's how we could afford to pay you. But we'll figure it out. It'll be okay."

It wasn't. In that moment, my heart knew, with absolute certainty, that I'd never be okay with Trevor going away. Ever.

I burst into tears, sobbing uncontrollably over my coffee cup. Tears gathered on top of the plastic lid, leaking into my drink. "I drove him away. I messed up. He thinks I don't... he thinks I... but I can't..."

Bess drew me into a hug, whispering into my ear. "You love him, right?"

"I love him," I sobbed. "I don't want him to go! I love him."

"I'm sorry I had to do it this way, but now you know."

I pulled away to look her in the eye. "Know what?"

Her smile sparkled, suspiciously bright. "I made it up. He's not going anywhere. He hasn't said anything like that. I don't think he's selling the house either. He made us do the paperwork to transfer half of his shares to you months ago, so that part is half-true. But you'd still have to agree to it." Her eyes glistened. "I just wanted you to see how you felt about him."

My breath caught in my throat, and I croaked in disbelief. Like a frog. I slapped her arm, then made another incoherent noise.

"Fuck, that was diabolical!" I huffed, hanging my head. "I feel like an idiot."

She grinned back. "Congratulations! You're in love."

♥ ♥ ♥

Two and half hours later, I arrived in Cozy Creek. The Valentine's Day decorations were finally gone, but the wintery scene was somehow every bit as magical, with gently floating snowflakes and snowcapped evergreens.

I parked Bess's little hatchback outside Trevor's cabin and ran towards the door. It felt weird that I'd never seen his place in Denver. We'd only ever spent time together in Cozy Creek. And now he apparently lived here.

In my frenzy to get to him, I knocked on the door and then froze, suddenly realizing he might not be alone. His car was in the driveway, but what if he'd driven here with someone else? What if Bess was mistaken, and he'd already moved on? I'd treated him horribly for months, assuming the worst. Sure, he'd hurt me, and sort of ruined my big break, but I understood him a little better now. More importantly, I had truly forgiven him. There wasn't even a small slice of grudge left in my soul, and it felt liberating. I felt lighter than air.

We'd both made mistakes. My instincts were fallible, just as fallible as Trevor's. Yet, I loved him. That ache in my chest had sharpened like flavor being teased out on low heat until it was all I could taste with every receptor in my body.

Bess's little theater piece had achieved two things: I knew how I felt, and I knew what I feared. On the way to Trevor's door, I'd scanned his yard for a 'for sale' sign, relieved there wasn't one. The alternate reality she'd painted of him selling the house and moving away wasn't that far-fetched. I'd believed it without a moment's hesitation. Maybe Trevor wasn't there yet, but if I kept pushing him away and breaking his heart, it might happen.

There's only so much rejection a man can take.

I knocked again and heard the faint sound of footsteps. Finally, the door opened. It was him. Barefoot, in gray slacks and a white tee, hair sticking out and mouth curving into a smile. The light flooding in through the tall windows framed him with an otherworldly halo as he leaned his arm on the doorframe, tilting his head at me. "Teresa."

He said my name like a caress, waiting for my move.

"Trevor," I said back, swallowing against the stickiness in my throat. "I'm ready."

"Ready for what?"

"For us."

He stepped aside to let me in. The cabin looked as inviting and grand as before, but there was a stack of boxes by the doorway. Next to them stood a huge office printer—the very same model I remembered cursing at Wilde Creative many times.

"Wait, are you moving?" My voice rang with fear.

Trevor looked confused. "Yeah. I'm moving here."

"Here," I repeated. "You're staying *here*?"

"Yes." He stood on the living room threshold, hands on his

hips, waiting for my next move.

My heart ached, but I tried to smile. "Is that your home printer?"

"Sort of," he said. "I bought it for the business, but it doesn't fit into our office in Denver, so I've been hosting it until we find a bigger office space."

"Why did I not know about that? I've been using the print shop down the road. This could have saved money."

He scratched his neck. "Because it was in my apartment, and I didn't think ye wanted to visit."

"Where was your apartment in Denver? I never even asked." My face flushed with shame.

"Two blocks from yours."

All the time we'd wasted, so close to each other... I nodded, looking at the giant gray box. "I hate the user interface on that thing, but the quality is pretty good. It does Spiro binding, right?"

"Did you come here to discuss office printing?" His smile was crooked, and a little sad.

I took off my shoes as he took my jacket. "No. I came to visit my couch."

"This way," he said, leading me to it. "Can I offer ye something? Coffee?"

I sank into the heavenly softness with a sigh. "No, it's okay." I pulled my passport out of my purse and handed it to him. "Here you go."

He made a show of inspecting it. "Teresa Dragonfly Shaw. Very good."

"It doesn't say that!" I huffed a small laugh as I tried to gather my thoughts. I'd imagined it all on the way here. I'd imagined throwing myself at him, not holding back. Showing him that I meant it. And now I'd already chickened out. What if he said "no"? What if he'd changed his mind?

He sat on the ottoman next to me, waiting. Watching.

"You know how I told you I've never been in love?" I said, sounding as breathless as I felt. Was I running out of oxygen? Would I faint again?

"Uh-huh."

"I've done a lot of thinking, and it turns out, that's not entirely true."

His mouth twitched and his eyes softened a little. "Oh, really?"

I tried to draw a steady breath. Remaining conscious would really help right now. "Really. Because, lately, it's been happening to me. Or maybe it's been happening for a long time, and I've finally caught on. And I don't want you to move away."

He looked at me quizzically. "I'm not going anywhere."

"Maybe not right now. But it's not something I'm willing to leave up to chance. Or circumstances."

He smiled, lifting my passport. "Would ye like to confiscate *my* passport?"

A blush warmed my face. "I'm not good at this. I'm not a copywriter or a poet!"

He shifted a little closer, reaching for my hand. "You're doing great."

Air escaped my lungs and words followed. "I think I'm in love with you, Trevor. I don't know how to be on my own anymore. It's not the same. It's like something is missing and I'll never be okay unless I'm with you."

"Don't look so scared. It's a good thing, I promise." He shifted next to me on the couch and pulled me against his chest, stroking my hair.

Judging by the storm raging inside of me, I probably did look terrified. But as he held me, the storm settled, and those waves turned into smaller waves, then tiny laps sloshing against my ribcage, as if all my insides had liquified. Maybe I was merging now, like ink spilling into a glass of water, swirling and diluting. I listened to his heartbeat and inhaled the slightly woodsy smell of his shirt, feeling safe. More okay than I'd felt in days.

If our lives were intertwined, he'd stay with me. I'd stay with him. No matter what happened to the house or the business, I'd have Trevor. And that was what I wanted.

"I don't want to go back to dating, though," I said. "Not the casual kind where I'm only sharing one piece of myself and keeping my life the same. I want the non-casual. The scary kind."

He chuckled softly into my hair. "That's what I want, too. The scary kind."

He kissed my curls, then brushed them off my face to trail his lips down my cheek. When they found my mouth, I held my breath. Every single time had felt amazing with him, but the layers of emotion bursting from my heart made the moment a hundred times more powerful. There was nothing standing between us anymore, neither of us holding back or questioning the magic.

We were submitting to it.

I parted my lips, drawing him in, hungry and desperate. I didn't even notice when we moved from vertical to horizontal, but at some point, I felt the pressure at the back of my head. I was lying on the couch, still kissing him. Every part of me was on fire. The good kind. The scary kind. One that cleansed without destroying.

"I love your smell," he murmured into my neck, inhaling deeply. "It's like a drug."

"Good," I whispered back. "Because I want to drug you and keep you."

"That's my line!" He laughed.

"No. I get to be obsessed with *you* now. You've put a spell on me and now I can't live without you." It was the cringiest thing anyone could have possibly said, and I'd said it with a straight face, grasping at his T-shirt.

"So, you're okay with me being a little obsessed with you? Because I've been holding back."

"Don't!" I tugged at his slacks until his hips were squarely against mine. "I want it all."

He grinned, gazing at me from under heavy eyelids. Dark eyes, unfocused and hungry. "Are you sure?"

He dived into my neck and kissed me hard, adding enough suction to probably leave a mark. I didn't care. I moaned.

Why had I ever settled for less than devotion? For being loved in that drunkenly obsessed way that left no room for doubt? No need for theatrics or performance. Only a desperate need to join with another person and bask in their presence. Now that I knew my heart could match his, I didn't need him to rein it in. I wanted everything.

"What have you always wanted to do with me? What have you fantasized about?" I asked.

I reached for his slacks, stretched taut by his erection, and stroked him through the fabric. I don't know what I'd expected, but the tears in his eyes took me by surprise.

"This," he choked out. "This is my fantasy."

"Having sex on a couch?"

He let out a wobbly laugh, then got off me and scooped me up so that we were standing. "This," he said again. "Being able to love you with all my heart."

"Let's do it," I said, catching his tear with my thumb. "Let's love excessively. Let's be over-the-top and cringe. It's taken me so long to get here, and I feel like I've missed out on too much."

"So, I can give you a house and you won't freak out?"

"Umm…"

"Because I put yer name on the deeds months ago. It's yours if you sign the papers."

My heart just about stopped, and I stared at him. "What?"

"It was always yours, Dragonfly." He glanced at the art print on the wall.

I took a deep breath and smiled, trying very hard not to freak out. Trevor scratched his beard. "I thought maybe it wasnae the right time to tell ye, so I kept it quiet. Let's talk about it later, aye?" He leaned in and whispered into my ear. "How about I give ye something else first? Something that comes with less paperwork... like an orgasm?"

My exhale turned into a shaky laugh. "Sounds good."

He placed his giant hand on my lower back, leading me towards the bedroom, and no part of me resisted.

"Do you have a kilt?" I asked. "Because the other two elements from my sex dream are... also available."

He froze in the bedroom doorway, casting me a look that spoke volumes. "Seriously? Here, in this house? Because I want to change my answer to your earlier question. My fantasy is to re-enact your dream. But I thought it was set on an alien planet."

I chuckled. "I told you it wasn't *that* strange, right?"

"Ye said, and I quote, 'It would never happen in real life.'"

"Well, how could I know you had a giant printer in your house? My dream featured the office one, and it seemed a bit far-fetched to sit on it naked while you fucked me in a kilt."

In two minutes, he'd changed into his kilt, grinning at me in blue-gray tartan and nothing else. "Every man dies; not every man really lives."

"Braveheart?"

He nodded, and I pulled off my black sweater, then my tank top, finally jiggling out of my jeans as I walked towards the office printer. I felt his gaze on my skin, as he gained on me, reaching me by the time I dropped my underwear on the floor by the bottom paper tray.

The front of his kilt bulged awkwardly. "You can't hide an erection in that, can you?" I smiled, beckoning him closer.

"Not well," he admitted, his eyes trailing down my body.

"What exactly happened in that dream? Why were you naked by the printer?"

"Dreams don't have to make sense."

"True. So, you were next to the printer?"

"Sitting on it," I said, biting my lip.

He hoisted me onto the printer, stepping between my knees. My hand rested on a button and the machine whirred.

"Sorry, it's on. I tested it earlier."

I smiled. "Perfect. I need it to know what's happening."

"So, what *is* happening?" he asked, eyelids heavy, voice pure gravel. "Describe the dream."

"I think we were in that stuffy little room at Wilde. It was always hot in there, so let's say I was naked because I was hot. And you came in..."

"Wearing a kilt," he finished.

I leaned my head against the wall of muscles that was his chest, feeling both embarrassed and excited. "And then you just had me right there."

"I've been wondering why I had this printer, and now I know. I bought it off Wilde when they upgraded."

I looked up in shock. "It's the same printer?"

"The very same one."

Uncontrollable laughter took over me. "I've had my arm inside it so many times!" I hiccupped.

"Paper jams?"

"Yeah. You have to pull out all these parts..."

"I know. I've done the same."

"I guess I always wanted to defile this machine in some way."

"Let's."

He trailed his mouth down my body, sucking my nipples, then moved down between my thighs. This was so much better than I'd ever imagined. In my dream, he'd been a sexy brute, lured in by my naked body. It'd been fast and forceful, an illicit office affair you could only ever have in your dreams if you wanted to keep your job and not overly complicate your life.

The real Trevor was something else entirely. He took his time, savoring every moment. He touched and teased me gently, responding to every sound I made.

"Dragonfly," he murmured.

I rocked with him, my body humming in response like I was the one plugged into a power socket, not the machine under me. The delicious tension gathered, building until I was truly floating somewhere high above, suspended between his hands and mouth, legs dangling in the air. I lost sense of time. Maybe I lost sense of myself, but it wasn't dangerous. It was perfect.

With his tongue dancing on my clit, I came apart, clutching onto his shoulders. I felt sunshine piercing my heart, as if I was floating above the clouds. Nothing had ever felt this good.

When he pushed the kilt aside and rolled on a condom, I gasped at the sight. It was my dream. He was making my dream come true. I throbbed in anticipation as he stepped closer, using an upturned plastic crate to reach the right height. Like in the dream, everything just worked out, and he pushed into me, taking over every bit of my body, releasing a low growl that resonated somewhere deep inside me.

I moved with him, drinking in the pure ecstasy I saw on his face and heard in his voice. I was so focused on his pleasure, I didn't even realize I was reaching another climax before it took over, delivering uncontrollable shakes. His head dropped onto my shoulder, and he sighed against my skin.

"I love you, Teresa."

"I love you, too."

I finally understood what it meant to have your heart so full it might split, because I could barely talk. He carried me away from the printer and into the bedroom. I was ready to fall now. Fall so hard that the world outside faded away. So madly that nothing else mattered.

I'd be pathetic and cringe and all the things I'd looked down on, as long as I got to be with him.

Trevor

10 MONTHS LATER

It was Christmas Eve, and Cozy Creek sparkled like a holiday card, the kind my nan used to send. The lights were so bright and plentiful we could see them from our living room window, from the cabin we both called home.

I couldn't believe my luck. My soulmate was finally mine, and somehow, I'd convinced her to live in a cabin in the mountains with me. Although, I would have sold the house in a heartbeat, had she asked me. I'd left the decision to her, knowing how difficult it was to return to a town that had once rejected her.

But Teresa was a resilient woman. She'd fought her way back, showing the Neville family she wasn't afraid of them. Together with Peony, she'd posted about Julian on the town discussion forum, asking for any other victims to contact them.

Legally, they had no recourse, but the publicity worked. Two other women came forward with their stories, and the town rumor mill took care of the rest.

Fortunately, one of the cases, Julian's former secretary, was fresh enough for the lawyers to deal with. Julian Neville had gone into hiding, waiting for his first trial. Whatever he'd planned to do to mess with Teresa must have been thwarted by the turning tide. He was quickly losing his influence and couldn't get others to carry out any dirty work for him.

Looking at the tall Christmas tree set up by the window and the decorations hanging all around us, I felt an incredible sense of calm. I was home. We were home. All the unhinged dreams I'd nurtured for so long had come true and now there was room for new ones. Dreams of a family we could raise here. The business we could build in this town.

"Bess said they'll be here in half an hour," Teresa said, handing me a glass of beer. "They're just packing their things. It'll be an hour with the baby and everything."

"That's okay. Let's heat up the food when they arrive."

Charlie and Bess lived in town, ten minutes away, within walking distance from our office. We'd signed the lease after the repairs were done and moved within a month. Teresa had taken a little longer to move in with me. We'd dated, driving back and forth before she sold her condo in Denver. To ease her transition, I'd installed a dancing pole in the spare room. Neither of us wanted to be apart, though, and our private chat pinged constantly when we were.

I'd never closed the chat, like Charlie had suggested. I couldn't imagine losing those early conversations. Our history. It was the story of us, every meme and comment part of the journey that finally brought us under the same roof, for real.

The doorbell rang. It was Kyle with a girlfriend he'd recently met in Cozy Creek. Right behind him, Peony beamed with two of her children, holding an intricately decorated Christmas cake. Two minutes later, Selma arrived with a bouquet of flowers. She'd been quite involved with our office move, supplying us with flowers and fruit bowls, gathering information for the town grapevine.

We'd invited everyone to our Christmas Eve party, and our spacious living room was starting to look full. Teresa had ordered a new table for the dining area to make sure there was enough seating. She'd painted our bedroom walls in Tyrian, and changed little things around the house, making it truly hers. Nothing made me happier than seeing her settle in. I'd tried to create a space she'd like, but this was so much better. This was her taking over and feeling at home.

I positioned myself behind the counter, serving mulled wine, coffees, and soda. The second living space was set up with the TV and cushions for the kids to hang out in. When Bess, Charlie, Celia, and baby Scott arrived, the noise level skyrocketed, drowning out the Christmas playlist.

Celia had made friends with Peony's kids and viewed our holiday gathering as her personal playdate. I didn't mind, but I did offer to set up their movie entertainment immediately, before they discovered other, more destructive activities.

Our business had survived the move and was slowly recovering as we found more local clients. Teresa had surprised everyone by joining the local business association and getting heavily involved in town matters. She was ignoring the haters and taking up space, gradually winning over the Nevilles' inner circle until they remained her only enemies. Next year, our business would be sponsoring the annual cardboard sled competition, along with a few of our clients. Charlie and Bess had bowed out, too overwhelmed by early parenthood, but Teresa and I would build a sled together with Celia. Babysitting was easier when you had a project.

Our guests gathered around Bess and the baby, who was just starting to make some coherent sounds. Not quite words, but it was fun to interpret them, anyway. Celia jumped in, placing her Santa hat on little Scott—whose name, I was assured, had nothing to do with my origins—and gave him a kiss.

"He looks like an elf now," she announced.

"Just like me!" Teresa appeared from our bedroom in her elf costume. "I had to get changed."

"Wow! That brings back memories," I mused, taking her hand, and spinning her around so that she jingled.

"When are you having a baby?" Celia asked her. "My mom says if you have a baby, she could be friends with Scott when he grows up."

Bess flushed beetroot red. "I... I—"

"She's very sleep deprived," Charlie replied for her. "Delirious, really." He yawned for good measure, and Bess ended up yawning with him.

Teresa laughed, looking a little flustered.

"Have ye heard the tale o' this elf costume?" I asked, laying on the brogue thick enough to make Celia giggle.

I could tell that story in my sleep, so I performed it again for a rapt audience.

As we settled around the table for the early dinner, it was getting dark outside. The sky was turning that intense blue I'd always missed in the city. Here, it was like a painting, brought out every night in our private gallery.

We ate, drank, and laughed until it was so dark only stars were visible outside, faint beyond the fairy lights Teresa had hung in the window.

After everyone had left and we'd loaded the dishes away, she joined me on the couch, releasing a deep sigh. "Today was perfect."

"Aye, it really was."

She snuggled under my arms, her voice thick and wobbly with emotion. "Thank you for not giving up on me."

I kissed her curls, not sure of what to say. I'd learned to wait and wait. If I stayed still, she came to me. She opened up. There'd always been something between us, and it wasn't one-sided. She'd been drawn to me in her own way, seeking me out even when she couldn't bear looking at me or didn't know how she felt. I had to trust that this connection would carry us forward. So, I relaxed, and waited. I was good at it now. I never mentioned marriage or kids, or even putting the house in her name. She'd let me know when she was ready.

When she finally turned to me, her eyes glossy with tears, I knew she'd arrived somewhere.

"I might want a baby." She bit her lip, watching me.

I smiled. "Ask me, and I'll give you anything."

"Just like that?"

"Just like that." My chest welled with emotion. It was time. My instinct, if I chose to take its advice, was nudging me to take the leap. "But there's something I need you to do for me."

"What?" She stared at me, perfectly still. The air crackled, like microscopic fairies were snapping their fingers.

"Marry me," I said. "Visit my family in Scotland. In either order."

Tears burst from her eyes. "I thought you'd never ask!"

Every muscle in my body relaxed. Muscles I didn't know I had, loosened, and I sank into the couch that was hers, in the house that was hers. My heart, which was also hers, swelled with happiness.

"Do you have a ring?" she asked. "You can tell me if you've had it for a while. I won't freak out."

"Since July," I said. "But I'm good at waiting."

"Can I see it?"

"It's with the jeweler, along with four backup options. Did ye think I was going to make a call about something visual without consulting you?" I lifted a brow. "Ye know I can't even pick curtains."

"Oh, thank God!" She breathed a sigh of relief and threw herself into my arms. "Although I admit I started a Pinterest board with my favorite ring designs. I thought you might see it." She laughed softly into my shirt and her elf shirt jingled.

"Ach, I should've checked yer account!" Now that she was with me, I wasn't online that much anymore.

"That's okay. I'll start another one for the wedding and invite you as a collaborator."

"Ye mean a silent observer?" I corrected.

"That works."

I placed a kiss on her lips, tasting a hint of salty tears. She was finally mine and I couldn't wait to share everything I had with her.

"We should celebrate," I said. "A toast or something."

I stood up, lifting her with me, trying to remember where I'd months ago stashed the champagne bottle. But as we reached the middle of the floor, she stopped me. "Can you write this down?" she asked. "Like you did after our first night? So, we don't forget."

"Sure."

"You can change stuff if you like."

"Like what?"

"Maybe... you save me from a real serial killer? And you decorate this house exactly to my taste because our tastes align perfectly. So, when I see it, I think we're meant to be?"

"Sounds a bit far-fetched, aye?"

She laughed. "Fine. You're the writer. Make yourself look like a fool." Her eyes sparkled like she was smuggling diamonds in there. "Don't forget to include a whole paragraph about your knitting. It's gold!"

"I'll write that story exactly as it happened, because it was perfect—it brought us together."

I spun her around the room, the jingle bells on her elf costume ringing like a Christmas carol gone rogue. Dizzy and laughing, I knew I didn't care if I looked like a lovesick fool. She didn't care either—we were too busy being madly in love.

ACKNOWLEDGMENTS

I'd like to thank my husband for loving me so madly that I still want to write about people falling in love. He feeds me. He fasts with me. He makes me feel like the hottest girl in the room. This time, he also taught me how the crypto market works and how crazy it really is.

Thank you, thank you, thank you to my author bestie Evie Alexander for her relentless encouragement and talent. She didn't just proofread for me. She made this book shine and made me believe in myself.

Lastly, a huge thank you to my business partner Beks, who's the best boss I've ever had. She supports my crazy writing obsession in many, many ways.

I may not have a huge team around me, but I have the best people.

ABOUT THE AUTHOR

Enni Amanda is a graphic designer moonlighting as a rom-com author, or maybe it's the other way around. In 2006, she and her husband moved from Finland to New Zealand and fell in love with the gorgeous islands and their laid-back people. They spent eight years traveling between the two rather inconveniently located countries, studying filmmaking and running a film festival.

Through all the filmmaking, Enni discovered a passion for screenwriting, which eventually led to writing books (a slippery slope). Her heart-warming, funny stories explore real-life issues like identity, found family, and the housing crisis. These days, she lives in the Waikato, close to the rolling hills of the Shire, raising two cute, rambunctious boys while writing away and ignoring housework.

Sign up for her newsletter here:

enniamanda.com/newsletter

ALSO BY ENNI AMANDA

A Tiny House on Wheels
Coffee on Waihi Beach
Christmas in July (novella)

LOVE NEW ZEALAND SERIES

Nest or Invest
Hidden Gem
Night and Day

LOVE ISTANBUL SERIES

My Lucky Star
My Turkish Fling

COZY CREEK COLLECTION

Falling Slowly
Falling Madly

You can find all of Enni's books and more information on her website: **enniamanda.com**